MAGICIANS'
CIRCLE

By the same editor for younger readers:

SCARY! Stories That Will Make You Scream
SCARY! 2 More Stories To Make You Scream
**THE WIZARDS' DEN Spellbinding Stories of Magic
& Magicians**

MAGICIANS' CIRCLE

More Spellbinding Stories of Wizards & Wizardry

Edited by

PETER HAINING

SOUVENIR PRESS

First published 2003 by
Souvenir Press Ltd,
43 Great Russell Street, London WC1B 3PD

ISBN 0 285 63681 2

Typeset by Photoprint, Torquay, Devon

Printed and bound in Great Britain by
Creative Print & Design, Ebbw Vale, Wales

This book is for

MATTHEW & JONATHAN

Two Little Magicians

If this be magic, let it be an art
Lawful as eating.

WILLIAM SHAKESPEARE
The Winter's Tale, c. 1610 or 1611

Engaging with a story is a magical feeling.

PHILIP PULLMAN
Sunday Times, January 2002

CONTENTS

THE SPELL OF MAGIC

Harry Potter is, of course, the most famous student wizard of modern times. But for many years that title belonged to the anonymous 'Magician's Apprentice', the hero of a classic poem by the eighteenth-century German writer, Johann Wolfgang von Goethe. If I say that this poem inspired the well-known sequence in Walt Disney's film, *Fantasia*, where Mickey Mouse uses one of his absent master's magic spells to make a broom do his chores, then you will know who I mean – although Goethe's apprentice is a boy and not a mouse.

Goethe was a fascinating man who actually dabbled in alchemy before becoming famous for his drama, *Faust* (1832), about a disillusioned scholar who calls on dark powers to make a pact with Satan to win the love of a girl who then dies tragically. The author obviously knew quite a lot about the workings of magic as these lines from 'The Magician's Apprentice' reveal:

> *Ho, thou battered broomstick! Take ye*
> *This seedy old coat and wear it –*
> *Ha, thou household drudge! I'll make ye*
> *Do my bidding; aye and fear it.*
> *Don a pair of legs, now;*
> *A head too, for the once!*

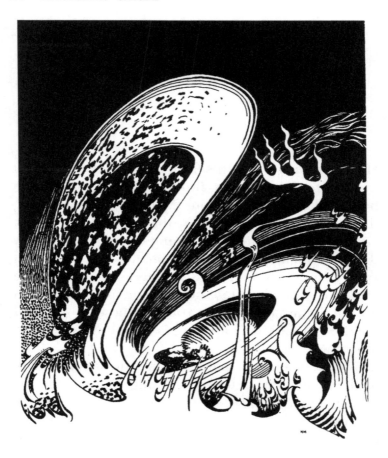

The powers of magic at work in the poem of 'The Magician's Apprentice'

To the river there, now
Bear the pail at once!
Hear ye! Hear ye! Be so spritely
Do your task most rightly
Toil, until the water clear, ye
Fill the bath to overflowing.

See, 'tis off – 'tis at the river
In the stream the bucket flashes;
Now 'tis back – and down, as ever
You can wink, the burden dashes.
Again, again, and quicker!
The floor is in a swim,
And every cup and beaker
Is running o'er the rim.
Stop, now stop! You have granted
All I wanted. Stop! Oh rot it!
Running still? I'm like to drop!
What's the magic word? I've clean forgot it!

Only the unexpected return of his master, the wise
old magician, who immediately puts a stop to the
spell, saves the young apprentice from completely
flooding the premises and drowning himself. Naturally, the Germans are very proud of their literary
forerunner to Harry Potter – a fact that has been
mentioned in many of their reviews of J.K. Rowling's
books as well as the films – although some people
were not too impressed by a toy version of the boy
wizard's flying broomstick, the Nimbus 2000, as it
contained some harmful ingredients that an expert
described as 'a time-bomb of harmful chemicals'.
Shades there of Goethe's young meddler needing to
be saved from the power he unleashed!

The people of New Zealand would also seem to
have a lot to be thankful for to their modern-day
'Magician of Christchurch'. New Zealand is the country where that other wonderful movie about wizards
and wizardry, *The Lord of the Rings*, was filmed a
couple of years ago. Long before that, in 1990, the
Prime Minister, Michael Moore, took a leaf out of

*The old-fashioned idea of a witch from
a story by George MacDonald*

the old books of folklore and legend and decided
that a bit of magic might be good for the country. He
decided to appoint an official wizard and issued
specifications as to what the man's job would be:

> To protect the Government, to bless new enter-
> prises, cast out evil spirits, upset fanatics, cheer up
> the population, attract tourists and, in particular,
> to design and promote a new and improved uni-
> verse which puts New Zealand on top of the world
> both physically and metaphysically.

Mr Moore said that an understanding of wizard
cosmology as well as a belief in fun were essential and

A modern witch is more likely to be enchanting and pretty to look at

offered the successful applicant the perk of living tax-free! Finally, the job went to an Englishman, Ian Channel, who had studied sociology and psychology in London, and had actually been made a wizard when he lived in Australia in the 1960s. Today, there are people in New Zealand who believe the 'Wizard of Christchurch's' magic *must* have been pretty good if the success of *The Lord of the Rings* is anything to go by – because the film not only emphasised what an enchantingly beautiful place the country is, but has put a spell on tourists from all over the world anxious to visit the locations where it was shot.

Both of these stories illustrate our enduring fascination with magic – and in this book you will find tales about it which range from ancient times to the present day, all written by some of the very best fantasy authors. Before we start, though, it is perhaps just worth asking what *is* magic that it can create such an interest?

A definition of magic is not easy to find, although it is known that the word derives from the Greek, *mageia*, to describe the secret practices of certain types of priests. Generally magic is said to be the art of controlling natural forces or demonic beings by supernatural means. According to *The Standard Dictionary of Folklore, Myth and Legend* (1975) this magic can be either positive or negative. Positive magic is intended to *do* something – a lucky talisman, for example, performs positive magic – while negative magic is meant to *prevent* something. Think of an amulet that can protect people by negative magic against demons, spells, witches and the other makers of positive magic. The *Dictionary* goes on:

> Magic may also be black or white. Black magic is evil, for it calls into play unsanctioned forces and beings, or aims at illness, death, injury or other unforeseen effects. White magic performs cures or wonders without the invocation of dark powers: astrology, alchemy, legerdemain and the like are all classified as white magic.

Ever since writers have been making up stories about magic they have all been working from the same assumption – that it *works*. In an entry on the subject, *The Encyclopedia of Fantasy* (1997) says that whenever magic is present in a story it can do almost *anything*, although it does obey certain rules according to its nature. Just *what* these rules are is generally left undefined. The *Encyclopedia* adds:

The primary assumption is that magic is possible in the world of fantasy and the exact nature of this ambient magic strongly influences the narrative. The way this influence works is most easily seen in one of the best-known worlds of magic, the Wonderland of *Alice's Adventures in Wonderland* by Lewis Carroll.

In a sentence then, when magic is present it can do almost anything – and examples of this happening in many different ways will be found in the stories in this book. Stories that range from George Mac-Donald and Sylvia Townsend Warner's adventures in

The crafty magician, Dr Danti Cadaverezzi, described by Philip Pullman

times long past, to Charles Dickens and Philip Pullman's historical dramas and Jacqueline Wilson and Roald Dahl's tales of magic at work today. In them you will meet not only magicians but also wizards, demons and witches – old and new – whose skills vary from the profound to the pathetic. Some will make you shiver, others will make you laugh, but all, I hope, will leave you enchanted.

My friend, Philip Pullman, whom I have known since he first became a published writer, once told me his formula for encouraging young people to read. As you have been reading this book so far, you probably won't need any further encouragement – but I would like to mention what he said all the same.

'Say, "This book's forbidden"', Philip advised. '"It's not for you. Don't touch it. It's this one here and I'm putting it up on the shelf and going out for a couple of hours".' Magic is supposed to be forbidden too, and there is plenty of it waiting to be discovered in the pages that follow. So give in to temptation, read on, and I am sure you will enjoy, at the very least, a couple of spellbinding hours . . .

PETER HAINING
Boxford, Suffolk
April 2003

A COURSE IN MAGIC

E. Nesbit

This story heralds the return of the master magician, Professor de Lara, who made his first appearance in my previous book, The Wizard's Den. *The crafty 'Professor of Magic and the Black Art' – as he describes himself – is once again loooking for pupils, but on this occasion is hoping to get an appointment to teach a special 'Course in Magic' at the posh Boarding School for Young Ladies run by Miss Fitzroy Robinson. Perhaps it's because he's rather scary-looking or because of his flashing black eyes and his hungry smile, but Miss Robinson feels it might be dangerous to let a magician anywhere near her girls – especially because they all belong to the nobility. So she says no – and in the blink of an eye the Professor has used his powers to make all her pupils disappear! What follows in the quest to find the girls is a real battle of wits – not to mention the use of some very extraordinary magic tricks . . .*

*   *   *

There was once a lady who found herself in middle life with but a slight income. Knowing herself to be insufficiently educated to be able to practise any other trade or calling, she of course decided, without hesitation, to enter the profession of teaching. She opened a very select Boarding School for Young Ladies. The highest references were given and required. And in order to keep her school as select as possible, Miss Fitzroy Robinson had a brass plate fastened on to the door, with an inscription in small polite lettering. (You have, of course, heard of the 'polite letters.' Well, it was with these that Miss Fitzroy Robinson's door-plate was engraved.)

'SELECT BOARDING ESTABLISHMENT FOR THE
DAUGHTERS OF RESPECTABLE MONARCHS.'

A great many kings who were not at all respectable would have given their royal ears to be allowed to send their daughters to this school, but Miss Fitzroy Robinson was very firm about references, and the consequence was that all the really high-class kings were only too pleased to be permitted to pay ten thousand pounds a year for their daughters' education. And so Miss Fitzroy Robinson was able to lay aside a few pounds as a provision for her old age. And all the money she saved was invested in land.

Only one monarch refused to send his daughter to Miss Fitzroy Robinson, on the ground that so cheap a school could not be a really select one, and it was found out afterwards that his references were not at all satisfactory.

There were only six boarders, and of course the best masters were engaged to teach the royal pupils everything which their parents wished them to learn, and as the girls were never asked to do lessons except when they felt quite inclined, they all said it was the nicest school in the world, and cried at the very thought of being taken away. Thus it happened that the six pupils were quite grown up and were just becoming parlour boarders when events began to occur. Princess Daisy, the daughter of King Fortunatus, the ruling sovereign, was the only little girl in the school.

Now it was when she had been at school about a year, that a ring came at the front door-bell, and the maid-servant came to the schoolroom with a visiting card held in the corner of her apron – for her hands were wet because it was washing-day.

'A gentleman to see you, Miss,' she said; and Miss Fitzroy Robinson was quite fluttered because she thought it might be a respectable monarch, with a daughter who wanted teaching.

But when she looked at the card she left off fluttering, and said, 'Dear me!' under her breath, because she was very genteel. If she had been vulgar like some of us she would have said 'Bother!' and if she had been more vulgar than, I hope, any of us are, she might have said 'Drat the man!' The card was large and shiny and had gold letters on it. Miss Fitzroy Robinson read:–

CHEVALIER DOLORO DE LARA
PROFESSOR OF MAGIC (WHITE)
AND THE BLACK ART.
PUPILS INSTRUCTED AT THEIR OWN RESIDENCES.
NO EXTRAS.
SPECIAL TERMS FOR SCHOOLS. EVENING PARTIES
ATTENDED.

Miss Fitzroy Robinson laid down her book – she never taught without a book – smoothed her yellow cap and her grey curls and went into the front parlour to see her visitor. He bowed low at sight of her. He was very tall and hungry-looking, with black eyes, and an indescribable mouth.

'It is indeed a pleasure,' said he, smiling so as to show every one of his thirty-two teeth – a very polite, but very difficult thing to do – 'it is indeed a pleasure to meet once more my old pupil.'

'The pleasure is mutual, I am sure,' said Miss Fitzroy Robinson. If it is sometimes impossible to be polite and truthful at the same moment, that is not my fault, nor Miss Fitzroy Robinson's.

'I have been travelling about,' said the Professor, still smiling immeasurably, 'increasing my stock of wisdom. Ah, dear lady – we live and learn, do we not? And now I am really a far more competent teacher than when I had the honour of instructing you. May I hope for an engagement as Professor in your Academy?'

'I have not yet been able to arrange for a regular course of Magic,' said the schoolmistress; 'it is a subject in which parents, especially royal ones, take but too little interest.'

'It was your favourite study,' said the professor.

'Yes – but – well, no doubt some day –'

'But I want an engagement *now*,' said he, looking hungrier than ever; 'a thousand pounds for thirteen lessons – to *you*, dear lady.'

'It's quite impossible,' said she, and she spoke firmly, for she knew from history how dangerous it is for a Magician to be allowed anywhere near a princess. Some harm almost always comes of it.

'Oh, very well!' said the Professor.

'You see my pupils are all princesses,' she went on, 'they don't require the use of magic, they can get all they want without it.'

'Then it's "*No*"?' said he.

'It's "No thank you kindly,"' said she.

Then, before she could stop him, he sprang past her out at the door, and she heard his boots on the oilcloth of the passage. She flew after him just in time to have the schoolroom door slammed and locked in her face.

'Well, I never!' said Miss Fitzroy Robinson. She hastened to the top of the house and hurried down the schoolroom chimney, which had been made with steps, in case of fire or other emergency. She stepped out of the grate on to the schoolroom hearthrug just one second too late. The seven Princesses were all gone, and the Professor of Magic stood alone among the ink-stained desks, smiling the largest smile Miss Fitzroy Robinson had seen yet.

'Oh, you naughty, bad, wicked man, you!' said she, shaking the school ruler at him.

The next day was Saturday, and the King of the country called as usual to take his daughter Daisy out to spend her half holiday. The servant who opened the door had a coarse apron on and cinders in her hair, and the King thought it was sackcloth and ashes, and said so a little anxiously, but the girl said, 'No, I've only been a-doing of the kitchen range – though, for the matter of that – but you'd best see missus herself.'

So the King was shown into the best parlour where the tasteful wax-flowers were, and the antimacassars and water-colour drawings executed by the pupils, and the wool mats which Miss Fitzroy Robinson's bed-ridden aunt made so beautifully. A delightful parlour full of the traces of the refining touch of a woman's hand.

Miss Fitzroy Robinson came in slowly and sadly. Her gown was neatly made of sackcloth – with an ingenious trimming of small cinders sewn on gold braid – and some larger-sized cinders dangled by silken threads from the edge of her lace cap.

The King saw at once that she was annoyed about something. 'I hope I'm not too early,' said he.

'Your Majesty,' she answered, 'not at all. You are always punctual, as stated in your references. Something has happened. I will not aggravate your misfortunes by breaking them to you. Your daughter Daisy, the pride and treasure of our little circle, has disappeared. Her six royal companions are with her. For the present all are safe, but at the moment I am unable to lay my hand on any one of the seven.'

The King sat down heavily on part of the handsome walnut and rep suite (ladies' and gentlemen's easy-chairs, couch and six occasional chairs) and gasped miserably, He could not find words. But the schoolmistress had written down what she was going to say on a slate and learned it off by heart, so she was able to go on fluently.

'Your Majesty, I am not wholly to blame – hang me if I am – I mean hang me if you must; but first allow me to have the honour of offering to you one or two explanatory remarks.'

With this she sat down and told him the whole story of the Professor's visit, only stopping exactly where I stopped when I was telling it to you just now.

The King listened, plucking nervously at the fringe of a purple and crimson antimacassar.

'I never *was* satisfied with the Professor's methods,' said Miss Fitzroy Robinson sadly; 'and I always had my doubts as to his moral character, doubts now set at rest for ever. After concluding my course of instruction with him some years ago I took a series of lessons from a far more efficient master, and thanks to those lessons, which were, I may mention, extremely costly, I was mercifully enabled to put a spoke in the wheel of the unprincipled ruffian –'

'Did you save the Princesses?' cried the King.

'No; but I can if your Majesty and the other parents will leave the matter entirely in my hands.'

'It's rather a serious matter,' said the King; 'my poor little Daisy –'

'I would ask you,' said the schoolmistress with dignity, 'not to attach too much importance to this event. Of course it is regrettable, but unpleasant accidents occur in all schools, and the consequences of them can usually be averted by the exercise of tact and judgment.'

'I ought to hang you, you know,' said the King doubtfully.

'No doubt,' said Miss Fitzroy Robinson, 'and if you do you'll never see your Daisy again. Your duty as a parent – yes – and your duty to me – conflicting duties are very painful things.'

'But can I trust you?'

'I may remind you,' said she, drawing herself up so that the cinders rattled again, 'that we exchanged satisfactory references at the commencement of our business relations.'

The King rose. 'Well, Miss Fitzroy Robinson,' he said, 'I have been entirely satisfied with Daisy's progress since she has been in your charge, and I feel I cannot do better than leave this matter entirely in your able hands.'

The schoolmistress made him a courtesy, and he went back to his marble palace a broken-hearted monarch, with his crown all on one side and his poor, dear nose red with weeping.

The select boarding establishment was shut up.

Time went on and no news came of the lost Princesses.

The King found but little comfort in the fact that his other child, Prince Denis, was still spared to him. Denis was all very well and a nice little boy in his way, but a boy is not a girl.

The Queen was much more broken-hearted than the King, but of course she had the housekeeping to see to and the making of the pickles and preserves and the young Prince's stockings to knit, so she had not much time for weeping, and after a year she said to the King –

'My dear, you ought to do something to distract your mind. It's unkinglike to sit and cry all day. Now, do make an effort; do something useful, if it's only opening a bazaar or laying a foundation stone.'

'I am frightened of bazaars,' said the King; 'they are like bees – they buzz and worry; but foundation stones –' And after that he began to sit and think sometimes, without crying, and to make notes on the backs of old envelopes. So the Queen felt that she had not spoken quite in vain.

A month later the suggestion of foundation stones bore fruit.

The King floated a company, and Fortunatus Rex & Co. became almost at once the largest speculative builders in the world.

Perhaps you do not know what a speculative builder is. I'll tell you what the King and his Co. did, and then you will know.

They bought all the pretty woods and fields they could get and cut them up into squares, and grubbed up the trees and the grass and put streets there and lamp-posts and ugly little yellow brick houses, in the hopes that people would want to live in them. And curiously enough people did. So the King and his Co. made quite a lot of money.

It is curious that nearly all the great fortunes are made by turning beautiful things into ugly ones. Making beauty out of ugliness is very ill-paid work.

The ugly little streets crawled further and further out of the town, eating up the green country like greedy yellow caterpillars, but at the foot of the Clover Hill they had to stop. For the owner of Clover Hill would not sell any land at all – for any price that Fortunatus Rex & Co. could offer. In vain the solicitors of the Company called on the solicitors of the owner, wearing their best cloaks and swords and shields, and took them out to lunch and gave them nice things to eat and drink. Clover Hill was not for sale.

At last, however, a little old woman all in grey called at the Company's shining brass and mahogany offices and had a private interview with the King himself.

'I am the owner of Clover Hill,' said she, 'and you may build on all its acres except the seven at the top and the fifteen acres that go round that seven, and you must build me a high wall round the seven acres

and another round the fifteen – of *red* brick, mind;
none of your cheap yellow stuff – and you must make
a brand new law that any one who steals my fruit is to
be hanged from the tree he stole it from. That's all.
What do you say?'

The King said 'Yes,' because since his trouble he
cared for nothing but building, and his royal soul
longed to see the green Clover Hill eaten up by
yellow brick caterpillars with slate tops. He did not at
all like building the two red brick walls, but he did
it.

Now, the old woman wanted the walls and the
acres to be this sort of shape –

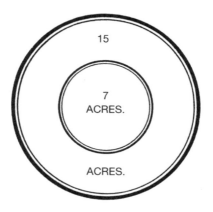

But it was such a bother getting the exact amount of
ground into the two circles that all the surveyors tore
out their hair by handfuls, and at last the King said,
'Oh bother! Do it this way,' and drew a plan on the
back of an old Act of Parliament. So they did, and it
was like this –

The old lady was very vexed when she found that there was only one wall between her orchard and the world, as you see was the case at the corner where the two 1's and the 15 meet; but the King said he couldn't afford to build it all over again and that she'd got her two walls as she had said. So she had to put up with it. Only she insisted on the King's getting her a fierce bulldog to fly at the throat of any one who should come over the wall at that weak point where the two 1's join on to the 15. So he got her a stout bulldog whose name was Martha, and brought it himself in a jewelled leash.

'Martha will fly at any one who is not of kingly blood,' said he. 'Of course she wouldn't dream of biting a royal person; but, then, on the other hand, royal people don't rob orchards.'

So the old woman had to be contented. She tied Martha up in the unprotected corner of her inner enclosure and then she planted little baby apple trees and had a house built and sat down in it and waited.

And the King was almost happy. The creepy, crawly yellow caterpillars ate up Clover Hill – all except the little green crown on the top, where the apple trees were and the two red brick walls and the little house and the old woman.

The poor Queen went on seeing to the jam and the pickles and the blanket washing and the spring cleaning, and every now and then she would say to her husband –

'Fortunatas, my love, do you *really* think Miss Fitzroy Robinson is trustworthy? Shall we ever see our Daisy again?'

And the King would rumple his fair hair with his hands till it stuck out like cheese straws under his crown, and answer –

'My dear, you must be patient; you know we had the very highest references.'

Now one day the new yellow brick town the King had built had a delightful experience. Six handsome Princes on beautiful white horses came riding through the dusty little streets. The housings of their chargers shone with silver embroidery and gleaming glowing jewels, and their gold armour flashed so gloriously in the sun that all the little children clapped their hands, and the Princes' faces were so young and kind and handsome that all the old women said: 'Bless their pretty hearts!'

Now, of course, you will not need to be told that these six Princes were looking for the six grown-up Princesses who had been so happy at the Select Boarding Establishment. Their six Royal fathers, who lived many years' journey away on the other side of the world, and had not yet heard that the Princesses were mislaid, had given Miss Fitzroy Robinson's address to these Princes, and instructed them to marry the six Princesses without delay, and bring them home.

But when they got to the Select Boarding Establishment for the Daughters of Respectable Monarchs,
the house was closed, and a card was in the window,
saying that this desirable villa residence was to be let
on moderate terms, furnished or otherwise. The wax
fruit under the glass shade still showed attractively
through the dusty panes. The six Princes looked
through the window by turns. They were charmed
with the furniture, and the refining touch of a
woman's hand drew them like a magnet. They took
the house, but they had their meals at the Palace by
the King's special invitation.

King Fortunatus told the Princes the dreadful story
of the disappearance of the entire Select School; and
each Prince swore by his sword-hilt and his honour
that he would find out the particular Princess that he
was to marry, or perish in the attempt. For, of course,
each Prince was to marry one Princess, mentioned by
name in his instructions, and not one of the others.

The first night that the Princes spent in the furnished house passed quietly enough, so did the second
and the third and the fourth, fifth and sixth, but on
the seventh night, as the Princes sat playing spilikins
in the schoolroom, they suddenly heard a voice that
was not any of theirs. It said, 'Open up Africa!'

The Princes looked here, there, and everywhere –
but they could see no one. They had not been
brought up to the exploring trade, and could not
have opened up Africa if they had wanted to.

'Or cut through the Isthmus of Panama,' said the
voice again.

Now, as it happened, none of the six Princes were
engineers. They confessed as much.

'Cut up China, then!' said the voice, desperately.

'It's like the ghost of a Tory newspaper,' said one of the Princes.

And then suddenly they knew that the voice came from one of the pair of globes which hung in frames at the end of the schoolroom. It was the terrestrial globe.

'I'm inside,' said the voice; 'I can't get out. Oh, cut the globe – anywhere – and let me out. But the African route is the most convenient.'

Prince Primus opened up Africa with his sword, and out tumbled half a Professor of Magic.

'My other half's in there,' he said, pointing to the Celestial globe. 'Let my legs out, do –'

But Prince Secundus said, 'Not so fast,' and Prince Tertius said, 'Why were you shut up?'

'I was shut up for as pretty a bit of parlour-magic as ever you saw in all your born days,' said the top half of the Professor of Magic.

'Oh, you were, were you?' said Prince Quartus; 'well, your legs aren't coming out just yet. We want to engage a competent magician. You'll do.'

'But I'm not all here,' said the Professor.

'Quite enough of you,' said Prince Quintus.

'Now look here,' said Prince Sextus; 'we want to find our six Princesses. We can give a very good guess as to how they were lost; but we'll let bygones be bygones. You tell us how to find them, and after our weddings we'll restore your legs to the light of day.'

'This half of me feels so faint,' said the half Professor of Magic.

'What are we to do?' said all the Princes, threateningly; 'if you don't tell us, you shall never have a leg to stand on.'

'Steal apples,' said the half Professor, hoarsely, and fainted away.

They left him lying on the bare boards between the inkstained desks, and off they went to steal apples. But this was not so easy. Because Fortunatus Rex & Co. had built, and built, and built, and apples do not grow freely in those parts of the country which have been 'opened up' by speculative builders.

So at last they asked the little Prince Denis where he went for apples when he wanted them. And Denis said –

'The old woman at the top of Clover Hill has apples in her seven acres, and in her fifteen acres, but there's a fierce bulldog in the seven acres, and I've stolen all the apples in the fifteen acres myself.'

'We'll try the seven acres,' said the Princes.

'Very well,' said Denis; 'You'll be hanged if you're caught. So, as I put you up to it, I'm coming too, and if you won't take me, I'll tell. So there!'

For Denis was a most honourable little Prince, and felt that you must not send others into danger unless you go yourself, and he would never have stolen apples if it had not been quite as dangerous as leading armies.

So the Princes had to agree, and the very next night Denis let himself down out of his window by a knotted rope made of all the stockings his mother had knitted for him, and the grown-up Princes were waiting under the window, and off they all went to the orchard on the top of Clover Hill.

They climbed the wall at the proper corner, and Martha, the bulldog, who was very well-bred, and knew a Prince when she saw one, wagged her kinked tail respectfully and wished them good luck.

The Princes stole over the dewy orchard grass and looked at tree after tree: there were no apples on any of them.

Only at last, in the very middle of the orchard there was a tree with a copper trunk and brass branches, and leaves of silver. And on it hung seven beautiful golden apples.

So each Prince took one of the golden apples, very quietly, and off they went, anxious to get back to the half-Professor of Magic, and learn what to do next. No one had any doubt as to the half-Professor having told the truth; for when your legs depend on your speaking the truth you will not willingly tell a falsehood.

They stole away as quietly as they could, each with a gold apple in his hand, but as they went Prince Denis could not resist his longing to take a bite out of his apple. He opened his mouth very wide so as to get a good bite, and the next moment he howled aloud, for the apple was as hard as stone, and the poor little boy had broken nearly all his first teeth.

He flung the apple away in a rage, and the next moment the old woman rushed out of her house. She screamed. Martha barked. Prince Denis howled. The whole town was aroused, and the six Princes were arrested, and taken under a strong guard to the Tower. Denis was let off, on the ground of his youth, and, besides, he had lost most of his teeth, which is a severe punishment, even for stealing apples.

The King sat in his Hall of Justice next morning, and the old woman and the Princes came before him. When the story had been told, he said –

'My dear fellows, I hope you'll excuse me – the laws of hospitality are strict – but business is business after all. I should not like to have any constitutional unpleasantness over a little thing like this; you must all be hanged to-morrow morning.'

The Princes were extremely vexed, but they did not want to make a fuss. They asked to see Denis, and told him what to do.

So Denis went to the furnished house which had once been a Select Boarding Establishment for the Daughters of Respectable Monarchs. The door was locked, but Denis knew a way in, because his sister had told him all about it one holiday. He got up on the roof and walked down the schoolroom chimney.

There, on the schoolroom floor, lay half a Professor of Magic, struggling feebly, and uttering sad, faint squeals.

'What are we to do now?' said Denis.

'Steal apples,' said the half-Professor in a weak whisper. 'Do let my legs out. Slice up the Great Bear – or the Milky Way would be a good one for them to come out by.'

But Denis knew better.

'Not till we get the lost Princesses,' said he, 'now, what's to be done?'

'Steal apples I tell you,' said the half-Professor, crossly; 'seven apples – there – seven kisses. Cut them down. Oh go along with you, do. Leave me to die, you heartless boy. I've got pins and needles in my legs.'

Then off ran Denis to the Seven Acre Orchard at the top of Clover Hill, and there were the six princes hanging to the apple tree, and the hangman had gone home to his dinner, and there was no one else about. And the Princes were not dead.

Denis climbed up the tree and cut the Princes down with the penknife of the gardener's boy. (You will often find this penknife mentioned in your German exercises; now you know why so much fuss is made about it.)

The Princes fell to the ground, and when they recovered their wits Denis told them what he had done.

'Oh why did you cut us down?' said the Princes, 'we were having such happy dreams.'

'Well,' said Denis, shutting up the penknife of the gardener's boy, 'of all the ungrateful chaps!' And he turned his back and marched off. But they ran quickly after him and thanked him and told him how they had been dreaming of walking arm in arm with the most dear and lovely Princesses in the world.

'Well,' said Denis, 'it's no use dreaming about *them*. You've got your own registered Princesses to find, and the half-Professor says, "Steal apples."'

'There aren't any more to steal,' said the Princes – but when they looked, there were the gold apples back on the tree just as before.

So once again they eack picked one. Denis chose a different one this time. He thought it might be softer. The last time he had chosen the biggest apple – but now he took the littlest apple of all.

'Seven kisses!' he cried, and began to kiss the little gold apple.

Each Prince kissed the apple he held, till the sound of kisses was like the whisper of the evening wind in leafy trees. And, of course, at the seventh kiss each Prince found that he had in his hand not an apple, but the fingers of a lovely Princess. As for Denis, he had got his little sister Daisy, and he was so glad he promised at once to give her his guinea-pigs and his whole collection of foreign postage stamps.

'What is your name, dear and lovely lady?' asked Prince Primus.

'Sexta,' said his Princess. And then it turned out that every single one of the Princes had picked the wrong apple, so that each one had a Princess who was not the one mentioned in his letter of instructions. Secundus had plucked the apple that held Quinta, and Tertius held Quarta, and so on – and everything was as criss-cross-crooked as it possibly could be.

And yet nobody wanted to change.

Then the old woman came out of her house and looked at them and chuckled, and she said –

'You must be contented with what you have.'

'We *are*,' said all twelve of them, 'but what about our parents?'

'They must put up with your choice,' said the old woman, 'it's the common lot of parents.'

'I think you ought to sort yourselves out properly,' said Denis; 'I'm the only one who's got his right Princess – because I wasn't greedy. I took the smallest.'

The tallest Princess showed him a red mark on her arm, where his little teeth had been two nights before, and everybody laughed.

But the old woman said –

'They can't change, my dear. When a Prince has picked a gold apple that has a Princess in it, and has kissed it till she comes out, no other Princess will ever do for him, any more than any other Prince will ever do for her.'

While she was speaking the old woman got younger and younger and younger, till as she spoke

the last words she was quite young, not more than
fifty-five. And it was Miss Fitzroy Robinson!

Her pupils stepped forward one by one with
respectful curtsies, and she allowed them to kiss her
on the cheek, just as if it was breaking-up day.

Then, all together, and very happily, they went
down to the furnished villa that had once been the
Select School, and when the half-professor had
promised on his honour as a Magician to give up
Magic and take to a respectable trade, they took his
legs out of the starry sphere, and gave them back to
him; and he joined himself together, and went off
full of earnest resolve to live and die an honest
plumber.

'My talents won't be quite wasted,' said he; 'a little
hanky-panky is useful in most trades.'

When the King asked Miss Fitzroy Robinson to
name her own reward for restoring the Princesses,
she said –

'Make the land green again, your Majesty.'

So Fortunatus Rex & Co. devoted themselves to
pulling down and carting off the yellow streets they
had built. And now the country there is almost as
green and pretty as it was before Princess Daisy and
the six parlour-boarders were turned into gold
apples.

'It was very clever of dear Miss Fitzroy Robinson to
shut up that Professor in those two globes,' said the
Queen; 'it shows the advantage of having lessons
from the *best* Masters.'

'Yes,' said the King, 'I always say that you cannot go
far wrong if you insist on the highest references!'

*   *   *

E – for Edith – NESBIT was a writer of fantasy stories for younger readers during the early years of the last century. Her tales combining magic and the supernatural proved very influential on many later authors. Notable among these was J.K. Rowling with her books about Hogwarts Academy and its staff of magicians including Professor McGonagall and Madam Hooch who taught Harry Potter and his class to fly. Rather like Rowling – who has also chosen to use her initials on her stories rather than her Christian name – Edith Nesbit also started writing to support her young daughter. She used her own childhood experiences in a series of three books (written between 1899 and 1904) about the Bastable children: *The Story of the Treasure-Seekers, The Wouldbe-goods,* and *The New Treasure-Seekers.* There followed *The Phoenix and the Carpet* (1904) and *The Railway Children* (1906), which helped to make her famous and have since been filmed and adapted for television. Magic and magicians appear in quite a number of her other stories, especially *The House of Arden* (1908) in which a magic spell raises the wonderful little pig-like creature, the Mouldiwarp, who helps a group of children find some buried treasure, plus *The Magic City* (1910) and its sequel, *The Magic World* (1912).

DOCTOR CADAVEREZZI'S MAGIC SHOW

Philip Pullman

Dr Danti Cadaverezzi in his flowing robe covered with the signs of the zodiac is either a very clever magician or a bit of a charlatan. He comes from Italy, claims that he is a Doctor of Philosophy at the University of Rio de Janeiro, and boasts that his 'Cabinet of Wonders' covered with projections, handles, eyepieces and mystic signs is one of the marvels of the world. According to him it can produce a whole variety of magical, spiritual and artistic phenomena, the like of which cannot be seen anywhere else in the world. Cadaverezzi is presently on tour in Karlstein, a little village lying in the shadow of the castle of the evil Count Karlstein. The Doctor is about to give a performance on All Souls' Eve – the night when Zamiel, the terrifying Demon Huntsman and his pack of ghostly hounds, are on the prowl looking for victims – and a time when most sensible people are indoors. This account of the Doctor's performance at the Jolly Huntsman *is one of the most enthralling if also amusing descriptions of a magic show you will read anywhere . . .*

*　　*　　*

Doctor Cadaverezzi's performance was arranged for nine o'clock, and when the great old wooden clock in the packed inn ticked and lurched its way round to that time, the air of excitement was so thick you could hardly see through it – though that might have been the smoke from the bright China pipes many of the customers were smoking. Silent, red-faced men, with an air of huge secret enjoyment, as if they were in on a joke that no one else suspected; men from far away in clothes that looked like costumes from a play; stout, slow-moving men, like elderly bears; brisk, dark-featured men, like monkeys; men who couldn't speak a word of German and who had to point to what they wanted and mime and make faces to explain; men with pale faces from the great forests further north; men with sunburned faces and bright narrow eyes, from the snowy glare of the mountains – all of them come for the shooting contest, of course. And then there were the villagers: the raucous boys, Peter's pals, sharp and easy and full of themselves, flirting with Elise and Hannerl; wide-eyed children at their mothers' skirts; middle-aged men who sipped their wine and talked energetically with their fellows; older men who took great care to settle themselves comfortably in a corner and get their pipes going nicely, reckoning that the height of their present ambitions.

And when all this company had crowded into the packed inn – Elise and Hannerl at the back, tea towels flung over one shoulder, arms folded, and an attentive young huntsman beside each of them in case they should need an escort to find their way outside during any interval that Doctor Cadaverezzi might allow for, and finally Ma and me, standing on a table by the streaming window – when all this was ready and the show about to begin, I had the first of two surprises that came my way that night.

Because the inn door opened, and, preceded by the beaming, sneezing, hand-wiping form of Herr Arturo Snivelwurst, hair pomaded Napoleonically and drippy little nose bright cherry-red, came the dark, glowering figure of my late employer, Count Karlstein. And he looked up at me, standing close enough for me to spit in his eye if I'd cared to, and – bowed! There was a nasty air of ironical triumph about him, as distinctive as the odour of cloves about someone with the toothache. The company fell silent; those who knew him because they did, and those who didn't because something about him told them they ought to.

'Good evening,' he said in his rasping voice, that metallic tone that appeared when he was trying to be genial. 'I have heard of the wonders of this Doctor Cadaverezzi and I have come to patronize his performance.'

Snivelwurst was motioning to some of the audience to move aside, and within a minute or two Count Karlstein, with his sniffling, snuffling, sneezing secretary beside him, was seated and provided with wine.

Then Doctor Cadaverezzi, who must have been watching the whole thing from behind the curtain, began his performance.

First of all, a gong was struck – a mighty, Chinese sound, somehow accompanied by invisible dragons and the fumes of opium. Then the curtains were whisked aside, and there beside the Cabinet, lit by some garish and sinister light, was the doctor himself – bowing suavely and fixing his glittering eyes on, seemingly, everyone at once. There was a burst of applause that he'd done nothing to deserve except stand there and look impressive; but some people are like that – you'd sooner watch *them* clean their boots than anyone else walk a tightrope across a cage of hungry tigers. Magnetism – that's what it is.

He held up his hand, and the applause halted.

'My friends: you have no doubt seen many travelling players – fortune-tellers, threadbare actors pretending to be Harlequin or Julius Caesar or Hamlet – of course you have. Please do not confuse me with people of that sort. I have spent a lifetime in the lonely pursuit of knowledge; I have been privileged to serve many monarchs. I was physician to the Great Mogul in India, I was Privy Councillor to the noble Alfonso, King of Brazil. I have risked my life in exploring distant regions of the earth, where no traveller's foot had been set before. And the fruits of all my researches, the treasures I have spent my life assembling, are here in this mystic Cabinet!'

A gong sounded again; the audience was hushed. 'First,' said the doctor, 'I shall introduce you to my personal attendant from the world of spirits – a devil from Lapland. Springer, to me!' He snapped his fingers. There was a puff of smoke from the Cabinet, a loud whizzing sound, and something small and red and horny and whiskery flew out of one of the apertures in the Cabinet and landed neatly in his hand.

And then there came an interruption.

'Nothing but a doll on a spring!' sneered Count Karlstein. 'The man's a fraud!'

One or two of the men in the audience nodded. Doctor Cadaverezzi looked like thunder. I thought he was going to lose them for a moment; they're a hard bunch to please, as many players have found to their cost. But I didn't know Doctor Cadaverezzi.

Suddenly a smile of childlike innocence spread over his features, like a bubble of pure delight.

'Next,' he said, 'I shall show you a trick that has baffled audiences from Paris to Peru. Has anyone got a watch that I may borrow?'

'Yes! Yes!' shouted Count Karlstein. 'Use this one!'

Doctor Cadaverezzi pretended to be unwilling, but as no one else offered a watch, he had to take Count Karlstein's.

'You'll see,' said the count gleefully as Doctor Cadaverezzi made his way back to the front, 'he'll pretend to smash it. I've seen this trick before!'

Doctor Cadaverezzi held up a large red-spotted handkerchief and placed the watch inside it. 'Your watch is in here, my lord,' he said, wrapping it up.

'Of course it is!' said the count, enjoying himself hugely.

'Now I shall take this very heavy mallet,' said the doctor, holding it up, 'and smash the watch to pieces.'

'Go on, then!' called the count, laughing loudly. 'I know how it's done, Snivelwurst! I've seen Goldini do this. Yes, go on, smash it!'

'With your permission, then,' said Doctor Cadaverezzi politely, 'I shall strike your watch with the mallet and break it to pieces.'

'Go on, go on!' Count Karlstein waved impatiently. Doctor Cadaverezzi put the wrapped-up watch on a small table next to him and struck it several heavy blows with the mallet.

In between the blows, the count was explaining to the audience that the watch wasn't there at all – that it was up Cadaverezzi's sleeve and that he'd shortly produce it from the other side of the room or from someone's hat. Snivelwurst, by this time, was nodding and beaming and rubbing his hands at Cadaverezzi's coming discomfiture; and poor Ma, by my side, was almost beside herself with bitterness at Count Karlstein's spoilsport behavior.

Finally, when the handkerchief had been well and truly battered, Doctor Cadaverezzi almost humbly picked it up and carried it to Count Karlstein, who was now roaring with laughter.

'Your watch, my lord,' he said.

'Ha ha! My watch! You don't think I fell for that, do you?' cried Count Karlstein, He took the handkerchief and held it high, showing it to everyone. 'Let's have a look, then,' he said, and opened it up. His expression changed as he pulled out a string of cogs, springs, bits of broken glass and bent silver, and a long watch chain. 'What's this?' he demanded.

'Your watch, as I explained,' said Doctor Cadaverezzi. 'I said I was going to smash it, and these ladies and gentlemen will bear witness to the fact that you told me to go ahead and do it.'

Murmurs of agreement and nods came from the audience, who didn't like the count.

'But – but –'

'So that is just what I have done.' Doctor Cadaverezzi shrugged, with all the melancholy politeness in the world; but a sparkle in his eyes told me, and the rest of the audience, that he'd won this little contest.

And the best was yet to come. As Count Karlstein sat down angrily and turned to Snivelwurst, the doctor produced an identical red handkerchief from somewhere else and took out of it . . . Count Karlstein's watch! He looked at it with droll pride, slipped in into his breast pocket, and patted it with satisfaction. This little mime took only a second, but the audience saw it and roared with approving laughter – which only annoyed Count Karlstein the more, as he didn't know what they were laughing at.

And so Doctor Cadaverezzi moved on, having captured his audience completely. They all knew, now, that he was a trickster – that if you turned your back on him, he'd pick your pocket; but it didn't seem to matter, as they were all in a high good humour. And he did it so well, with such a delight in his own tricks, that you couldn't help but enjoy it. So now we saw what all the strange knobs and handles and levers on the Cabinet were for: this one, for instance, worked a device called the Chromoeido-phusikon, and Hans Pfafferl was shoved up out of the front row by his pals and made to press his face close to the eyepiece while Doctor Cadaverezzi turned a handle and a little windmill on top of the Cabinet revolved, and loud bangs and whizzing sounds and whistles came from inside. Hans was seeing, the doctor assured us, a clockwork representation of the Battle of Bodelheim, with musical, optical, and bal-listical effects – and when Hans staggered away from the Cabinet, his face was printed a medley of colours that made him look like a savage from one of the heathen lands Doctor Cadaverezzi claimed to have visited.

He didn't understand the laughter at all.

*   *   *

PHILIP PULLMAN has become one of the best-selling authors in the world with his sequence of novels, *Northern Lights* (1995), *The Subtle Knife* (1997) and *The Amber Spyglass* (2000) that form the trilogy known as *His Dark Materials*. The story of the epic quest of young Lyra and Eric is packed with magical figures – in particular the graceful witches who can fly beyond the Northern Lights – and has been described by the fantasy writer Terry Jones of *Monty Python* fame as 'one of the marvellous creations of fantastic literature'. Philip Pullman who lives in Oxford – and for years, like Roald Dahl, wrote his books in a shed at the bottom of his garden – has won numerous awards, including the Whitbread Book of the Year, and attracted a huge army of fans. This success is a world away from his early years as a middle school teacher in Oxford where it seems one of his pleasures was writing a school play each year. The story of Dr Cadaverezzi formed part of one of these dramas, *Count Karlstein*, and Philip Pullman remembers it with great affection – both for the cleverly constructed magical cabinet and the enthusiasm of all the pupils who took part. A scene that remains particularly etched in his memory concerns Ben Brandon, the boy who played Cadaverezzi:

At one point he was supposed to pull a string and out from the Cabinet of Wonders would fly a little demon who would shoot across the stage with a loud whizzing sound. In the final performance, Ben pulled the string – and nothing happened. With a beam of audacity, he turned to the audience and said, 'Of course, it is completely invisible to the foolish.'

THE MAGIC FISH-BONE

Charles Dickens

Grandmarina is a short-tempered, sharp-tongued old lady who dresses in rich silks and smells of lavender. Sometimes she refers to herself as a Good Fairy and there is no doubt she has the power to make herself invisible and cast spells for any children who are genuinely in need of her help. The family of King Watkins – nineteen children and always more on the way – are just the sort of people to attract her attention: in particular the eldest daughter, Alicia, who spends her life taking care of all her brothers and sisters. Grandmarina presents the girl with a salmon bone that she says must be polished until it shines like mother-of-pearl. It is a magic fish-bone and will satisfy any wish – but just one and only if wished for at the right time. What happens is full of surprises and those readers who have read Charles Dickens' novel, David Copperfield, *will probably see similarities between the talkative and improvident Mr Wilkins Micawber and his family and King Watkins' scatty clan.*

* * *

There was once a King, and he had a Queen, and he was the manliest of his sex, and she was the loveliest of hers. The King was, in his private profession, Under Government. The Queen's father had been a medical man out of town.

They had nineteen children, and were always having more. Seventeen of these children took care of the baby, and Alicia, the eldest, took care of them all. Their ages varied from seven years to seven months.

Let us now resume our story.

One day the King was going to the Office, when he stopped at the fishmonger's to buy a pound and a half of salmon not too near the tail, which the Queen (who was a careful housekeeper) had requested him to send home. Mr Pickles, the fishmonger, said, 'Certainly, sir, is there any other article, good morning.'

The King went on towards the Office in a melancholy mood, for Quarter Day was such a long way off, and several of the dear children were growing out of their clothes. He had not proceeded far, when Mr Pickles's errand-boy came running after him, and said, 'Sir, you didn't notice the old lady in our shop.'

'What old lady?' inquired the King. 'I saw none.'

Now, the King has not seen any old lady, because this old lady had been invisible to him, though visible to Mr Pickles's boy. Probably because he messed and splashed the water about to that degree, and flopped the pairs of soles down in that violent manner, that, if she had not been visible to him, he would have spoilt her clothes.

Just then the old lady came trotting up. She was dressed in shot-silk of the richest quality, smelling of dried lavender.

'King Watkins the First, I believe?' said the old lady.

'Watkins,' replied the King, 'is my name.'

'Papa, if I am not mistaken, of the beautiful Princess Alicia?' said the old lady.

'And of eighteen other darlings,' replied the King.

'Listen. You are going to the Office,' said the old lady.

It instantly flashed upon the King that she must be a Fairy, or how could she know that?

'You are right,' said the old lady, answering his thoughts, 'I am the Good Fairy Grandmarina. Attend. When you return home to dinner, politely invite the Princess Alicia to have some of the salmon you bought just now.'

'It may disagree with her,' said the King.

The old lady became so very angry at this absurd idea, that the King was quite alarmed, and humbly begged her pardon.

'We hear a great deal too much about this thing disagreeing and that thing disagreeing,' said the old lady, with the greatest contempt it was possible to express. 'Don't be greedy. I think you want it all yourself.'

The King hung his head under this reproof, and said he wouldn't talk about things disagreeing, any more.

'Be good then,' said the Fairy Grandmarina, 'and don't! When the beautiful Princess Alicia consents to partake of the salmon – as I think she will – you will find she will leave a fish-bone on her plate. Tell her to dry it, and to rub it, and to polish it till it shines like mother-of-pearl, and to take care of it as a present from me.'

'Is that all?' asked the King.

'Don't be impatient, sir,' returned the Fairy Grand-marina, scolding him severely, 'Don't catch people short, before they have done speaking. Just the way with you grown-up persons. You are always doing it.'

The King again hung his head, and said he wouldn't do so any more.

'Be good then,' said the Fairy Grandmarina, 'and don't! Tell the Princess Alicia, with my love, that the fish-bone is a magic present which can only be used once; but that it will bring her, that once, whatever she wishes for, PROVIDED SHE WISHES FOR IT AT THE RIGHT TIME. That is the message. Take care of it.'

The King was beginning, 'Might I ask the reason –?' When the Fairy became absolutely furious.

'*Will* you be good, sir?' she exclaimed, stamping her foot on the ground. 'The reason for this, and the reason for that, indeed! You are always wanting the reason. No reason. There! Hoity toity me! I am sick of your grown-up reasons.'

The King was extremely frightened by the old lady's flying into such a passion, and said he was very sorry to have offended her, and he wouldn't ask for reasons any more.

'Be good then,' said the old lady, 'and don't!'

With those words, Grandmarina vanished, and the King went on and on and on, till he came to the Office. There he wrote and wrote and wrote, till it was time to go home again. Then he politely invited the Princess Alicia, as the Fairy had directed him, to partake of the salmon. And when she had enjoyed it very much, he saw the fish-bone on her plate, as the Fairy had told him he would, and he delivered the Fairy's message, and the Princess Alicia took care to dry the bone, and to rub it, and to polish it till it shone like mother-of-pearl.

And so when the Queen was going to get up in the morning, she said, 'O dear me, dear me, my head, my head!' And then she fainted away.

The Princess Alicia, who happened to be looking in at the chamber door, asking about breakfast, was very much alarmed when she saw her Royal Mamma in this state, and she rang the bell for Peggy – which was the name of the Lord Chamberlain. But remembering where the smelling-bottle was, she climbed on a chair and got it, and after that she climbed on another chair by the bedside and held the smelling-bottle to the Queen's nose, and after that she jumped down and got some water, and after that she jumped up again and wetted the Queen's forehead, and, in short, when the Lord Chamberlain came in, that dear old woman said to the little Princess, 'What a Trot you are! I couldn't have done it better myself!'

But that was not the worst of the good Queen's illness. O no! She was very ill indeed, for a long time. The Princess Alicia kept the seventeen young Princes and Princesses quiet, and dressed and undressed and danced the baby, and made the kettle boil, and heated the soup, and swept the hearth, and poured out the medicine, and nursed the Queen, and did all that ever she could, and was as busy busy busy, as busy could be. For there were not many servants at that Palace, for three reasons; because the King was short of money, because a rise in his office never seemed to come, and because quarter-day was so far off that it looked almost as far off and as little as one of the stars.

But on the morning when the Queen fainted away, where was the magic fish-bone? Why, there it was in the Princess Alicia's pocket. She had almost taken it out to bring the Queen to life again, when she put it back, and looked for the smelling-bottle.

After the Queen had come out of her swoon that morning, and was dozing, the Princess Alicia hurried up stairs to tell a most particular secret to a most particularly confidential friend of hers, who was a Duchess. People did suppose her to be a Doll, but she was really a Duchess, though nobody knew it except the Princess.

This most particular secret was the secret about the magic fish-bone, the history of which was well known to the Duchess, because the Princess told her everything. The Princess kneeled down by the bed on which the Duchess was lying, full dressed and wide-awake, and whispered the secret to her. The Duchess smiled and nodded. People might have supposed that she never smiled and nodded, but she often did, though nobody knew it except the Princess.

Then the Princess Alicia hurried down stairs again, to keep watch in the Queen's room. She often kept watch by herself in the Queen's room; but every evening, while the illness lasted, she sat there watching with the King. And every evening the King sat looking at her with a cross look, wondering why she never brought out the magic fish-bone. As often as she noticed this, she ran up stairs, whispered the secret to the Duchess over again, and said to the Duchess besides, 'They think we children never have a reason or a meaning!' And the Duchess, though the most fashionable Duchess that ever was heard of, winked her eye.

'Alicia,' said the King, one evening when she wished him Good Night.

'Yes, Papa.'

'What has become of the magic fish-bone?'

'In my pocket, Papa.'

'I thought you had lost it?'

'O no, Papa!'

'Or forgotten it?'

'No, indeed, Papa!'

And so another time the dreadful little snapping pug-dog next door made a rush at one of the young Princes as he stood on the steps coming home from school, and terrified him out of his wits, and he put his hand through a pane of glass, and bled bled bled. When the seventeen other young Princes and Princesses saw him bleed bleed bleed, they were terrified out of their wits too, and screamed themselves black in their seventeen faces all at once. But the Princess Alicia put her hands over all their seventeen mouths, one after another, and persuaded them to be quiet because of the sick Queen. And then she put the wounded Prince's hand in a basin of fresh cold water, while they stared with their twice seventeen are thirty-four put down four and carry three eyes, and then she looked in the hand for bits of glass, and there were fortunately no bits of glass there. And then she said to two chubby-legged Princes who were sturdy though small, 'Bring me in the Royal rag-bag; I must snip and stitch and cut and contrive.' So those two young Princes tugged at the Royal rag-bag and lugged it in, and the Princess Alicia sat down on the floor with a large pair of scissors and a needle and thread, and snipped and stitched and cut and contrived, and made a bandage and put it on, and it fitted beautifully, and so when it was all done she saw the King her Papa looking on by the door.

'Alicia.'

'Yes, Papa.'

'What have you been doing?'

'Snipping stitching cutting and contriving, Papa.'

'Where is the magic fish-bone?'

'In my pocket, Papa.'

'I thought you had lost it?'

'O no, Papa!'

'Or forgotten it?'

'No, indeed, Papa!'

After that, she ran up stairs to the Duchess and told her what had passed, and told her the secret over again, and the Duchess shook her flaxen curls and laughed with her rosy lips.

Well! and so another time the baby fell under the grate. The seventeen young Princes and Princesses were used to it, for they were almost always falling under the grate or down the stairs, but the baby was not used to it yet, and it gave him a swelled face and a black eye. The way the poor little darling came to tumble was that he slid out of the Princess Alicia's lap just as she was sitting, in a great coarse apron that quite smothered her, in front of the kitchen fire, beginning to peel the turnips for the broth for dinner; and the way she came to be doing that was that the King's cook had run away that morning with her own true love, who was a very tall but very tipsy soldier. Then, the seventeen young Princes and Princesses, who cried at everything that happened, cried and roared. But the Princess Alicia (who couldn't help crying a little herself) quietly called to them to be still, on account of not throwing back the Queen up stairs, who was fast getting well, and said, 'Hold your tongues you wicked little monkeys, every one of you, while I examine baby!' Then she examined baby, and found that he hadn't broken anything, and she held cold iron to his poor dear eye, and smoothed his poor dear face, and he presently fell asleep in her arms. Then she said to the seventeen Princes and Princesses, 'I am afraid to lay him down yet, lest he should wake and feel pain, be good and you shall all be cooks.' They jumped for joy when they heard that, and began making themselves cooks' caps out of old newspapers. So to one she gave the salt-box, and to one she gave the barley, and to one she gave the herbs, and to one she gave the turnips, and to one she gave the carrots, and to one she gave the onions, and to one she gave the spice-box, till they were all cooks, and all running about at work, she sitting in the middle, smothered in the great coarse apron, nursing baby. By and by the broth was done, and the baby woke up, smiling like an angel, and was trusted to the sedatest Princess to hold, while the other Princes and Princesses were squeezed into a far-off corner to look at the Princess Alicia turning out the saucepan-full of broth, for fear (as they were always getting into trouble) they should get splashed and scalded. When the broth came tumbling out, steaming beautifully, and smelling like a nosegay good to eat, they clapped their hands. That made the baby clap his hands; and that, and his looking as if he had a comic toothache, made all the Princes and Princesses laugh. So the Princess Alicia said, 'Laugh and be good, and after dinner we will make him a nest on the floor in a corner, and he shall sit in his nest and see a dance of eighteen cooks.' That delighted the young Princes and Princesses, and they ate up all the broth, and washed up all the plates and dishes, and cleared away, and pushed the table into a

corner, and then they in their cooks' caps, and the
Princess Alicia in the smothering coarse apron that
belonged to the cook that had run away with her own
true love that was the very tall but very tipsy soldier,
danced a dance of eighteen cooks before the angelic
baby, who forgot his swelled face and his black eye,
and crowed with joy.

And so then, once more the Princess Alicia saw
King Watkins the First, her father, standing in the
doorway looking on, and he said: 'What have you
been doing, Alicia?'

'Cooking and contriving, Papa.'

'What else have you been doing, Alicia?'

'Keeping the children light-hearted, Papa.'

'Where is the magic fish-bone, Alicia?'

'In my pocket, Papa.'

'I thought you had lost it?'

'O no, Papa!'

'Or forgotten it?'

'No, indeed, Papa!'

The King then sighed so heavily, and seemed so
low-spirited, and sat down so miserably, leaning his
head upon his hand, and his elbow upon the kitchen
table pushed away in the corner, that the seventeen
Princes and Princesses crept softly out of the kitchen,
and left him alone with the Princess Alicia and the
angelic baby.

'What is the matter, Papa?'

'I am dreadfully poor, my child.'

'Have you no money at all, Papa?'

'None, my child.'

'Is there no way left of getting any, Papa?'

'No way,' said the King. 'I have tried very hard, and
I have tried all ways.'

When she heard those last words, the Princess Alicia began to put her hand into the pocket where she kept the magic fish-bone.

'Papa,' said she, 'when we have tried very hard, and tried all ways, we must have done our very very best?'

'No doubt, Alicia.'

'When we have done our very very best, Papa, and that is not enough, then I think the right time must have come for asking help of others.' This was the very secret connected with the magic fish-bone, which she had found out for herself from the good fairy Grandmarina's words, and which she had so often whispered to her beautiful and fashionable friend the Duchess.

So she took out of her pocket the magic fish-bone that had been dried and rubbed and polished till it shone like mother-of-pearl, and she gave it one little kiss and wished it was quarter-day. And immediately it *was* Quarter-Day, and the King's quarter's salary came rattling down the chimney, and bounced into the middle of the floor.

But this was not half of what happened, no not a quarter, for immediately afterwards the good fairy Grandmarina came riding in, in a carriage and four (Peacocks), with Mr Pickles's boy up behind, dressed in silver and gold, with a cocked-hat, powdered hair, pink silk stockings, a jewelled cane, and a nosegay. Down jumped Mr Pickles's boy with his cocked-hat in his hand and wonderfully polite (being entirely changed by enchantment), and handed Grandmarina out, and there she stood, in her rich shot-silk smelling of dried lavender, fanning herself with a sparkling fan.

'Alicia, my dear,' said this charming old Fairy, 'how do you do, I hope I see you pretty well, give me a kiss.'

The Princess Alicia embraced her, and then Grandmarina turned to the King, and said rather sharply: 'Are you good?'

The King said he hoped so.

'I suppose you know the reason, *now*, why my god-Daughter here,' kissing the Princess again, 'did not apply to the fish-bone sooner?' said the Fairy.

The King made her a shy bow.

'Ah! But you didn't *then*!' said the Fairy.

The King made her a shyer bow.

'Any more reasons to ask for?' said the Fairy.

The King said no, and he was very sorry.

'Be good then,' said the Fairy, 'and live happy ever afterwards.'

Then, Grandmarina waved her fan, and the Queen came in most splendidly dressed, and the seventeen young Princes and Princesses, no longer grown out of their clothes, came in, newly fitted out from top to toe, with tucks in everything to admit of its being let out. After that, the Fairy tapped the Princess Alicia with her fan, and the smothering coarse apron flew away, and she appeared exquisitely dressed, like a little Bride, with a wreath of orange-flowers, and a silver veil. After that, the kitchen dresser changed of itself into a wardrobe, made of beautiful woods and gold and looking-glass, which was full of dresses of all sorts, all for her and all exactly fitting her. After that, the angelic baby came in, running alone, with his face and eye not a bit the worse but much the better. Then, Grandmarina begged to be introduced to the

Duchess, and when the Duchess was brought down many compliments passed between them.

A little whispering took place between the Fairy and the Duchess, and then the Fairy said out loud, 'Yes. I thought she would have told you.' Grandmarina then turned to the King and Queen, and said, 'We are going in search of Prince Certainpersonio. The pleasure of your company is requested at church in half an hour precisely.' So she and the Princess Alicia got into the carriage, and Mr Pickles's boy handed in the Duchess who sat by herself on the opposite seat, and then Mr Pickles's boy put up the steps and got up behind, and the Peacocks flew away with their tails spread.

Prince Certainpersonio was sitting by himself, eating barley-sugar and waiting to be ninety. When he saw the Peacocks followed by the carriage coming in at the window, it immediately occurred to him that something uncommon was going to happen.

'Prince,' said Grandmarina, 'I bring you your Bride.'

The moment the Fairy said those words, Prince Certainpersonio's face left off being sticky, and his hair curled, and a cap and feather flew in like a bird and settled on his head. He got into the carriage by the Fairy's invitation, and there he renewed his acquaintance with the Duchess whom he had seen before.

In the church were the Prince's relations and friends, and the Princess Alicia's relations and friends, and the seventeen Princes and Princesses, and the baby, and a crowd of neighbors. The marriage was beautiful beyond expression. The Duchess was bridesmaid, and beheld the ceremony from the pulpit where she was supported by the cushion of the desk.

Grandmarina gave a magnificent wedding feast afterwards, in which there was everything and more to eat, and everything and more to drink. The wedding cake was delicately ornamented with white satin ribbons, frosted silver and white lilies, and was forty-two yards round.

When Grandmarina had drunk her love to the young couple, and Prince Certainpersonio had made a speech, and everybody had cried Hip Hip Hip Hurrah! Grandmarina announced to the King and Queen that in future there would be eight Quarter-Days in every year, except in a leap-year, when there would be ten. She then turned to Certainpersonio and Alicia, and said, 'My dears, you will have thirty-five children, and they will all be good and beautiful. Seventeen of your children will be boys, and eighteen will be girls. The hair of the whole of your children will curl naturally. They will never have the measles, and will have recovered from the whooping-cough before being born.'

On hearing such good news, everybody cried out 'Hip Hip Hip Hurrah!' again.

'It only remains,' said Grandmarina in conclusion, 'to make an end of the fish-bone.'

So she took it from the hand of the Princess Alicia, and it instantly flew down the throat of the dreadful little snapping pug-dog next door and choked him, and he expired in convulsions.

*   *   *

CHARLES DICKENS is one of the most famous of all British authors and among his many books – of which a number were written especially for younger readers – there are several with fantasy themes that have been influential on modern writers including Philip Pullman and J.K. Rowling. Ghost stories are, in fact, to be found in the pages of his earliest success, *Pickwick Papers* (1836–7), while *A Christmas Carol* (1843) with its gripping account of the haunting of Ebenezer Scrooge by the spirits of Christmas past, present and future has been a favourite with every generation of younger readers. The best of Dickens' fantasy fiction is to be found in the omnibus volume, *Christmas Books*, published in 1852. 'The Magic Fish-bone' was first published in 1858 in an American magazine, *Our Young Folks*, with Dickens signing it as the work of 'Miss Alice Rainbird, Aged 7'. I think it brilliantly captures the working of a young mind, but is also rather intriguing because when the author wrote it *he* had a sick wife, ten children and was also desperate for money!

THE MAGICIAN OF KARAKOSK

Peter S. Beagle

Lanak does not look anything like a traditional wizard, although people say he is a magician 'too good at magic'. He is short, thickset and going bald, but he has kind eyes and strong, friendly hands. Lanak was born the son of a peasant in the town of Karakosk and was still only a child when he realised that he possessed special powers. From the simple magic of making his father's beer stronger or calming a stallion that has been stung, he graduated to getting horses working twice as hard, orchards doubling their fruit yield and even stopping the snow so that spring came early to his little community. Unlike most wizards – who live alone – Lanak has taken a wife and is dedicated to using his powers to help his neighbours. But when the Queen hears of his talent and decides he must be her personal wizard, Lanak realises that he will need all the power at his command to prevent his simple life being changed for ever . . .

*   *   *

What, what – is it my turn? No, I was not asleep – I would never be so unmannerly as to doze off when someone else was telling a story. I was thinking only, thinking about how long it has been since I sat like this with friends – oh, with anyone, really – listening to wonders and sillinesses and wonders again by firelight. I have lived an odd sort of life, and I am afraid that it has left me with little to tell that would not bore the young ones here and antagonize the old; and I would not do either tonight for worlds. You must indulge me – I promise to keep the tale short, and leave plenty of evening for Gri and Chashi and Mistress Kydra here. I am as eager as anyone else to be done with my rambling mumbles.

Well, then. Once, a very long time ago, in the land I come from, there was a magician who was too good at magic. Ah, you stare, you look at each other, you snicker, but it's so – it is quite possible to be too good at anything, and especially magic. Consider – if you only need a gentle shower to restore your thirsty fields, what good is a wizard who can bring nothing but storms that will wash them away? If you ask for a little kitchen charm to keep your man faithful, what's the use of a spell that will have him underfoot and at your heel every hour of every day, until you could scream for a single moment to yourself? No, no, when it comes to magic, give me a humble medi-ocrity, always. Believe me, I know what I am saying.

Now the magician of whom I speak was a humble man in every way. He was of low birth, the son of a *rishu*-herder, and although he gave evidence of his abilities quite young, as most wizards do, there was never any possibility of his receiving the proper training in its use. Even if he could have had access to the teaching scrolls of Am-Nemil or Kirisinja, such as are preserved in the great thaumaturgic library at Cheth na'Bata, I much doubt that he could even have read them. He was a peasant with a gift, nothing more. His name was Lanak.

What did he look like? Well, if your notion of a magician is someone tall, lean, and commanding, swirling a black cape around his shoulders, you would have been greatly disappointed in Lanak. He was short and thickset, like all the men of his family, with their tendency to early baldness, I am afraid. But he had nice eyes, or so I have heard, and quite good manners, and large, friendly brown hands.

I repeat, because it is important: this Lanak was a humble man with no high dreams at all – most unusual in a wizard of any origin. He lived in Karakosk, a town notable only for its workhorses and its black beer, which suited our Lanak down to the ground, as you might say, for he understood both of those good creatures in his bones. In fact, the first spell he ever attempted successfully was one to strengthen his father's rather watery home brew, and the second was to calm a stallion maddened by the pain of a sand-spider bite. Left to himself, he'd likely never have asked to do anything grander than that with his magical gift. Spending his life as a town conjuror, no different from the town baker or cobbler – aye, that would have suited him right down to the ground.

But magic has a way of not leaving you to yourself, by its own nature. Magic has an ambition to be used, even if you don't. Our Lanak went along happily for many years, liked and respected by all who knew him – he even married a Karakosk woman, and I can count on the fingers of one hand those wizards who have ever wed. They simply do *not*; wizards live immensely alone, and there it is. But Lanak never really thought of himself as a wizard, you see. Lanak thought of himself as a Karakosk man, nothing more.

And if his talent had been as modest as he, likely enough he would have spent his life in perfect tranquility, casting his backyard spells over fields, gardens, ovens, finding strayed children and live-stock impartially, blessing marriage beds and melon beds alike – and yes, why not? bringing a bit of rain now and then. But it was not to be.

He was simply too good. Do you begin to under-stand me now? The colicky old horses he put his hands on and whispered to did not merely recover – they became twice the workers they had been in their prime, as the orchards he enchanted bore so much fruit that the small farmers of Karakosk found them-selves exporting to cities like Bitava, Leishai, even Fors na'Shachim, for the first time in the town's history. There was a hard winter, I remember, when Lanak cast a spell meant only to ease the snowfall, just for the children, so their shoes would last longer – and what was the result? Spring came to Karakosk a good two months before a single green shoot stuck up its head anywhere else in the entire land. This is the sort of thing that gets itself noticed.

And noticed it was, first by the local warlord – I forget his name, it will come to me in a moment – who swept down on Karakosk one day with his scabby troop at his heels. You know the sort, you doubtless have a Night Visitor or a Protector of your own, am I right in that? Aye, well, then you've an idea what it was like for Karakosk when their particular bravo and his gang came swaggering into the market square months before their yearly tribute was due. There were close on forty of them: all loud, stupid and brutal, except for their commander, who was not stupid, but made up for it by being twice as brutal as the rest. His name was Bourjic, I remember now.

Well, this Bourjic demanded to see the great wizard folk had been telling him about; and when the townspeople appeared reluctant to fetch their Lanak on a bandit's whim, he promptly snatched the headman's little son up to his saddle and threatened to cut his throat on the spot if someone didn't produce a wizard in the next five minutes. There was nothing for it – Bourjic had made similar threats in the past, and carried them all through – so the headman himself ran to the very edge of town to find Lanak in his barn, where he was once more redesigning his firework display for the Thieves' Day festival. Lanak's fireworks were the pride of the region for twenty miles around, but he was forever certain that he could improve them with just a little effort.

When he understood the danger to the headman's son, he flushed red as a *taiya*-bush with outrage. Rather pink-faced as he was by nature, no one had ever seen him turn just that shade of redness before. He put his arm around the headman's shoulders, spoke three words – and there they were in the market square, face-to-face with a startled Bourjic trying to control his even more startled horse. Bourjic said, 'Hey!' and the horse said, '*Wheee!*' and Lanak said the little boy's name and one other word. The boy vanished from Bourjic's saddle and reappeared in his father's arms, none the worse for the experience, and the spoiled envy of all his schoolmates for the next six months. Lanak set his hands on his hips and waited for Bourjic's horse to calm down.

I've told you that Bourjic's men were all as stupid as gateposts? Yes, well, one of them cranked up his crossbow and let a quarrel fly straight for Lanak's left eye, as he was bending over the boy to make certain that he was unharmed. Lanak snatched the bolt out of the air without looking up, kissed it – of all things to do – and hurled it back at Bourjic's man, where it whipped around his neck like a noose and clung very tight indeed. Not tight enough to strangle, but enough so that he fell off his horse and lay there on the ground kicking and croaking. Bourjic looked down at him once, and not again.

'The very fellow I wanted to see,' says he with a wide, white smile. Bourjic was a gentleman born, after all, and had a bit of manners when it suited him. He said now, 'I've grand news for you, young Lanak. You're to come straightway to the castle and work for me.'

Lanak answered him, 'I'm not young, and your castle is a tumbledown hogpen, and I work for the folk of Karakosk and no one beside. Leave us now.'

Bourjic reached for his sword hilt, but checked himself, keeping that smile strapped onto his face. 'Let us talk,' he said. 'It seems to me that if *I* were offered a choice between life as a nobleman's personal wizard and seeing my town, my fields, my friends all burned to blowing ashes – well, I must say I might be a bit more inclined toward seeing reason. Of course, that's just me.'

Lanak nodded toward the man writhing in the dirt. Bourjic laughed down at him. 'Ah, but that has just made me want you more, you see. And I simply must have what I want, that's why I am what I am. So float up here behind me, or magic yourself up a horse, whichever you choose, and let's be on our way.'

Lanak shook his head and turned away. Bourjic said nothing more, but there came a sound behind him that made Lanak wheel round instantly, It was the sound of forty men striking flint against steel at once and setting light to tallow-stiff torches they'd had ready at their saddles. The townsfolk looking on gasped and wailed; a few bravely, hopelessly, picked up clods to throw. But Lanak fixed his mild, washed-out-looking blue eyes on Bourjic and said only, 'I told you to leave us.'

'And so indeed I shall,' the warlord answered him cheerfully. 'With you or without you. The decision is yours for another ten seconds.'

Lanak stood fast. Bourjic sighed ostentatiously and said, 'So be it, then.' He turned in the saddle to signal his men.

'Get back,' Lanak said to the folk of Karakosk. They scrambled to obey him, as Bourjic's grinning soldiers raised their torches. Lanak folded his arms, bowed deeply – to the earth itself, as it seemed – and began to sing what sounded like no more than a nonsensical nursery rhyme. Bourjic, suddenly alarmed, shouted to his men, 'Burn! Now!'

But even as he uttered those two words, the ground before him began to heave and stretch itself and grumble, like an old man finally deciding to throw off his quilt and get out of bed. Where it stretched, it split, and some bits fell in and down and deep out of sight, and other bits swelled right up to the height of storm waves heading for shore. Bourjic's horse reared and danced back from the chasm that has just opened between him and Lanak,

while all his men fought to control their own terrified beasts, and the folk of Karakosk clung to their
children, to each other, to anything that seemed at
all solid. The earth went on splitting, left and right,
as though it were shedding its skin: raw red canyons
were opening everywhere, and you could see fire
crawling away and away in their depths. Shops and
houses all around the square were toppling, bursting
apart, and the angry, juddering, groaning sound kept
getting louder, louder. Lanak himself covered his
ears.

Bourjic and his lot crumbled like dry cheese. They
yanked their horses' heads round and were gone, a
good bit faster than they'd come, and it was hard to
say who was doing the more screaming, man or
mount. The ground began to quiet, by little and
little, as soon as they were out of sight, and the
townsfolk were amazed to see the fearful wounds in
the earth silently closing before their eyes, the scars
healing without a trace, the buildings somehow float-
ing back together, and the Karakosk market square
demurely returning to the dusty, homely patch of
ground it had always been. And there stood Lanak in
the middle of it, stamping out a few smoldering
torches, wiping his forehead, blowing his nose.

'There,' he said. 'There. Nothing but an illusion,
as you see, but one that should keep friend Bourjic
well clear of us for some while. Glad to be of help, I'll
be off home now.' He started away; then glanced
around at his dumbstruck neighbors and repeated,
'An illusion, that's all. No more. The fireworks, now,
those are real.'

But the citizens of Karakosk had all seen one of
Bourjic's soldiers – the one with the crossbow quarrel

wrapped so snugly around his neck – plummet straight down into a bottomless crevasse that opened where he lay, and that closed over him a moment later. And if *that* was an illusion, you could never have proved it by that man.

As I'm sure you can well imagine, the whole business made things even more difficult for poor Lanak. Bourjic was probably as interested as he in keeping the story from getting around; but get around it did, and it was heard in towns and cities a long way from black-beer Karakosk. Sirit Byar made a song out of it, I think. Lissi Jair did, I know that much – a good song, too. There were others.

And the Queen, in her black castle in Fors na'Shachim, heard them all.

None of you know much about the Queen in Fors, do you? No, I thought not, and no reason why you should. Well, there is always a Queen, which really means little more than the hereditary ruler of Fors na'Shachim itself and a scatter of surrounding provinces and towns – including Karakosk – and even particular manors. Most of the Queens have proved harmless enough over the years; one of two have been surprisingly benign and visionary, and a very few have turned out plain wicked. The one I speak of, unfortunately, was one of those last.

Which does not mean that she was a stupid woman. On the contrary, she was easily the cleverest Queen Fors na'Shachim has ever had, and it is quite an old city. She listened to new songs as intently as she did to the words of her ministers and her spies; and it is told that she walked often among her subjects in various guises, and so learned many things that many would have kept from her. And when she had heard enough ballads about the wizard Lanak of little Karakosk, she said to her greatest captain, the Lord Durgh, 'That one. Get him for me.'

Well now, this Durgh was no fool himself, and he had heard the songs, too. He'd no mind at all to have as many people laughing and singing about *his* humiliation by some bumpkin trickster as were still laughing at Bourjic. So when he went down to Karakosk, he went unarmed, with only two of his most closemouthed lieutenants for company. He asked politely to be directed to the home of a gentleman named Lanak, and rode there slowly enough to let the rumors of his arrival and destination reach the house before he did. He'd been born in the country himself, Lord Durgh had.

And when he was at last facing Lanak in the wizard's front garden, he got off his horse and bowed formally to him, and made his men do so, too. He said, 'Sir, I am come to you from the Queen on a mission of grave urgency for the realm. Will it please you to attend on her?'

Yes, of course, it was a trick, and all of us here would doubtless have seen through it instantly. But no high personage had ever spoken to Lanak in such a humble manner before. He asked only, 'May I be told Her Majesty's need?' to which Lord Durgh replied, 'I am not privileged to know such things,' which was certainly true. Then Lanak bowed in his turn, and went into his house to tell Dwyla, his wife, that he had been summoned to the Queen's aid and would return in plenty of time for the Priests' Moon, which is when the folk around Karakosk do their spring sowing. Dwyla packed the few garments he requested and kissed him farewell, making him promise to bring their little daughter something pretty from Fors.

There's been a new road cut long since, but it is still three hard-riding days from the market square at Karakosk to the black castle. Durgh made a diffident half-suggestion that the wizard might like to call up a wind to whisk them there instantly, but Lanak said it would frighten the horses. He rode pillion behind Lord Durgh, and enjoyed the journey immensely, however the others felt about it. You must remember, Lanak had never been five miles from Karakosk in his life.

Trotting over his first real cobblestones in the streets of Fors na'Shachim, he almost disjointed his neck turning it in every direction, this gawking peasant who could chase away winter and make the earth rend itself under bandits' feet. He was so busy memorizing everything he saw for Dwyla's benefit – the marketplace as big as his entire town; the legendary Glass Orchard; divisions of the Queen's household guard in their silver livery wheeling right about and saluting as the Lord Durgh cantered by – that the black castle was looming over him before he realized that they had arrived. He did, however, notice Lord Durgh's poorly concealed sigh of relief as they dismounted and gave their horses over to the grooms.

Does anyone here know Fors at all, by any chance? Ah, your father did, Mistress Kydra? Well, I'm sure it hadn't changed much from Lanak's time when your father saw it, nor would it be greatly different today. Fors na'Shachim never really changes. For all its color, for all the bustle, the musicians and tumblers and dancers on every corner, the sharpers and the alley girls, the street barrows where you can buy anything from *namph* still wet from the fields to steaming lamprey pies – those *are* good – for all that, as I say, one never truly escapes the taste of iron underneath, of dutiful abandon working overtime to mask the cold face of power. And even if that power casts no shadow beyond the city gates, I can assure you that it is real enough in Fors na'Shachim. I have been there often enough to know.

But Lanak had never been to Fors, and he was thrilled enough for any dozen bumpkins to be marching up those obsidian stairs with Lord Durgh's hand closed gently enough just above his left elbow, and all those silver-clad men-at-arms falling in behind them. He was not taken directly to see the Queen – no one ever is. Indeed, that's rather the whole point of being Queen, as you might say. There have been those who forced their way into the presence, mind you; but these were a different sort of people from our modest Lanak. Most of them ended quite differently, too.

Lanak was perfectly content to be shown to his quarters in what used to be called the Hill Tower because you can just make out the haze over the Ghost Range from the upper windows. They call it the Wizard's Tower now. There was food and drink and hot water waiting, and he used the time to wash, change from his grimy traveling clothes into something more suitable for meeting the Queen, and then to begin a long letter to Dwyla at home. He was still hard at it that evening when Lord Durgh came to fetch him.

What is the black castle really like? Well, it is as

grand as you imagine, Hramath, but perhaps not exactly in the *way* you imagine. It began as a fortress, you know, in the old times when Fors was nothing more than a military outpost; which is why it is black, being mostly built of dressed *almuri* stone from the quarries near Chun. Every queen for the last five hundred years has tried in turn to make the castle a bit more luxurious for herself, if no less forbidding to her subjects: so there are a great many windows and rich carpets, and countness chandeliers, even in places where you would never expect more than a rushlight. There is always music, and always sounding just at your shoulder, even if the players are a dozen galleries distant – that's a trick of *almuri*, no other stone does that. And of course the walls of every room and every corridor are hung with real paintings, not merely the usual rusty shields and pieces of armor – and the paintings are done on real cloth and canvas, not bark or raw wood, as we do here. The food and wine served to the Queen's guests is the best to be had south of the Durli Hills; the ladies of her court have Stimezst silk for their everyday wear; the beds are almost too comfortable for comfort, if you understand me. Oh, you would want for nothing you know how to dream of in the black castle at Fors, Hramath.

Even so, just like the city itself, it is always the stone fortress it always was, with the Silver Guard never more than a room away, and Lanak was not bumpkin enough to miss that for long. Not that he was especially on his guard when Lord Durgh bowed him into the Queen's presence – perhaps what I mean is that he was attempting from the first to see his marvelous adventure through his wife's eyes, and

Dwyla was a shrewd countrywoman who missed very little. Wizard or no, he did well to marry her, Lanak did.

Yes, yes, yes, the Queen. She received Lanak in her most private chambers, with no one in attendance but Lord Durgh himself, and she packed *him* off on some errand or other before Lanak had finished bowing. I am told that she was quite a small woman, daintily made, with a great deal of dark hair, a sweetly curved mouth, skin as smooth as water, and eyes as shiny and cold as the gleaming black walls of her castle. She seemed no older than Lanak himself, but of course you never know with queens.

Well, then. She greeted Lanak most royally and courteously, even saying to him with an appealing air of shyness, 'Sir, I have never received a great wizard in these rooms before. You must pardon me if I hardly know how to behave.'

Those were her very words, as I was told them, and of course she could have said nothing more calculated to reach the heart of Lanak, who really *was* shy. He swallowed hard several times, finally managing to reply, 'Majesty, I am no great wizard, but only a journeyman from a town of journeymen. As honored as I am, I cannot imagine why you have summoned me, who have your pick of masters.'

And he meant it, and the Queen could see that he meant it, and she smiled the way a cat smiles in its sleep. She said, 'Indeed, I must confess that I have made some small study of wizards. I know very well who the masters in this realm are, and who the journeymen – every one – and which lay claim to mastery who would be hard put to turn cream into butter. And nowhere have I heard tales to equal the word I have of you, good Lanak. Without even stirring from your dear little town whose name I keep forgetting, you have become the envy of magicians whose names I am sure you cannot know. What have you to say of that, I wonder?'

Lanak did not know at all what to say. He looked at his hands, stared away at the pale-rose canopy over the Queen's bed, and finally mumbled, 'I think it is no good thing to be envied. if what you tell me is true, it distresses me greatly, but I cannot believe it is so. How could a Rhyssa, a K'Shas, a Tombry Dar envy Lanak of Karakosk? You are mistaken, Majesty, surely.'

'Queens are never mistaken,' the Queen answered him, 'as even great wizards must remember.' But she went on smiling kindly and thoughtfully at Lanak. 'Well, I will test your skill then, though for your reassurance, not my own. The water of my domain is not of the best, as you know.'

Lanak did know. As you here cannot, even the oldest among us. In the time of which I tell you, the water of Fors na'Shachim and the country round about was renowned for its bitterness. It was not vile enough to be undrinkable, nor foul enough to cause sickness or plague, but it tasted like copper coins and harness polish, with a slight touch of candle wax. Clothes washed in any stream turned a pale, splotchy yellow which came quickly to identify their owners to amused outsiders; indeed, citizens of Fors were often referred to as 'pissbreeches' in those days. The term is still used now and then, even today, though no one in the city could tell you why.

The Queen said, 'I have requested several wizards to improve the water of Fors na'Shachim. I will not embarrass such an unassuming man by revealing their names. Suffice it to say that not one succeeded, though all proved most wondrously gifted at vanishing when I showed my displeasure.' She leaned forward and touched Lanak's rough brown hand. 'I am confident that it will be quite otherwise with you.'

Lanak answered helplessly, 'I will do my best, Majesty. But I fear sorely that I will disappoint you, like my colleagues.'

'Then I hope you are at least their equal at disappearing,' the Queen replied. She laughed, to show him that this was meant humorously, and stood up to indicate that the interview was at an end. As Lanak was backing out of the room (Dwyla had read somewhere about the proper way to take leave of royalty), she added, 'Sleep well, good friend. For myself, I will certainly be awake all night, imagining my subjects' surprise and pleasure when they brew their afternoon tea tomorrow.'

But Lanak never even lay down in the grand, soft bed which had been prepared for him. He paced his room in the moonlight, trying as hard as he could to imagine which magicians had already tried their skills on For's water, and which charms they might have attempted. For there is a common language of magic, you know, just as there is in music: it is the one particular singer, the one particular *chayad*-player, the one particular wizard who makes the difference in the song or the spell. Lanak walked in circles, muttering to himself, that whole night, and at last he stood very still, staring blankly out of the window at the dark courtyard below. And when morning came, he ate the handsome breakfast that the Queen's own butler had brought to him, washed it down with the eyewash that still passes for ale in Fors, then belched comfortably, leaned back in his chair, and turned the water of the realm sweeter than any to be found without crossing an ocean. And so it remains to this day, though apparently he could do nothing with the ale.

The Queen was mightily pleased. She brought Lanak out on a high balcony and embarrassed him immensely by showing him to her fold as the wonder-worker who had done for them what the mightiest sorcerers in all the land had incessantly promised and failed to do. They cheered him deliriously, celebrated him all that day and the next, and were generally useless as subjects until the Silver Guard harried them back to work. Most of that last was done out of Lanak's sight, but not all.

'There,' said the Queen. 'Have you not satisfied yourself now that you are wizard enough to serve me?'

But Lanak said, 'Majesty, it was merely my good fortune that I understand water. Water, in its nature, does not like to feel itself foul; it recoils from its own taste as much as you do. All I needed to do was to *become* the water of Fors na'Shachim, to feel my way down into the source of its old bitterness and become that too. Your other wizards cannot have been country people, or they would have known this, too. In the country, spells and glamours are the very least of magic – understanding, becoming what you understand, that is all of it, truly. My Queen, you need a wizard who will understand the world of queens, ministers, captains, campaigns. Forgive me, I am not that man.'

'Do not speak to me of my needs,' the Queen answered him, and her tone was hard for the first time. 'Speak of my desires, as I bid you.' But she quickly hid her impatience and patted Lanak's hand again. She said, 'Very well, then, very well, let me set you one last unnecessary test. It is known to be beyond any doubt that three high officers of my incorruptible Silver Guard are in the pay of a foreign lord whose name does not matter. I cannot prove this, but *that* would not matter' – and she showed just the tops of her teeth – 'if I but knew who they were. Find these traitors out for me, simple country Lanak, and be assured forever of my favor.'

Now even in Karakosk, Lanak had resisted all efforts to make him, with his magical talents, a sheriff, a constable, a thief-taker. He wanted no part of the Queen's request, but even he could see that there was no courteous way to decline without offending her hospitality. So he said at last, 'So be it, but give me the night once again to take counsel with my spirits.' And this being just the sort of talk the Queen wanted to hear, and not any prattle of under-standing and becoming, she smiled her warmest smile and left Lanak to himself. But she also left two trusted men-at-arms clanking back and forth outside his door that night, and another under his window, because you never know with wizards either.

And there went another night's sleep for our poor Lanak, who had been so peacefully accustomed to snuggling close to Dwyla, with his arm over her and her cold feet tucked in between his. As before, he brooded and pondered, proposing courses of action aloud to himself and each time breaking in to deride himself for an incompetent fool. But somewhere between deep midnight and dawn, as before, he grew very still, as only a wizard can be still; and by and by, he began to draw odd lines and shapes in the dust on the windowsill, and then he began to say words. They made no more sense than the dust trails he was tracing; nor was there anything grandly ominous in the sound of them. By and by, he stopped speaking and just leaned his head against the window like a child on a rainy day, gazing silently down at the courtyard. I think he even slept a little, with his eyes half-open, for he was quite weary.

And presently what do you suppose? – here came a sound of quick hoofbeats on stone, and a horseman in the glinting livery of the Silver Guard clattered across the courtyard, past the inner gatehouse without so much as a glance for the drowsy sentry, and away for the portcullis at full gallop. Nothing stirred within the black castle, least of all the wizard Lanak.

An hour, maybe less, and by all the seagoing gods of the terrible Goro folk, here's another rider heading away from Fors as fast as he can go. Panting on his heels comes another, and what Lanak can see of his face in the icy moonlight is taut with fear, wooden with fear. No more after them, but Lanak leans at that window all the rest of that night, maybe sleeping, maybe not.

In the morning he went to the Queen in her throne room and told her to turn out the Silver Guard for review. Since she was used to doing this no more than once a week, she looked at Lanak in some surprise, but she did what he said. And when she noticed that three of her highest-ranking officers were notable for not being there, nor anywhere she sent to find them, she turned on Lanak and raged in his face, 'You warned them! You helped them escape me!'

'I did no such thing,' Lanak answered calmly. Even a wide-eyed countryman can take the measure of royalty, give him time enough, and he had the Queen's by now. 'Seeking to learn who your turn-coats might be, I sent a spell of fear over your entire garrison, a spell of guilt and unreasoning terror of discovery. Those three panicked and fled in the night, and can do you no more harm.'

'I wanted them,' the Queen said. Her own face was very pale now, and her voice was gentle as gentle. 'I wanted to see them with their bones broken and their skin stripped off, hanging from my balcony, still a little alive, blackening in the sun. I am very dis-appointed, Lanak.'

'Well,' Lanak murmured apologetically, 'I did tell you I was not the right sort of wizard for a Queen.' He kept his face and his manner downcast, even somber, trying hard to keep his jubilation from spilling over. The Queen would be bound to dismiss him from her service on the pot, and on his own, unburdened by mounted companions, he could be home in Karakosk for lunch, bouncing his daughter on his knee and telling Dwyla what it was like to dine in the black castle with musicians playing for you. But the Queen confounded him.

'No, you are not,' she said, and there was no expression at all in her voice. 'None of you are, not a preening, posturing one of you. But I realized that long ago, as I realized what I would have to do to attain my desire.' She was staring at him from far behind her dark, shiny eyes; and Lanak, who –

without ever thinking about it, feared very little –
looked back at her and was afraid.

'You will teach me,' the Queen said. 'You will teach
me your magic – all of it, all of it, every spell, every
gesture, every rune, every rhyme of power. Do you
understand me?'

Lanak tried to speak, but she waved him silent,
showing him the tips of her teeth again. She said, 'Do
you understand? You will not leave this place until
I know everything you know. Everything.'

'It will take your lifetime,' Lanak whispered. 'It is
not a business of learning one spell or learning a
dozen. One is always becoming a wizard, always –'

'*Becoming* again,' the Queen snapped contemptuously. 'I did not order you to teach me the philosophy of magic – it is your magic itself I desire and
I will have it, be very sure of that.' Now she softened
her tone, speaking in soothing counterfeit of the way
in which she had first greeted him. 'It will not take
nearly as long as all that, good Lanak. You will find
me quite a good pupil – I learn swiftly when the
matter is of interest to me. We will begin tomorrow,
and I promise to surprise you by the end of the very
first day. And Lanak' – and here her voice turned flat
and hard once again – 'please do not let even the
shadow of a thought of taking wizard's leave of me
cross your mind. Your wife and child in quaint little
Karakosk would not thank you for it.'

Lanak, who had been within two short phrases and
one stamp of his foot of taking that very course, felt
himself turning to stone where he stood. His voice
sounded far away in his own ears, empty as her voice,
saying, 'If you have harmed them, I will have every

stone of this castle down to make your funeral barrow. I can do this.'

'I should hope you can,' the Queen answered him. 'Why would I want to study with a wizard who could do any less? And yes, you could have your dear family safe in your arms days before I could get any word to the men who have been keeping friendly watch over them since you left home. And you could destroy those same men with a wave of our hand if they and a thousand like them came against you, and another thousand after those – I know all that, believe me, I do.' Her sleeping-cat smile was growing wider and warmer as she spoke.

'But for how long, Lanak? For how long could you keep them safe, do you think? Never mind the legions, I am not such a fool as to put my faith in lances and armor against such a man. I am speaking of the knife in the marketplace, the runaway coach in the crowded street, the twilight arrow in the kitchen garden. Is your magic – no, is your *attention* powerful enough to protect those you love every minute of the rest of their lives? Because it had better be, Lanak. I have my failings, queen or no queen, but no one has ever said of me that I was not patient. I will not grow weary of waiting for my opportunity, and I will not forget. Think very well on this, wizard, before you bid me farewell.'

Lanak did not answer her for a long time. They stood facing one another, alone in the great cold throne room, hung with the ceremonial shields and banners of a hundred queens before this Queen, and what passed between their eyes I cannot tell you. But Lanak said at last, 'So be it. I will teach you what I know.'

'I am grateful and most honored,' replied the Queen, and there was almost no mockery in her tone. 'When you have completed your task, you may go in peace, laden to exasperation with a queen's gifts to your family. Until tomorrow, then.' And she inclined her head graciously for Lanak to bow himself out of the room.

If no one would mind, I'll pass quickly over what Lanak thought that night, and over what he felt and did in solitude – even over whether he slept or not, which I certainly hope he did. I doubt very much that any of you could have slept, or I myself, but magicians are very different people from you and me. It was the Queen's misfortune that, clever as she was, she could not imagine just how different magicians are.

In any case, she appeared in Lanak's quarters early the next morning, just like any other eager student hoping to make a good impression on her teacher. And the truth is that she did exactly that. She had not been boasting when she called herself a quick learner: by afternoon he had already taken her through the First Principles of magic, which are at once as simple as a nursery rhyme and as slippery as buttered ice. Many's the wizard who will tell you that nothing afterward in his training was ever as difficult as comprehending First Principles. Kirisinja herself took eight months – so the tale has it, anyway.

And the Queen did indeed surprise Lanak greatly that day when, illustrating the Sixth Principle, he made a winter-apple fade out of existence, and she promptly reversed his gesture and called the apple into being again. Elementary, certainly; but since the Sixth Principle involves bringing back, not the vanished object itself, but the last actual moment when the object existed, it is easy to understand why Lanak was a good deal more than surprised. A great many people have at least a small gift for magic, but most die without ever realizing this. The Queen knew.

Now I will tell you, the appalling thing for Lanak was that he found himself enjoying teaching her; even rather looking forward to their lessons. He had never taught his art before, nor had he ever had much opportunity to discuss it with other wizards. Dwyla was as knowledgeable as one could wish about the daily practicalities of living with magic, but as indifferent as the Queen to the larger reality behind the chalked circles and pentacles that she scrubbed off the floor many mornings. But the Queen at least was hungry to know every factor that might possibly affect the casting or the success of even the smallest spell. Lanak felt distinctly guilty at times to be enjoying his work with her as much as he was.

Because he had no illusions at all regarding what she proposed to do with the skills she was acquiring from him. She said it herself, more than once: 'This whole realm south of the Durlis should be a true kingdom, an empire – and what is it? Nothing but a rusty clutter of overgrown family estates, with not even energy enough for a decent war. Well, when I am a wizard, we will see about *that*. Believe me, we will.'

'Majesty, you will never be a wizard,' Lanak would answer her plainly. 'When we are done, you may have a wizard's abilities, yes. It is not at all the same thing.'

The Queen would laugh then: a child's spluttering giggle that never quite concealed the iron delight beneath. 'It will serve me just as well, my dear Lanak. Everything will serve me, soon enough.'

And *soon enough* would arrive altogether too soon, Lanak realized, if the Queen kept up her astonishing pace of study. She was not so much learning as devouring, annexing the enchantments he taught her, as she planned to annex every one of the little city-states, provinces, and principalities she derided. He had no doubt that she could do it: any competent wizard could have done so straightforward a thing long before, if wizards were at all concerned with that sort of power, which they are not. Even the most evil wizard has no real interest in land or riches or great glory in the mortal world. That is a game for kings, and for queens – what those others covet is a tale I will not tell here.

This tale, now – it might have had a very different ending if Lanak had not been a married man. As I have said, magicians almost never take wives or husbands; when they lie sleepless, it is because they are brooding mightily over the ethics of conjuration, the logical basis of illusion, the influence of the stars on shape-lifting. But Lanak's nights were haunted by his constant worry about Dwyla and the little one, and about Dwyla's worry about him (he had not dared attempt to communicate with her for weeks, even by magical means, for fear of provoking her watchers), and the deep-growing anger of a mild man. And this last is very much to be wary of, whether your man is a wizard or no. But the Queen had never had to consider such things. No more than had Lanak, when you come to think about it.

So. So the Queen came to know more spells than anyone but a wizard ever has known; and, also, that she learned them far faster than a true apprentice wizard ever would have done. She walked through the walls of her castle, utterly terrifying her servants and soldiers, who took her for her own ghost; she caused the dishes being prepared for her in the great kitchens to rise and float solemnly through the halls to her dining table; at times she left a smiling, regal shadow to debate with ministers and counselors, and herself slipped away unnoticed to gaze from her highest tower far over the lands she intended to rule. There is a legend – no more than that – that as she grew even more accomplished, she took to prowling the midnight alleys of the city in the lean, man-faced form of a *lourijakh*, straight out of the Barrens. Further, it is told that she did not go hungry in that form, but that I do not believe. Lanak would never have allowed it, of that much I am sure.

Finally Lanak said to her, 'I have kept our agreement, Majesty. You now know what I know – every spell, every gesture, every rune, every rhyme. Except, perhaps –' and he suddenly coughed and looked away, so plainly trying to swallow back the betraying word. But it was too late.

'*Except*,' repeated the Queen. Her voice was light, her tone no more than respectfully curious, but her eyes were bright stone. 'Except what, my master?' When Lanak did not answer, she spoke once again, and all she said was, 'Lanak.'

Lanak sighed, still not looking at her. 'Sendings,' he mumbled. 'I did not teach you about sendings, because I do not use them myself. I would never employ a sending, for any reason. Never.'

The Queen said, 'But you know how it is done.'

'Yes, yes,' Lanak answered her. He rubbed his

hands hard together and shivered, though it was a hot day for the time of year. He said, 'A sending is death. That is its only purpose – whether it ever touches its victim or not, its presence kills. It may appear as an ordinary man or woman, as any animal from a snake to a *shukri* to a rock-*targ* – but it is in truth born of the very essence of the magician who controls it. And yet it is *not* the magician, not at all.' His voice grew more urgent, and he did look straight at the Queen now. 'Majesty, magic is neither good nor bad in itself, but a sending is evil in its nature, always. How you will use what I have taught is your own affair – but ask me no more about sendings. I implore you, ask me no more.'

'Oh, but I must,' replied the Queen prettily. 'I simply must ask, since you have so aroused my curiosity. And you must tell me, good Lanak.' They stared at each other, and I think there was something in Lanak's eyes that made the Queen add, 'Of course, I have no intention of ever using such a thing. You are my master, after all, and I take your words most seriously. That is why I would hear all of them. All of them, Lanak.'

So Lanak taught her about sendings.

It took him more than two weeks: still far less time than it should have, when you consider the memorizing alone, never mind the embarrassing rituals, the herbs that have to gathered and cooked into stinking brews, the merciless discipling of your mind – and all that for a single sending! But the Queen took it in as though it were no more than another lesson in predicting the sex of a child or the best month for planting. Truly, she was a remarkable woman, that one, and no mistake.

At the end, she said, 'Well, Lanak, you have indeed kept your word, and I will keep mine. You may depart for home and hearth this very moment, if you desire, though I would be truly honored if you chose to dine with me this one last night. I do not imagine that we will meet again, and I would do you tribute if I may. Because I may have mocked you somewhat at times, but never when I call you *master*.' And she looked so young when she said this, and so earnest and so anxious, that Lanak could do nothing in the world but nod.

That night the Queen served Lanak a dinner such as he never had again in his life, and he lived to be very old and more celebrated than he liked. They drank a great deal of wine together – yes, you are quite right, Chashi, the vineyards of this province have always supplied the black castle – and both of them laughed more than you might think; and Lanak even sang a few bars of an old song that the folk of Karakosk sing about their rulers in Fors na'Shachim, which made the Queen laugh until she spilled her drink. Nevertheless, when Lanak went off to his quarters, he was dreadfully, freezingly sober, and he knew that the Queen was, too. He turned in the doorway and said to her, 'Above all, remember the very last word of the spell. It is a sure safeguard, should anything go ill.'

'I have it perfectly,' answered the Queen. 'Not that I would ever need it.'

'And remember this, too,' Lanak said. 'Sendings call no one *master*. No one.'

'Yes,' said the Queen. 'Yes. Good night, Lanak.'

Lanak did not go to bed that night. By candlelight he carefully folded the clothes that Dwyla had packed for him – how long ago – and put them back into his traveling bag, along with the gifts and little keepsakes that he had bought for her and their daughter, or been given for them by the Queen. When he had finished, the moon was low in the east, and he could hear a new shift of guards tramping to their posts on the castle walls. But he did not lie down.

If you had been there, you would have watched in wonder as he wrapped his arms around his own shoulders, just as precisely as he had packed his bag; and even if you missed the words he murmured, you would have seen him stand up on his toes – a little too high, you might have thought – and then begin to spin around in a curious way, faster and faster, until he rose into the air and floated up towards the arched ceiling, vanishing into a corner where the candlelight did not go. And how he remained there, and for how long, I cannot say.

By and by, when all the candles save one had burned out, and every other sound in the black castle had long been swallowed by other high, cold corners, there came the faint scratching of claws on stone in the corridor just outside his door. There was no rattling of the knob, no trying of the lock – which Lanak had left unturned – there was simply a thing in the room. The shadows by the door concealed it at first, but you would have known it was there, whether you could see it or not.

It took a step forward, halfway into the shivering light. It stood on two legs, but looked as though it might drop back down onto four at any moment. The legs were too long, and they bent in the wrong places, while the arms – or front legs, whichever they were – were thick and jointless, and the claws made them look too short. There were rust-green scales glinting, and there was a heavy swag to belly and breast – like a *sheknath*, yes, Gri, but there was a sick softness to it as well, such as no one ever saw on a living *sheknath*. It was not dead, and not alive, and it smelled like wet, rotting leaves.

Then it took another step, and the candlelight twitched across its face. It was the face of the Queen.

Not altogether her face, no, for the delicate features had blurred, as though under layers of old cobwebs, and the rusty skin of it seemed to be running away from her eyes, like water crawling under a little wind. But there were tears on it, a few, golden where the light caught them.

In the darkness, Lanak spoke very quietly. 'I have done a terrible thing.' The Queen, or what remained of the Queen, turned ponderously toward his voice, her blank black eyes searching for him. Lanak said, 'But I saw no other way.'

The creature lifted its ruinous head toward the sound, so that Lanak could see for the first time just what had happened to the Queen's hair. The mouth was squirming dreadfully, showing splintery brown teeth, and the eyes had grown suddenly wide and deadly bright at the sound of his voice.

'A terrible thing,' Lanak said again. 'There was no need for me to mention sendings, knowing you as I do. I knew very well that you would command that I teach you to summon them, and that you would set about it as soon as I was out of your sight. For whom this first one was meant, I have no idea. Perhaps for the Council in Suk'kai, over the hills – perhaps for the Jiril of Derridow – perhaps even for me, why not? Sendings call no one *master*, after all, and you might easily feel that it might be safer to silence me. Was that the way of it, Majesty?'

The Queen-thing made a sound. It might have melted your bones and mine with terror, or broken our hearts, who can say? Lanak went on. 'The last word of the summoning. I did not lie to you, not exactly. It is indeed a ward against the sending – but not for the sender. Rather, it balks and nullifies the entire enchantment by protecting the target itself against the malice of the enemy. Thus you set your arrow to the string, and let it fly, and struck it aside, all in the same spell. My doing.' His voice was slow and weary, I should imagine.

'But sendings call no one *master*. I did warn you. Finding itself thwarted from its very birth, it turned back in fury toward its source and its one home – you. And when it could not unmake itself, could not unite with the soul from which it was spun, then it chose to merge with your body, as best it might. And so. So.'

Somewhere in the town a cock crowed, though there was no sign of morning in the sky. The Queen-thing lumbered this way and that, looking up at Lanak in raging supplication. He said heavily, 'Oh, this is all so bad, there is no good in it anywhere. I do not think I will ever be able to tell Dwyla about this. Majesty, I have no love for you, but I cannot hate you, seeing you so. I cannot undo what you and I have done together, but what I can I will do now.' He spoke several harsh words, pronouncing them with great care. If there were gestures to accompany them, of course these could not be seen.

The Queen-thing began to glow. It blazed up brighter and brighter, first around its edges and then inward, until Lanak himself had to shut his eyes. Even then the image clung pitilessly to the inside of his lids, like the sticky burning the Dariki tribesmen make in their caves south of Grannach Harbor. He saw the outlines of the Queen and her sending, separate and together at once: her in her pride and beauty and cunning, and the other – *that other* – embracing her in fire. Then it was gone, but I think that Lanak never really stopped seeing it ever again. I could be wrong.

The room was indeed growing a bit light now, and the cock outside was joined by the wail of a Nounouri at his dawn prayers. There are a lot of Nounos in Fors, or there used to be. Into the silence that was not emptiness, Lanak said, 'No one else will ever see you. I cannot end your suffering, but you need not endure it in the view of all men. And if a greater than I can do more, I will send him here. Forgive me, Majesty, and farewell.'

Well, that is all of it, and longer than I meant, for which I ask pardon in my turn. Lanak went home to Karakosk, to Dwyla and his daughter, and to his fields, his black beer, and his fireworks; and he did the very best he could to vanish from all other tales and remembrances. He was not wholly successful – but there, that's what happens when you are too good at something for your own ambitions. But I will say nothing more about him, which would have made him happy to know.

As for the Queen. When I was last in Fors na'Shachim, not too long ago, there were still a few street vendors offering charms to anyone bound as a guest to the black castle. They are supposed to protect you from the sad and vengeful spirit that wanders those halls even now. Highly illegal they are, by the way – you can lose a hand for buying and a head for selling. I myself have spent nights at the castle without such protection, and no harm has ever come to me. Unless you count my dreams, of course.

*   *   *

PETER S. BEAGLE was writing stories of fantasy when he was in his teens – his first published story, 'Telephone Call' appeared when he was just sixteen – and he was acknowledged as a major talent when his debut novel, *A Fine and Private Place* was published in 1960 before he was twenty-one. The tale of the reclusive Jonathan Rebeck who lived in a Bronx graveyard with his talking raven and shares his existence with two ghosts set a new benchmark in fantasy fiction. *The Last Unicorn* (1968) was also a ground-breaking story with its account of the life of Schmendrick, an imcompetent magician, who can never grow old until he has mastered his art. The old crone, Molly Grue, who dogs his footsteps is an unforgettable character. Schmendrick is also present in *The Innkeeper's Song* (1993) about another magus who calls on his students to help him fight off demons from the underworld. Sadly, Peter Beagle has only written a few short stories of which 'The Magician of Karkosk' rates, in my opinion, as one of the very best.

ELPHENOR AND WEASEL

Sylvia Townsend Warner

Master Elisha Blackbone has a good business in necro-mancy, divination and magic. He travels far and wide with his book of spells, alembics, skull and chart of the heavens in order to practise his skills. Master Blackbone is especially busy in spring when the need for love charms and salves to stop itching exceeds the demand for raising the Devil. On one journey in Suffolk he stumbles across young Elphenor and offers him a job as his assistant. The boy learns quickly, but this is perhaps not surprising for someone who comes from the Kingdom of Elphin where the inhabitants have wings and pursue such activities as cat-racing, table-turning and flying out to sea to view shipwrecks. Soon Master Blackbone begins to dream of opening a consulting room for magic in London – but he has not bargained on his assistant's own powers nor what happens when the boy meets Weasel, a beautiful young girl who is a very pretty shade of green . . .

*   *   *

The ship had sailed barely three leagues from IJmuiden when the wind backed into the east and rose to gale force. If the captain had been an older man he would have returned to port. But he had a mistress in Lowestoft and was impatient to get to her; the following wind, the waves thwacking the stern of the boat as though it were the rump of a donkey and tearing on ahead, abetted his desires. By nightfall, the ship was wallowing broken-backed at the mercy of the storm. Her decks were awash and clutted with shifting debris. As she lurched lower, Elphenor thrust the confidential letter inside his shirt, the wallet of mortal money deeper in his pocket, and gave his mind to keeping his wings undamaged by blows from ripped sails and the clutches of his fellow-passengers. Judging his moment, he took off just before the ship went down, and was alone with the wind.

His wings were insignificant: he flew by the force of the gale. If for a moment it slackened he dropped within earshot of the hissing waves, then was scooped up and hurled onward. In one of these descents he felt the letter, heavy with seals, fall out of his breast. It would be forever private now, and the world of Elfin unchanged by its contents. On a later descent, the wallet followed it. His clothes were torn to shreds, he was benumbed with cold, he was wet to the skin. If the wind had let him drown he would have drowned willingly, folded his useless wings and heard the waves hiss over his head. The force of the gale enclosed him, he could hardly breath. There was no effort of flight; the effort lay in being powerlessly and violently and almost senselessly conveyed – a fragment of existence in the drive of the storm. Once or twice he was asleep till a slackening of the wind jolted him awake with the salt smell of the sea beneath him. Wakened more forcibly, he saw a vague glimmer on the face of the water and supposed it might be the light of dawn; but he could not turn his head. He saw the staggering flight of a gull, and thought there must be land not far off.

The growing light showed a tumult of breakers ahead, close on each other's heels, devouring each other's bulk. They roared, and a pebble beach screamed back at them, but the wind carried him over, and on over a dusky flat landscape that might be anywhere. So far, he had not been afraid. But when a billow of darkness reared up in front of him, and the noise of tossing trees swooped on his hearing, he was suddenly in panic, and clung to a bough like a drowning man. He had landed in a thick grove of ilex trees, planted as a windbreak. He squirmed into the shelter of their midst, and heard the wind go on without him.

Somehow, he must have fallen out of the tree without noticing. When he woke, a man with mustachios was looking down on him.

'I know what you are. You're a fairy. There were fairies all round my father's place in Suffolk. Thieving pests, they were, bad as gypsies. But I half liked them. They were company for me, being an only child. How did you get here?'

Elphenor realized that he was still wearing the visibility he had put on during the voyage as a measure against being jostled. It was too late to discard it – though the shift between visible and invisible is a press-button affair. He repressed his indignation at being classed with gypsies and explained how the ship from IJmuiden had sunk and the wind carried him on.

'From IJmuiden, you say? What happened to the rest of them?'

'They were drowned.'

'Drowned? And my new assistant was on that ship! It's one calamity after another. Sim's hanged, and

Jacob Kats gets drowned. Seems as though my stars meant me to have you.'

It seemed as though Elphenor's stars were of the same mind. To tease public opinion he had studied English as his second language; he was penniless, purposeless, breakfastless, and the wind had blown his shoes off. 'If I could get you out of any difficulties –' he said.

'But I can't take you to Walsham Borealis looking like that. We'll go to old Bella, and she'll fit you out.'

Dressed in secondhand clothes too large for him and filled with pork pie, Elphenor entered Walsham Borealis riding pillion behind Master Elisha Blackbone. By then he knew he was to be assistant to a quack in several arts, including medicine, necromancy, divination, and procuring.

Hitherto, Elphenor, nephew to the Master of Ceremonies at the Elfin Court of Zuy, had spent his days in making himself polite and, as far as in his tailor lay, ornamental. Now he had to make himself useful. After the cautious pleasures of Zuy everything in this new life, from observing the planets to analyzing specimens of urine, entertained him. It was all so agreeably terminal: one finished one thing and went on to another. When Master Blackbone's clients overlapped, Elphenor placated those kept waiting by building card houses, playing the mandora, and sympathetic conversation – in which he learned a great deal that was valuable to Master Blackbone in casting horoscopes.

For his part, Master Blackbone was delighted with an assistant who was so quick to learn, so free from prejudice, and, above all, a fairy. To employ a fairy was a step up in the world. In London practice every reputable necromancer kept a spiritual appurtenance – fairy, familiar, talking toad, airy consultant. When he had accumulated the money, he would set up in London, where there is always room for another marvel. For the present, he did not mention his assistant's origin, merely stating that he was the seventh son of a seventh son, on whom any gratuities would be well bestowed. Elphenor was on the footing of an apprentice; his keep and training were sufficient wages. A less generous master would have demanded the gratuities, but Master Blackone had his eye on a golden future, and did not care to imperil it by more than a modest scriptural tithe.

With a fairy as an assistant, he branched out into larger developments of necromancy and took to raising the Devil as a favour. The midnight hour was essential and holy ground desirable – especially disused holy ground: ruined churches, disinhabited religious foundations. The necromancer and the favoured clients would ride under cover of night to Bromholm or St. Benet's in the marshes. Elphenor, flying invisibly and dressed for the part, accompanied them. At the Word of Power, he became visible, pranced, menaced, and lashed his tail till the necromancer ordered him back to the pit. This was for moonlight nights. When there was no moon, he hovered invisibly, whispering blasphemies and guilty secrets. His blasphemies lacked unction; being a fairy he did not believe in God. But the guilty secrets curdled many a good man's blood. A conscience-stricken clothier from a neighbouring parish spread such scandals about the iniquities done in Walsham Borealis that Master Blackbone thought it wisest to make off before he and Elphenor were thrown into jail.

They packed his equipment – alembics, chart of the heavens, book of spells, skull, etc. – and were off before the first calm light of an April morning. As they travelled southward Elphenor counted windmills and church towers and found windmills slightly predominating. Church towers were more profitable, observed Master Blackbone. Millers were rogues and cheats, but wherever there was a church you could be sure of fools; if Elphanor were not a fairy and ignorant of Holy Writ he would know that fools are the portion appointed for the wise. But for the present they would lie a little low, shun the Devil, and keep to love philtres and salves for the itch, for which there is always a demand in spring. He talked on about the herbs they would need, and the henbane that grew round Needham in Suffolk, where he was born and played with fairies, and whither they were bound. 'What were they like?' Elphenor asked. He did not suppose Master Blackbone's fairies were anything resplendent. Master Blackbone replied that they came out of a hill and were green. Searching his memory, he added that they smelled like elderflowers. At Zuy, elderflowers were used to flavour gooseberry jam – an inelegant conserve.

At Zuy, by now, the gardeners would be bringing the tubs of myrtle out of the conversatories, his uncle would be conducting ladies along the sanded walks to admire the hyacinths, and he would be forgotten; for in good society failures are smoothly forgotten, and as nothing had resulted from the confidential letter it would be assumed he had failed to deliver it. He would never be able to go back. He did not want

to. There was better entertainment in the mortal
world. Mortals packed more variety into their brief
lives – perhaps because they knew them to be brief.
There was always something going on and being
taken seriously: love, hate, ambition, plotting, fear,
and all the rest of it. He had more power as a quack's
assistant than ever he would have attained to in Zuy.
To have a great deal of power and no concern was
the life for him.

Hog's grease was a regrettable interpolation in his
career. Master Blackbone based his salves and oint-
ments on hog's grease, which he bought in a crude
state from pork butchers. It was Elphenor's task to
clarify it before it was tinctured with juices expressed
from herbs. Wash as he might, his hands remained
greasy and the smell of grease hung in his nostrils.
Even the rankest-smelling herbs were a welcome
change, and a bundle of water peppermint threw
him into a rapture. As Master Blackbone disliked
stooping, most of the gathering fell to him.

It is a fallacy that henbane must be gathered at
midnight. Sunlight raises its virtues (notably effica-
cious against toothache, insomnia, and lice), and to
be at its best it should be gathered in the afternoon
of a hot day. Elphenor was gathering it in a sloping
meadow that faced south. He was working invisibly –
Master Blackbone did not wish every Tom, Dick, and
Harry to know what went into his preparations.
Consequently, a lamb at play collided with him and
knocked the basket out of his hand. As it stood
astonished at this sudden shower of henbane,
Elphenor seized it by the ear and cuffed it. Hearing
her lamb bleat so piteously, its mother came charging
to the rescue. She also collided with Elphenor and,

being heavy with her winter fleece, sent him sprawling. He was still flat on his back when a girl appeared from nowhere, stooped over him, and slapped his face, hard and accurately. To assert his manly dignity he pulled her down on top of him – and saw that she was green.

She was a very pretty shade of green – a pure delicate tint, such as might have been cast on a white eggshell by the sun shining through the young foliage of a beech tree. Her hair, brows, and lashes were a darker shade; her lashes lay on her green cheek like a miniature fern frond. Her teeth were perfectly white. Her skin was so nearly transparent that the blue veins on her wrists and breasts showed through like some exquisitely marbled cheese.

As they lay in an interval of repose, she stroked the bruise beginning to show on his cheek with triumphant moans of compassion. Love did not heighten or diminish her colour. She remained precisely the same shade of green. The smell, of course, was that smell of elderflowers. It was strange to think that exactly like this she may have been one of the fairies who played with Elisha Blackbone in his bragged-of boyhood, forty, fifty years back. He pushed the speculation away, and began kissing her behind the ear, and behind the other ear, to make sure which was the more sensitive. But from that hour love struck root in him.

Eventually he asked her name. She told him it was Weasel. 'I shall call you Mustela,' he said, complying with the lover's imperative to rename the loved one; but in the main he called her Weasel. They sat up, and saw that time had gone on as usual, that dusk had fallen and the henbane begun to wilt.

When they parted, the sheep were circling gravely to the top of the hill, the small grassy hill of her tribe. He flew leisurely back, swinging the unfilled basket. The meagre show of henbane would be a pretext for going off on the morrow to a place where it grew more abundantly; he would have found such a place, but by then it was growing too dark for picking, and looking one way while flying another he had bruised his cheek against a low-growing bough. At Zuy this artless tale would not have supported a moment's scrutiny; but it would pass with a mortal, though it might be wise to substantiate it with a request for the woundwort salve. For a mortal, Master Blackbone was capable of unexpected intuitions.

The intuitions had not extended to the reverence for age and learning which induced Elphenor to sleep on a pallet to the windward. Toward morning, he dreamed that he was at the foot of the ilex; but it was Weasel who was looking down at him, and if he did not move she would slap his face. He moved, and woke. Weasel lay asleep beside him. But at the same time they were under the ilex, for the waves crashed on the screaming pebble beach and were Master Blackbones snores.

At Zuy, the English Elfindom was spoken of with admiring reprehension: its magnificence, wastefulness, and misrule, its bravado and eccentricity. The eccentricity of being green and living under a hill was not included. A hill, yes. Antiquarians talked of hill dwellings, and found evidence of them in potsherds and beads. But never, at any time, green. The beauties of Zuy, all of them white as bolsters, would have swooned at the hypothesis. Repudiating the memory of past bolsters, he looked at Weasel, curled against him like a caterpillar in a rose leaf, green as spring, fresh as spring, and completely contemporary.

She stirred, opened her eyes, and laughed.

'Shush!'

Though invisible, she might not be inaudible, and her voice was ringing and assertive as a wren's. She had come so trustingly it would be the act of an ingrate to send her away. Not being an ingrate he went with her, leaving Master Blackbone to make what he would of an early-rising assistant. They breakfasted on wild strawberries and a hunk of bread he had had the presence of mind to take from the bread crock. It was not enough for Weasel, and when they came to a brook she twitched up a handful of minnows and ate them raw. Love is a hungry emotion, and by midday he wished he had not been so conventional about the minnows. As a tactful approach, he began questioning her about life in the hill, its amenities, its daily routine. She suddenly became evasive: he would not like it; it was dull, old-fashioned, unsociable.

'All the same, I should like to visit it. I have never been inside a hill.'

'No! You can't come. It's impossible. They'd set on you, you'd be driven out. *You're not green.*'

Etiquette.

'Don't you understand?'

'I was wondering what they would do to you if they found out where you woke this morning.'

'Oh that! They'd have to put up with it. Green folk don't draw green blood. But they'd tear *you* in pieces.'

'It's the same where I come from. If I took you to Zuy, they might be rather politer, but they'd never forgive you for being green. But I won't take you, Weasel. We'll stay in Suffolk. And if it rains and rains and rains –'

'I don't mind rain –'

'We'll find a warm, dry badger sett.'

They escaped into childishness and were happy again, with a sharpened happiness because for a moment they had so nearly touched despair.

As summer became midsummer, and the elder blossom outlasted the wild roses and faded in its turn till the only true elderflower scent came from her, and the next full moon had a broader face and shone on cocks of hay in silvery fields, they settled in to an unhurried love and strolled from day to day as through a familiar landscape. By now they were seldom hungry, for there was a large crop of mushrooms, and Elphenor put more system into his attendances on Master Blackbone, breakfasting soundly and visibly while conveying mouthfuls to the invisible Weasel (it was for the breakfasts that they slept there). Being young and perfectly happy and pledged to love each other till the remote end of their days, they naturally talked of death and discussed how to contrive that neither should survive each other. Elphenor favoured being struck by lightning as they lay in each other's arms, but Weasel was terrified by thunder – she winced and covered her ears at the slightest distant rumble – and though he talked soothingly of the electric fluid and told her of recent experiments with amber and a couple of silk stockings, one black, one white, she refused to die by lightning strike.

And Master Blackbone, scarcely able to believe his ears, madly casting horoscopes and invoking the goddess Fortuna, increasingly tolerant of Elphenor's inattention, patiently compounding his salves unassisted, smiling on the disappearance from his larder, was day after day, night after night, more sure of his surmise – till convinced of his amazing good fortune he fell into the melancholy of not knowing what best to do about it, whether to grasp fame single-handed or call in the help of an expert and self-effacingly retire on the profits. He wrote a letter to an old friend. Elphenor was not entrusted with this letter, but he know it had been written and was directed to London. Weasel was sure Master Blackbone was up to no good – she had detested him at first sight. They decied to keep a watch on him. But their watch was desultory, and the stranger was already sitting in Master Blackbone's lodgings and conversing with him when they flew in and perched on a beam.

The stranger was a stout man with a careworn expression. Master Blackbone was talking in his best procuring voice.

'It's a Golconda, an absolute Golconda! A pair of them, young, in perfect condition. Any manager would snap at them. But I have kept it dark till now. I wanted you to have the first option.'

'Thanks, I'm sure,' said the stranger. 'But it's taking a considerable chance.'

'Oh no, it isn't. People would flock to see them, You could double the charges – in fact you should, for it's something unique – and there wouldn't be an empty seat in the house. Besides, it's a scientific rarity. You'd have all the illuminati. Nobs from the colleges. Ladies of fashion. Royal patronage.'

The stranger said he didn't like buying pigs in pokes.

'But I give you my word. A brace of fairies – lovely, young, amorous fairies. Your fortune would be made.'

'How much do you want?'

'Two-thirds of the takings. You can't say that's exorbitant. Not two-thirds of the profits, mind. Two-thirds of the takings and a written agreement.'

The stranger repeated that he didn't like buying pigs in pokes, the more so when he had no warrant the pigs were within.

'Wait till tonight! They come every night and cuddle on that pallet there. They trust me like a father. Wait till they're asleep and throw a net over them, and they're yours.'

'But when I've got them to London, suppose they are awkward, and won't perform? People aren't going to pay for what they can't see. How can I be sure they'll be visible?'

Master Blackbone said there were ways and means, as with performing animals.

'Come, Weasel. We'll be off.'

The voice was right overhead, loud and clear. Some cobwebs drifted down.

Elphenor and Weasel were too pleased with themselves to think beyond the moment. They had turned habitually toward their usual haunts and were dabbling their feet in the brook before it occurred to Elphenor that they had no reason to stay in the neighbourhood and good reason to go elsewhere. Weasel's relations would murder him because he was not green, Master Blackbone designed to sell them because they were fairies. Master Blackbone might have further designs: he was a necromancer, though a poor one; it would be prudent to get beyond his magic circle. Elphenor had congratulated himself on leaving prudence behind at Zuy. Now it reasserted itself and had its charm. Prudence had no charm whatever for Weasel; it was only by representing the move as reckless that he persuaded her to make it.

With the world before them, he flew up for a survey and caught sight of the sea, looking as if ships would not melt in its mouth – which rather weakened the effect of his previous narrative of the journey from IJmuiden to the ilexes. Following the coastline they came to Great Yarmouth, where they spent several weeks. It was ideal for their vagrant purposes, full of vigorous, cheerful people, with food to be had for the taking – hot pies and winkles in the market-place, herring on the quayside where the fishing boats unloaded. The air was rought and cold, and he stole a pair of shipboy's trousers and a knitted muffler for Weasel from a marine store near the Custom House. He was sorry to leave this kind place. But Weasel showed such a strong inclination to go to sea, and found it so amusing to flaunt her trousers on the quayside and startle her admirers with her green face, that she was becoming notorious, and he was afraid Master Blackbone might hear of her. From Yarmouth they flew inland, steering their course by church towers. Where there is a church tower you can be sure of fools, Master Blackbone had said. True enough; but Elphenor tired of thieving – though it called for more skill in villages – and he thought he would try turning an honest penny, for a change. By now he was so coarsened and brown-handed that he could pass as a labouring man. In one place he

sacked potatoes, in another baled reeds for thatch-
ing. At a village called Scottow, where the sexton had
rheumatism, he dug a grave. Honest-pennying was
no pleasure to Weasel, who had to hang about
invisibly, passing the time with shrivelled blackber-
ries. In these rustic places which had never seen a
circus or an Indian peddler, her lovely green face
would have brought stones rattling on their heels.

Winter came late that year and stealthily, but the
nights were cold. Nights were never cold in Suffolk,
she said. He knew this was due to the steady tem-
perature under the hill, but hoping all the same she
might be right he turned southward. He had earned
more than enough to pay for a night at an inn. At
Bury St. Edmunds he bought her a cloak with a deep
hood, and telling her to pull the hood well forward
and keep close to his heels he went at dusk to a
respectable inn and hired the best bedroom they
had. All went well, except that they seemed to look at
him doubtfully. In his anxiety to control the situation
he had reverted to his upper-class manner, which his
clothes did not match with. The four-poster bed was
so comfortable that he hired the room for a second
night, telling the chambermaid his wife had a headache and must not be disturbed. It was certainly an
elopement, she reported; even before she had left
the room, the little gentleman had parted the bed
curtains and climbed in beside the lady. After the
second night there was no more money.

They left on foot, and continued to walk, for there
was a shifting, drizzling fog which made it difficult to
keep each other in sight if they flew. Once again they
stole a dinner, but it was so inadequate that Elphenor
decided to try begging. He was rehearsing a beggar's

whine when they saw a ruddy glow through the fog and heard a hammer ring on an anvil. Weasel as usual clapped her hands to her ears; but when they came to a wayside forge the warmth persuaded her to follow Elphenor, who went in shivering ostentatiously and asked if he and his wife could stand near the blaze: they would not get in the way, they would not stay long. The blacksmith was shaping horseshoes. He nodded, and went on with his work. Elphenor was preparing another whine when the blacksmith remarked it was no day to be out, and encouraged Weasel, who stood in the doorway, to come nearer the fire.

'Poor soul, she could do with a little kindness,' said Elphenor. 'And we haven't met with much of it today. We passed an inn, farther back' – it was there they had stolen the heel of a Suffolk cheese – 'but they said they had no room for us.'

Weasel interrupted. 'What's that black thing ahead, that keeps on showing and going?'

The blacksmith pulled his forelock. 'Madam. That's the church.'

They thanked him and went away, Elphenor thinking he must learn to beg more feelingly. The blacksmith stood looking after them. At this very time of year, too. He wished he had not let slip the opportunity of a Hail Mary not likely to come his way again.

The brief December day was closing when they came to the church. The south porch, large as a room, was sheltered from the wind, and they sat there, huddled in Weasel's cloak. 'We can't sleep here,' Elphenor said. For all that, he got up and tried the church door. It was locked. He immediately determined to get in by a window. They flew round the church, fingering the cold panes of glass, and had almost completed their round and seen the great bulk of the tower threatening down on them, when Weasel heard a clatter overhead. It came from one of the clerestory windows, where a missing pane had been replaced by a shutter. They wrenched the shutter open, and flew in, and circled downward through darkness, and stood on a flagstone pavement. Outlined against a window was a tall structure with a peak. Fingering it, they found it was wood, carved, and swelling out of a stem like a goblet. A railed flight of steps half encircled the stem. They mounted the steps and found themselves in the goblet. It was an octagonal cupboard, minus a top but carpeted. By curling round each other, there would be room to lie down. The smell of wood gave them a sense of security, and they spent the night in the pulpit.

He woke to the sound of Weasel laughing. Daylight was streaming in, and Weasel was flitting about the roof, laughing at the wooden figures that supported the crossbeams – carved imitations of fairies, twelve foot high, with outstretched turkey wings and gaunt faces, each uglier than the last. 'So that's what they think we're like,' she said. 'And look at *her*!' She pointed to the fairy above the pulpit, struggling with a trumpet.

Exploring at floor level, Elphenor read the Ten Commandments, and found half a bottle of wine and some lozenges. It would pass for a breakfast; later, he would stroll into the village and see what could be got from there. While he was being raised as the Devil at Walsham Borealis, he had learned some facts about the Church of England, one of them that the reigning monarch, symbolically represented as a lion and a unicorn is worshipped noisily on one day of the week and that for the rest of the week churches are unmolested. There was much to be said for spending the winter here. The building was windproof and weatherproof, Weasel was delighted with it, and, for himself, he found its loftiness and spaciousness congenial, as though he were back in Zuy – a Zuy improved by a total removal of its inhabitants. He had opened a little door and discovered a winding stone stairway behind it when his confidence in Church of England weekdays was shaken by the entrance of two women with brooms and buckets. He beckoned to Weasel, snatched her cloak from the pulpit, and preceded her up the winding stairs, holding the bottle and the lozenges. The steps were worn; there was a dead crow on one of them. They groped their way up into darkness, then into light; a window showed a landing and a door open on a small room where some ropes dangled from the ceiling. Weasel seized a rope and gave it a tug, and would have tugged more energetically if Elphenor had not intervened, promising that when the women had gone away she could tug to her heart's content. Looking out of the cobwebbed window he saw the churchyard far below and realised they must be a long way up the tower. But the steps wound on into another darkness and a dimmer lightness, and to another landing and another door open on another room. This room had louvred windows high up in the wall, and most of its floor space was taken up by a frame supporting eight bells, four of them upside down with their clappers lolling in their iron mouths. This was the bell chamber, he explained. The ropes went from the bells into the room below, which was the ringing chamber. There was a similar tower near Zuy; mortals thought highly of it, and his tutor had taken him to see it.

Weasel began to stroke one of the bells. As though she were caressing some savage sleeping animal, it presently responded with a noise between a soft growl and a purr. Elphenor stroked another. It answered at a different pitch, deeper and harsher, as though it were a more savage animal. But they were hungry. The bells could wait. The light from the louvred windows flickered between bright and sombre as the wind tossed the clouds. It was blowing up for a storm.

They would be out of the wind tonight and for many nights to come. January is a dying season, there would be graves to dig, and with luck and management, thought Elphenor, he might earn a livelihood and be a friend to sextons here and around. Weasel would spare crumbs from the bread he earned, scatter them for birds, catch the birds, pluck and eat them: she still preferred raw food, with the life still lively in it. On Sundays, she said, they would get their week's provisions; with everybody making a noise in church, stealing would be child's play. The pulpit would be the better for a pillow, and she could soon collect enough feathers for a pillow, for a feather mattress even: one can always twitch a pillowcase from the washing line. The wind had gone to their heads; they outbid each other with grand plans of how they would lie in the church, and laughed them down, and imagined more. They would polish the wooden fairies' noses till they shone like drunkards' noses; they would grow water-cresses in the font;

Elphenor would tell the complete story of his life before they met. Let him begin now! Was he born with a hook nose and red hair? He began, obediently and prosily. Weasel clamped her eyes open, and suppressed yawns. He lost the thread of his narrative. Drowsy with wine, they fell asleep.

He woke to two appalling sounds. Weasel screaming with terror, a clash of metal. The bell ringers had come to practise their Christmas peal, and prefaced it by sounding all the bells at once. The echo was heavy on the air as they began to ring a set of changes, first the scale descending evenly to the whack of the tenor bell, then in patterened steps to the same battleaxe blow. The pattern altered; the tenor bell sounded midway, jolting an arbitrary finality into the regular measure of eight. With each change of position the tenor bell accumulated a more threatening insistency, and the other bells shifted round it like a baaing flock of sheep.

Weasel cowered in Elphenor's arms. She had no strength left to scream with; she could only tremble before the impact of the next flailing blow. He felt his senses coming adrift. The booming echo was a darkness on his sight through which he saw the bells in their frame heaving and evading, evading and heaving, under a dark sky. The implacable assault of the changing changes pursued him as the waves had pursued the boat from IJmuiden. But here there was no escape, for it was he who wallowed broken-backed at the mercy of the storm. Weasel lay in his arms like something at a distance. He felt his protectiveness, his compassion, ebbing away; he watched her with a bloodless, skeleton love. She still trembled, but in a disjointed way, as though she were falling to pieces.

He saw the lovely green fade out of her face. 'My darling,' he said, 'death by lightning would have been easier.' He could not hear himself speak.

The frost lasted on into mid-March. No one went to the bell chamber till the carpenter came to mend the louvres in April. The two bodies, one bowed over the other, had fallen into decay. No one could account for them, or for the curious weightless fragments of a substance rather like sheet gelatine which the wind had scattered over the floor. They were buried in the same grave. Because of their small stature and light bones they were entered in the Register of Burials as *Two Stranger Children*.

*   *   *

SYLVIA TOWNSEND WARNER was a trained musician who turned to writing poetry and stories and created one of the most unusual fantasy novels of the last century, *Lolly Willowes*, published in 1926. It tells the story of a middle-aged spinster living in London who grows tired of her stifling existence and moves to the depth of the country where she becomes a witch and discovers unsuspected powers in herself. Sylvia Townsend Warner continued to explore her interest in magic in *The Cat's-Cradle Book* (1940) that drew on traditional fairy tales for a series of stories all told to children by *cats*. Her last, and most famous book, *The Kingdom of Elphin* (1977), describes the lives of fairies living in worlds just apart from the human race who are unnoticed by adults but not usually by children.

THE RULE OF NAMES

Ursula Le Guin

Mr Underhill is a cheerful little fat man who looks almost comical with his bow-legs and black tights. But he is still a wizard – the only one on Sattins Island where the people treat him with a mixture of respect and affection. He is certainly not great at magic – the tomatoes he tries to make grow larger rarely get bigger than melons while any warts he charms invariably return after three days. Mostly Mr Underhill likes to keep himself to himself in his cave, though occasionally the braver children will try to sneak inside when he is away. One thing he always does is to keep out of sight when any ships dock in the harbour because, it is said, he is afraid of the evil eye. However, life on Sattins Island changes dramatically on the day when a handsome stranger arrives in port and starts to beguile the population – the women in particular. In no time the word is being whispered around: has Mr Underhill got a rival magician in his domain?

*   *   *

Mr Underhill came out from under his hill, smiling and breathing hard. Each breath shot out of his nostrils as a double puff of steam, snow-white in the morning sunshine. Mr Underhill looked up at the bright December sky and smiled wider than ever, showing snow-white teeth. Then he went down to the village.

'Morning Mr Underhill,' said the villagers as he passed them in the narrow street between houses with conical, overhanging roofs like the fat red caps of toadstools. 'Morning, morning!' he replied to each. (It was of course bad luck to wish anyone a *good* morning; a simple statement of the time of day was quite enough, in a place so permeated with Influences as Sattins Island, where a careless adjective might change the weather for a week.) All of them spoke to him, some with affection, some with affectionate disdain. He was all the little island had in the way of a wizard, and so deserved respect – but how could you respect a little fat man of fifty who waddled along with his toes turned in, breathing steam and smiling? He was no great shakes as a workman either. His fireworks were fairly elaborate but his elixirs were weak. Warts he charmed off frequently reappeared after three days; tomatoes he enchanted grew no bigger than canteloupes; and those rare times when a strange ship stopped at Sattins harbor, Mr Underhill always stayed under his hill – for fear, he explained, of the evil eye. He was, in other words, a wizard the way wall-eyed Gan was a carpenter: by default. The villagers made do with badly-hung doors and inefficient spells, for this generation, and relieved their annoyance by treating Mr Underhill quite familiarly, as a mere fellow-villager. They even asked him to dinner. Once he asked some of them to dinner, and served a splendid repast, with silver, crystal, damask, roast goose, sparkling Andrades '639, and plum pudding with hard sauce; but he was so nervous all through the meal that it took the joy out of it, and besides, everybody was hungry again half an hour afterward. He did not like anyone to visit his cave, not even the anteroom, beyond which in fact nobody had ever got. When he saw people approaching the hill he always came trotting to meet them. 'Let's sit out here under the pine trees!' he would say, smiling and waving towards the fir-grove, or if it was raining, 'Let's go have a drink at the inn, eh?' though everybody knew he drank nothing stronger than well-water.

Some of the village children, teased by that locked cave, poked and pried and made raids while Mr Underhill was away; but the small door that led into the inner chamber was spell-shut, and it seemed for once to be an effective spell. Once a couple of boys, thinking the wizard was over on the West Shore curing Mrs Ruuna's sick donkey, brought a crowbar and a hatchet up there, but at the first whack of the hatchet on the door there came a roar of wrath from inside, and a cloud of purple steam. Mr Underhill had got home early. The boys fled. He did not come out, and the boys came to no harm, though they said you couldn't believe what a huge hooting howling hissing horrible bellow that little fat man could make unless you'd heard it.

His business in town this day was three dozen fresh eggs and a pound of liver; also a stop at Seacaptain Fogeno's cottage to renew the seeing-charm on the old man's eyes (quite useless when applied to a case of detached retina, but Mr Underhill kept trying), and finally a chat with old Goody Guld the concertina-maker's widow. Mr Underhill's friends were mostly old people. He was timid with the strong young men of the village, and the girls were shy of him. 'He makes me nervous, he smiles so much,' they all said, pouting, twisting silky ringlets round a finger. 'Nervous' was a new-fangled word, and their mothers all replied grimly, 'Nervous my foot, silliness is the word for it. Mr Underhill is a very respectable wizard!'

After leaving Goody Guld, Mr Underhill passed by the school, which was being held this day out on the common. Since no one on Sattins Island was literate, there were no books to learn to read from and no desks to carve initials on and no blackboards to erase, and in fact no schoolhouse. On rainy days the children met in the loft of the Communal Barn, and got hay in their pants; on sunny days the school-teacher, Palani, took them anywhere she felt like. Today, surrounded by thirty interested children under twelve and forty uninterested sheep under five, she was teaching an important item on the curriculum: the Rules of Names. Mr Underhill, smiling shyly, paused to listen and watch. Palani, a plump, pretty girl of twenty, made a charming picture there in the wintry sunlight, sheep and children around her, a leafless oak above her, and behind her the dunes and sea and clear, pale sky. She spoke earnestly, her face flushed pink by wind and words. 'Now you know the Rules of Names already, children. There are two, and they're the same on every island in the world. What's one of them?'

'It ain't polite to ask anybody what his name is,' shouted a fat, quick boy, interrupted by a little girl shrieking, 'You can't never tell your own name to nobody my ma says!'

'Yes, Suba. Yes, Popi dear, don't screech. That's right. You never ask anybody his name. You never tell your own. Now think about that a minute and then tell me why we call our wizard Mr Underhill.' She smiled across the curly heads and the woolly backs at Mr Underhill, who beamed, and nervously clutched his sack of eggs.

'Cause he lives under a hill!' said half the children.

'But is it his truename?'

'No!' said the fat boy, echoed by little Popi shrieking, 'No!'

'How do you know it's not?'

'Cause he came here all alone and so there wasn't anybody knew his truename so they could not tell us, and *he* couldn't –'

'Very good, Suba. Popi, don't shout. That's right. Even a wizard can't tell his truename. When you children are through school and go through the Passage, you'll leave your childnames behind and keep only your truenames, which you must never ask for and never give away. Why is that the rule?'

The children were silent. The sheep bleated gently. Mr Underhill answered the question: 'Because the name is the thing,' he said, in his shy, soft, husky voice, 'and the truename is the true thing. To speak the name is to control the thing. Am I right, Schoolmistress?'

She smiled and curtseyed, evidently a little embarrassed by his participation. And he trotted off towards his hill, clutching the eggs to his bosom. Somehow the minute spent watching Palani and the children had made him very hungry. He locked his inner door behind him with a hasty incantation, but there must have been a leak or two in the spell, for soon the bare anteroom of the cave was rich with the smell of frying eggs and sizzling liver.

The wind that day was light and fresh out of the west, and on it at noon a little boat came skimming the bright waves into Sattins harbor. Even as it rounded the point a sharp-eyed boy spotted it, and knowing, like every child on the island, every sail and spar of the forty boats of the fishing fleet, he ran down the street calling out, 'A foreign boat, a foreign boat!' Very seldom was the lonely isle visited by a boat from some equally lonely isle of the East Reach, or an adventurous trader from the Archipelago. By the time the boat was at the pier half the village was there to greet it, and fishermen were following it home-wards, and cowherds and clamdigggers and herb-hunters were puffing up and down all the rocky hills, heading towards the habor.

But Mr Underhill's door stayed shut.

There was only one man aboard the boat. Old Seacaptain Fogeno, when they told him that, drew down a bristle of white brows over his unseeing eyes. 'There's only one kind of man,' he said, 'that sails the Outer Reach alone. A wizard, or a warlock, or a Mage . . .'

So the villagers were breathless hoping to see for once in their lives a Mage, one of the mighty White Magicians of the rich, towered, crowded inner islands of the Archipelago. They were disappointed, for the voyager was quite young, a handsome black-bearded fellow who hailed them cheerfully from his boat, and leaped ashore like any sailor glad to have made port. He introduced himself at once as a sea-peddlar. But when they told Seacaptain Fogeno that he carried an oaken walking-stick around with him,

the old man nodded. 'Two wizards in one town,' he
said. 'Bad!' And his mouth snapped shut like an old
carp's.

As the stranger could not give them his name, they
gave him one right away: Blackbeard. And they gave
him plenty of attention. He had a small mixed cargo
of cloth and sandals and *piswi* feathers for trimming
cloaks and cheap incense and levity stones and fine
herbs and great glass beads from Venway – the usual
peddlar's lot. Everyone on Sattins Island came to
look, to chat with the voyager, and perhaps to buy
something – 'Just to remember him by!' cackled
Goody Guld, who like all the women and girls of the
village was smitten with Blackbeard's bold good
looks. All the boys hung round him too, to hear him
tell of his voyages to far, strange islands of the Reach
or describe the great rich islands of the Archipelago,
the Inner Lanes, the roadsteads white with ships, and
the golden roofs of Havnor. The men willingly listened to his tales; but some of them wondered why a
trader should sail alone, and kept their eyes thoughtfully upon his oaken staff.

But all this time Mr Underhill stayed under his
hill.

'This is the first island I've ever seen that had no
wizard,' said Blackbeard one evening to Goody Guld,
who had invited him and her nephew and Palani in
for a cup of rushwash tea. 'What do you do when you
get a toothache, or the cow goes dry?'

'Why, we've got Mr Underhill!' said the old
woman.

'For what that's worth,' muttered her nephew Birt,
and then blushed purple and spilled his tea. Birt was

a fisherman, a large, brave, wordless young man. He loved the schoolmistress, but the nearest he had come to telling her of his love was to give baskets of fresh mackerel to her father's cook.

'Oh, you do have a wizard?' Blackbeard asked. 'Is he invisible?'

'No, he's just very shy,' said Palani. 'You've only been here a week, you know, and we see so few strangers here . . .' She also blushed a little, but did not spill her tea.

Blackbeard smiled at her. 'He's a good Sattinsman, then, eh?'

'No,' said Goody Guld, 'no more than you are. Another cup, nevvy? keep it in the cup this time. No, my dear, he came in a little bit of a boat, four years ago was it? just a day after the end of the shad run, I recall, for they was taking up the nets over in East Creek, and Pondi Cowherd broke his leg that very morning – five years ago it must be. No, four. No, five it is, 'twas the year the garlic didn't sprout. So he sails in on a bit of a sloop loaded full up with great chests and boxes and says to Seacaptain Fogeno, who wasn't blind then, though old enough goodness knows to be blind twice over, 'I hear tell,' he says, 'you've got no wizard nor warlock at all, might you be wanting one?' – 'Indeed, if the magic's white!' says the Captain, and before you could say cuttlefish Mr Underhill had settled down in the cave under the hill and was charming the mange off Goody Beltow's cat. Though the fur grew in grey, and 'twas an orange cat. Queer-looking thing it was after that. It died last winter in the cold spell. Goody Beltow took on so at that cat's death, poor thing, worse than when her man was drowned on the Long Banks, the year of the long herring-runs, when nevvy Birt here was but a babe in petticoats.' Here Birt spilled his tea again, and Blackbeard grinned, but Goody Guld proceeded undismayed, and talked on till nightfall.

Next day Blackbeard was down at the pier, seeing after the sprung board in his boat which he seemed to take a long time fixing, and as usual drawing the taciturn Sattinsmen into talk. 'Now which of these is your wizard's craft?' he asked. 'Or has he got one of those the Mages fold up into a walnut shell when they're not using it?'

'Nay,' said a stolid fisherman. 'She's oop in his cave, under hill.'

'He carried the boat he came in up to his cave?'

'Aye. Clear oop. I helped. Heavier as lead she was. Full oop with great boxes, and they full oop with books o' spells, he says. Heavier as lead she was.' And the stolid fisherman turned his back, sighing stolidly. Goody Guld's nephew, mending a net nearby, looked up from his work and asked with equal stolidity, 'Would ye like to meet Mr Underhill, maybe?'

Blackbeard returned Birt's look. Clever black eyes met candid blue ones for a long moment; then Blackbeard smiled and said, 'Yes. Will you take me up to the hill, Birt?'

'Aye, when I'm done with this,' said the fisherman. And when the net was mended, he and the Archipelagan set off up the village street towards the high green hill above it. But as they crossed the common Blackbeard said, 'Hold on a while, friend Birt. I have a tale to tell you, before we meet your wizard.'

'Tell away,' says Birt, sitting down in the shade of a live-oak.

'It's a story that started a hundred years ago, and isn't finished yet – though it soon will be, very soon . . . In the heart of the Archipelago, where the islands crowd thick as flies on honey, there's a little isle called Pendor. The sealords of Pendor were mighty men, in the old days of war before the League. Loot and ransom and tribute came pouring into Pendor, and they gathered a great treasure there, long ago. Then from somewhere away out in the West Reach, where dragons breed on the lava isles, came one day a very mighty dragon. Not one of those overgrown lizards most of you Outer Reach folk call dragons, but a big, black, winged, wise, cunning monster, full of strength and subtlety, and like all dragons loving gold and precious stones above all things. He killed the Sealord and his soldiers, and the people of Pendor fled in their ships by night. They all fled away and left the dragon coiled up in Pendor Towers. And there he stayed for a hundred years, dragging his scaly belly over the emeralds and sapphires and coins of gold, coming forth only once in a year or two when he must eat. He'd raid nearby islands for his food. You know what dragons eat?'

Birt nodded and said in a whisper, 'Maidens.'

'Right,' said Blackbeard. 'Well, that couldn't be endured forever, nor the thought of him sitting on all that treasure. So after the League grew strong, and the Archipelago wasn't so busy with wars and piracy, it was decided to attack Pendor, drive out the dragon, and get the gold and jewels for the treasury of the League. They're forever wanting money, the League is. So a huge fleet gathered from fifty islands, and seven Mages stood in the prows of the seven strongest ships, and they sailed towards Pendor . . .

They got there. They landed. Nothing stirred. The houses all stood empty, the dishes on the tables full of a hundred years' dust. The bones of the old Sealord and his men lay about in the castle courts and on the stairs. And the Tower rooms reeked of dragon. But there was no dragon. And no treasure, not a diamond the size of a poppyseed, not a single silver bead . . . Knowing that he couldn't stand up to seven Mages, the dragon had skipped out. They tracked him, and found he'd flown to a deserted island up north called Udrath; they followed his trail there, and what did they find? Bones again. His bones – the dragon's. But no treasure. A wizard, some unknown wizard from somewhere, must have met him singlehanded, and defeated him – and then made off with the treasure, right under the League's nose!'

The fisherman listened, attentive and expressionless.

'Now that must have been a powerful wizard and a clever one, first to kill a dragon, and second to get off without leaving a trace. The lords and Mages of the Archipelago couldn't track him at all, neither where he'd come from nor where he'd made off to. They were about to give up. That was last spring; I'd been off on a three-year voyage up in the North Reach, and got back about that time. And they asked me to help them find the unknown wizard. That was clever of them. Because I'm not only a wizard myself, as I think some of the oafs here have guessed, but I am also a descendant of the Lords of Pendor. That treasure is mine. It's mine, and knows that it's mine. Those fools of the League couldn't find it, because it's not theirs. It belongs to the House of Pendor, and the great emerald, the star of the hoard, Inalkil the Greenstone, knows its master. Behold!' Blackbeard raised his oaken staff and cried aloud, 'Inalkil!' The tip of the staff began to glow green, a fiery green radiance, a dazzling haze the color of April grass, and at the same moment the staff tipped in the wizard's hand, leaning, slanting till it pointed straight at the side of the hill above them.

'It wasn't so bright a glow, far away in Havnor,' Blackbeard murmured, 'but the staff pointed true. Inalkil answered when I called. The jewel knows its master. And I know the thief, and I shall conquer him. He's a mighty wizard, who could overcome a dragon. But I am mightier. Do you want to know why, oaf? Because I know his name!'

As Blackbeard's tone got more arrogant, Birt had looked duller and duller, blanker and blanker; but at this he gave a twitch, shut his mouth, and stared at the Archipelagan. 'How did you ... learn it?' he asked very slowly.

Blackbeard grinned, and did not answer.

'Black magic?'

'How else?'

Birt looked pale, and said nothing.

'I am the Sealord of Pendor, oaf, and I will have the gold my fathers won, and the jewels my mothers wore, and the Greenstone! For they are mine. – Now, you can tell your village boobies the whole story after I have defeated this wizard and gone. Wait here: Or you can come and watch, if you're not afraid. You'll never get the chance again to see a great wizard in all his power.' Blackbeard turned, and without a backward glance strode off up the hill towards the entrance to the cave.

Very slowly, Birt followed. A good distance from the cave he stopped, sat down under a hawthorn tree, and watched. The Archipelagan had stopped; a stiff, dark figure alone on the green swell of the hill before the gaping cave-mouth, he stood perfectly still. All at once he swung his staff up over his head, and the emerald radiance shone about him as he shouted, 'Thief, thief of the Hoard of Pendor, come forth!'

There was a crash, as of dropped crockery, from inside the cave, and a lot of dust came spewing out. Scared, Birt ducked. When he looked again he saw Blackbeard still standing motionless, and at the mouth of the cave, dusty and dishevelled, stood Mr Underhill. He looked small and pitiful, with his toes turned in as usual, and his little bowlegs in black tights, and no staff – he never had had one, Birt suddenly thought. Mr Underhill spoke. 'Who are you —' he said in his husky little voice.

'I am the Sealord of Pendor, thief, come to claim my treasure!'

At that, Mr Underhill slowly turned pink, as he always did when people were rude to him. But he then turned something else. He turned yellow. His hair bristled out, he gave a coughing roar – and was a yellow lion leaping down the hill at Blackbeard, white fangs gleaming.

But Blackbeard no longer stood there. A gigantic tiger, color of night and lightning, bounded to meet the lion . . .

The lion was gone. Below the cave all of a sudden stood a high grove of trees, black in the winter sunshine. The tiger, checking himself in mid-leap just before he entered the shadow of the trees, caught fire in the air, became a tongue of flame lashing out at the dry black branches . . .

But where the trees had stood a sudden cataract leaped from the hillside, an arch of silvery crashing water, thundering down upon the fire. But the fire was gone . . .

For just a moment before the fisherman's staring eyes two hills rose – the green one he knew, and a new one, a bare, brown hillock ready to drink up the rushing waterfall. That passed so quickly it made Birt blink, and after blinking he blinked again, and moaned, for what he saw now was a great deal worse. Where the cataract had been there hovered a dragon. Black wings darkened all the hill, steel claws reached groping, and from the dark, scaly, gaping lips fire and steam shot out.

Beneath the monstrous creature stood Blackbeard, laughing.

'Take any shape you please, little Mr Underhill!' he taunted. 'I can match you. But the game grows tiresome. I want to look upon my treasure, upon Inalkil. Now, big dragon, little wizard, take your true shape. I command you by the power of your true name – Yevaud!'

Birt could not move at all, not even to blink. He cowered staring whether he would or not. He saw the black dragon hang there in the air above Blackbeard. He saw the fire lick like many tongues from the scaly mouth, the steam jet from the red nostrils. He saw

Blackbeard's face grow white, white as chalk, and the beard-fringed lips trembling.

'Your name is Yevaud!'

'Yes,' said a great, husky, hissing voice. 'My true-name is Yevaud, and my true shape is this shape.'

'But the dragon was killed – they found dragon-bones on Udrath Island –'

'That was another dragon,' said the dragon, and then stooped like a hawk, talons outstretched. And Birt shut his eyes.

When he opened them the sky was clear, the hillside empty, except for a reddish-blackish, trampled spot, and a few talon-marks in the grass.

Birt the fisherman got to his feet and ran. He ran across the common, scattering sheep to right and left, and straight down the village street to Palani's father's house. Palani was out in the garden weeding the nasturtiums. 'Come with me!' Birt gasped. She stared. He grapped her wrist and dragged her with him. She screeched a little, but did not resist. He ran with her straight to the pier, pushed her into his fishing-sloop, the *Queenie*, untied the painter, took up the oars and set off rowing like a demon. The last that Sattins Island saw of him and Palani was the *Queenie*'s sail vanishing in the direction of the nearest island westward.

The villagers thought they would never stop talking about it, how Goody Guld's nephew Birt has lost his mind and sailed off with the schoolmistress on the very same day that the peddlar Blackbeard disappeared without a trace, leaving all his feathers and beads behind. But they did stop talking about it, three days later. They had other things to talk about, when Mr Underhill finally came out of his cave.

Mr Underhill had decided that since his truename was no longer a secret, he might as well drop his disguise. Walking was a lot harder than flying, and besides, it was a long, long time since he had had a real meal.

*   *   *

URSULA LE GUIN has been described as one of the two or three most important contemporary American science fiction writers and her award-winning sequence of Earthsea novels for younger readers are certainly among the most deeply influential fantasy works of the twentieth century. Beginning with *A Wizard of Earthsea* (1968), the saga traces the adventures of young Ged Sparrowhawk who is sent to a school for wizards on Roke Island – years before Harry Potter – graduates as a Magus and enters into a power-struggle with the ominous Shadow. Like the other books in the series, *The Tombs of Atuan* (1971), *The Farthest Shore* (1972), *Tehanu* (1990), *Tales from Earthsea* (2001) and *The Other Wind* (2002) the narrative describes life on an archipelago of islands where magic works and dragons are real and there is a constant battle between good and evil. But magic also has a cost – for, according to the lore of Earthsea, everything must be kept in balance and it has the power to corrupt as well as to cure. Ursula Le Guin is another writer for the younger generation whose stories are also read by adults and her fascination with magic can be enjoyed in other short stories including 'April in Paris', 'Semley's Necklace' and 'The Word of Unbinding', which are all crowded with wizards, sorcerers and magicians.

THE MAGIC SHOP

H.G. Wells

'The Magic Shopman' is a curious, dark figure with an extraordinarily long body, one ear bigger than the other and a chin like the toe-cap of a boot. But behind his suave smile – 'a playground of unspeakable emotions' – there lurks the mind of a man who knows about wizardry. This impression is, indeed, soon demonstrated to customers by the man's long, magic fingers which can produce colourful sparks and make them disappear into the shadows of his mysterious little shop in London's Regent Street. The narrator of the story says the shop is a modest-sized place, but I have never been able to find it. Little Gip and his father are rather luckier, however. Once inside, it soon becomes evident to them that the Magic Shopman is very particular about his customers – he turns away one fractious child and informs Gip that he will only serve 'the right sort of boy'. Those who meet the criteria can expect untold surprises, the man says, but when he offers to make Gip disappear, the magic starts to becomes just too real for his dad . . .

*　　*　　*

I had seen the Magic Shop from afar several times; I had passed it once or twice, a shop window of alluring little objects, magic balls, magic hens, wonderful cones, ventriloquist dolls, the material of the basket trick, packs of cards that *looked* all right, and all that sort of thing, but never had I thought of going in until one day, almost without warning, Gip hauled me by my finger right up to the window, and so conducted himself that there was nothing for it but to take him in. I had not thought the place was there, to tell the truth – a modest-sized frontage in Regent Street, between the picture shop and the place where the chicks run about just out of patent incubators – but there it was sure enough. I had fancied it was down nearer the Circus, or around the corner in Oxford Street, or even in Holborn; always over the way and a little inaccessible it had been, with something of the mirage in its position; but here it was now quite indisputably, and the fat end of Gip's pointing finger made a noise upon the glass.

'If I was rich,' said Gip, dabbing a finger at the Disappearing Egg, 'I'd buy myself that. And that' – which was The Crying Baby, Very Human – 'and that,' which was a mystery, and called, so a neat card asserted, 'Buy One and Astonish Your Friends.'

'Anything,' said Gip, 'will disappear under one of those cones. I have read about it in a book.

'And there, Dad, is the Vanishing Halfpenny – only they've put it this way up so's we can't see how it's done.'

Gip, dear boy, inherits his mother's breeding, and he did not propose to enter the shop or worry in any way; only, you know, quite unconsciously he lugged my finger doorward, and he made his interest clear.

'That,' he said, and pointed to the Magic Bottle.

'If you had that?' I said; at which promising inquiry he looked up with a sudden radiance.

'I could show it to Jessie,' he said, thoughtful as ever of others.

'It's less than a hundred days to your birthday,

Gibbles,' I said, and laid my hand on the door-handle.

Gip made no answer, but his grip tightened on my finger, and so we came into the shop.

It was no common shop this; it was a magic shop and all the prancing precedence Gip would have taken in the matter of mere toys was wanting. He left the burden of the conversation to me.

It was a little, narrow shop, not very well lit, and the doorbell pinged again with a plaintive note as we closed it behind us. For a moment or so we were alone and could glance about us. There was a tiger in *papier-mâché* on the glass case that covered the low counter – a grave, kind-eyed tiger that waggled his head in a methodical manner; there were several crystal spheres, a china hand holding magic cards, a stock of magic fish-bowls in various sizes, and an immodest magic hat that shamelessly displayed its springs. On the floor were magic mirrors; one to draw you out long and thin, one to swell your head and vanish your legs, and one to make you short and fat like a draught; and while we were laughing at these the shopman, as I suppose, came in.

At any rate, there he was behind the counter – a curious, sallow, dark man, with one ear larger than the other and a chin like the toe-cap of a boot.

'What can we have the pleasure?' he said, spreading his long, magic fingers on the glass case; and so with a start we were aware of him.

'I want,' I said, 'to buy my little boy a few simple tricks.'

'Legerdemain?' he asked. 'Mechanical? Domestic?'

'Anything amusing?' said I.

'Um!' said the shopman, and scratched his head for a moment as if thinking. Then, quite distinctly, he drew from his head a glass ball. 'Something in this way?' he said, and held it out.

The action was unexpected. I had seen the trick done at entertainments endless times before – it's part of the common stock of conjurers – but I had not expected it here. 'That's good,' I said, with a laugh.

'Isn't it?' said the shopman.

Gip stretched out his disengaged hand to take this object and found merely a blank palm.

'It's in your pocket,' said the shopman, and there it was!

'How much will that be?' I asked.

'We make no charge for glass balls,' said the shopman, politely. 'We get them' – he picked one out of his elbow as he spoke – 'free.' He produced another from the back of his neck, and laid it beside its predecessor on the counter. Gip regarded his glass ball sagely, then directed a look of inquiry at the two on the counter, and finally brought his round-eyed scrutiny to the shopman, who smiled. 'You may have those, too,' said the shopman, 'and if you *don't* mind, one from my mouth – *So!*'

Gip counselled me mutely for a moment, and then in a profound silence put away the four balls, resumed my reassuring finger, and nerved himself for the next event.

'We get all our smaller tricks in that way,' the shopman remarked.

I laughed in the manner of one who subscribes to a jest. 'Instead of going to the wholesale shop,' I said. 'Of course, it's cheaper.

'In a way,' the shopman said. 'Though we pay in the end. But not so heavily – as people suppose. . . . Our larger tricks, and our daily provisions and all the other things we want, we get out of that hat. . . . And you know, sir, if you'll excuse my saying it, there *isn't* a wholesale shop, not for Genuine Magic goods, sir. I don't know if you noticed our inscription – the Genuine Magic shop.' He drew a business-card from his cheek and handed it to me. 'Genuine,' he said, with his finger on the word, and added, 'There is absolutely no deception, sir.'

He seemed to be carrying out the joke pretty thoroughly, I thought.

He turned to Gip with a smile of remarkable affability. 'You, you know, are the Right Sort of Boy.'

I was surprised at his knowing that, because, in the interests of discipline, we keep it rather a secret even at home; but Gip received it in unflinching silence, keeping a steadfast eye on him.

'It's only the Right Sort of Boy gets through that doorway.'

And as if by way of illustration, there came a rattling at the door, and a squeaking little voice could be faintly heard. 'Nyar! I *warn* a' go in there, Dad, I WARN a' go in there. Ny-a-a-ah!' and then the accents of a down-trodden parent, urging consolations and propitiations. 'It's locked, Edward,' he said.

'But it isn't,' said I.

'It is, sir,' said the shopman, 'always – for that sort of child,' and as he spoke we had a glimpse of the other youngster, a small, white face, pallid from sweet-eating and over-fatty food, and distorted by evil passions, a ruthless little egotist, pawing at the enchanted pane. 'It's no good, sir,' said the shopman, as I moved, with my natural helpfulness, door-ward, and presently the spoilt child was carried off howling.

'How do you manage that?' I said, breathing more freely.

'Magic!' said the shopman, with a careless wave of the hand, and behold! sparks of coloured fire flew out of his fingers and vanished into the shadows of the shop.

'You were saying,' he said, addressing himself to Gip, 'before you came in, that you would like one of our "Buy One and Astonish your Friends' boxes?'

Gip, after a gallant effort, said 'Yes.'

'It's in your pocket.'

And leaning over the counter – he really had an extraordinarily long body – this amazing person produced the article in the customary conjurer's manner. 'Paper,' he said, and took a sheet out of the empty hat with the springs; 'string', and behold his mouth was a string-box, from which he drew an unending thread, which when he had tied his parcel he bit off – and, it seemed to me, swallowed the ball of string. And then he lit a candle at the nose of one of the ventriloquist's dummies, stuck one of his fingers (which had become sealing-wax red) into the flame, and so sealed the parcel. 'Then there was the Disappearing Egg,' he remarked, and produced one from within my coat-breast and packed it, and also The Crying Baby, Very Human. I handed each parcel to Gip as it was ready, and he clasped them to his chest. He said very little, but his eyes were eloquent; the clutch of his arms was eloquent. He was the playground of unspeakable emotions. These, you know, were *real* Magics.

Then, with a start, I discovered something moving about in my hat – something soft and jumpy. I whipped it off, and a ruffled pigeon – no doubt a confederate – dropped out and ran on the counter, and went, I fancy, into a cardboard box behind the *papier-mâché* tiger.

'Tut, tut!' said the shopman, dexterously relieving me of my headdress; 'careless bird, and – as I live – nesting!'

He shook my hat, and shook out into his extended hand two or three eggs, a large marble, a watch, about half-a-dozen of the inevitable glass balls, and then crumpled, crinkled paper, more and more and more, talking all the time of the way in which people neglect to brush their hats *inside* as well as out, politely, of course, but with a certain personal appli-cation. 'All sorts of things accumulate, sir . . . Not *you*, of course, in particular . . . Nearly every customer . . . Astonishing what they carry about with them . . .' The crumpled paper rose and billowed on the counter more and more and more, until he was nearly hidden from us, until he was altogether hidden, and still his voice went on and on. 'We none of us know what the fair semblance of a human being may conceal, sir. Are we all then no better than brushed exteriors, whited sepulchres –'

His voice stopped – exactly like when you hit a neighbour's gramophone with a well-aimed brick, the same instant silence, and the rustle of the paper stopped, and everything was still . . .

'Have you done with my hat?' I said, after an interval.

There was no answer.

I stared at Gip, and Gip stared at me; and there were our distortions in the magic mirrors, looking very rum, and grave, and quiet . . .

'I think we'll go now,' I said. 'Will you tell me how much all this comes to? . . .

'I say,' I said, on a rather louder note, 'I want the bill; and my hat, please.'

It might have been a sniff from behind the paper pile. . . .

'Let's look behind the counter, Gip,' I said. 'He's making fun of us.'

I led Gip round the head-wagging tiger, and what do you think there was behind the counter? No one at all! Only my hat on the floor, and a common conjurer's lop-eared white rabbit lost in meditation, and looking as stupid and crumpled as only a conjurer's rabbit can do. I resumed my hat, and the rabbit lolloped a lollop or so out of my way.

'Dad!' said Gip, in a guilty whisper.

'What is it, Gip?' said I.

'I *do* like this shop, Dad.'

'So should I,' I said to myself, 'if the counter wouldn't suddenly extend itself to shut one off from the door.' But I didn't call Gip's attention to that. 'Pussy!' he said, with a hand out to the rabbit as it came lolloping past us; 'Pussy, do Gip a magic!' and his eyes followed it as it squeezed through a door I had certainly not noticed a moment before. Then this door opened wider, and the man with one ear larger than the other appeared again. He was smiling still, but his eye met mine with something between amusement and defiance. 'You'd like to see our showroom, sir,' he said, with an innocent suavity. Gip tugged my finger forward. I glanced at the counter and met the shopman's eye again. I was beginning to think the magic just a little too genuine. 'We haven't *very* much time,' I said. But somehow we were inside the showroom before I could finish that.

'All goods of the same quality, said the shopman, rubbing his flexible hands together, 'and that is the Best. Nothing in the place that isn't genuine Magic, and warranted thoroughly rum. Excuse me, sir!'

I felt him pull at something that clung to my coat-sleeve, and then I saw he held a little, wriggling red demon by the tail – the little creature bit and fought and tried to get at his hand – and in a moment he tossed it carelessly behind a counter. No doubt the thing was only an image of twisted india-rubber, but for the moment! And his gesture was exactly that of a man who handles some petty biting bit of vermin. I glanced at Gip, but Gip was looking at a magic rocking-horse. I was glad he hadn't seen the thing. 'I say,' I said, in an undertone, and indicating Gip and the red demon with my eyes, 'you haven't many things like *that* about, have you?'

'None of ours! Probably brought it with you,' said the shopman – also in an undertone, and with a more dazzling smile than ever. 'Astonishing what people *will* carry about with them unawares!' And then to Gip, 'Do you see anything you fancy here?'

There were many things that Gip fancied there.

He turned to this astonishing tradesman with mingled confidence and respect. 'Is that a Magic Sword?' he said.

'A Magic Toy Sword. It neither bends, breaks, nor cuts the fingers. It renders the bearer invincible in battle against anyone under eighteen. Half-a-crown to seven and sixpence, according to size. These panoplies on cards are for juvenile knights-errant and very useful – shield of safety, sandals of swiftness, helmet of invisibility.'

'Oh, Dad!' gasped Gip.

I tried to find out what they cost, but the shopman did not heed me. He had got Gip now; he had got him away from my finger; he had embarked upon the exposition of all his confounded stock, and nothing was going to stop him. Presently I saw with a qualm of distrust and something very like jealousy that Gip had hold of this person's finger as usually he has hold of mine. No doubt the fellow was interesting, I thought, and had an interestingly faked lot of stuff, really *good* faked stuff, still –

I wandered after them, saying very little, but keeping an eye on this prestidigital fellow. After all, Gip was enjoying it. And no doubt when the time came to go we should be able to go quite easily.

It was a long, rambling place, that showroom, a gallery broken up by stands and stalls and pillars, with archways leading off to other departments, in which the queerest-looking assistants loafed and stared at one, and with perplexing mirrors and curtains. So perplexing, indeed, were these that I was presently unable to make out the door by which we had come.

The shopman showed Gip magic trains that ran without steam or clockwork, just as you set the signals, and then some very, very valuable boxes of soldiers that all came alive directly you took off the lid and said – I myself haven't a very quick ear and it was a tongue-twisting sound, but Gip – he has his mother's ear – got it in no time. 'Bravo!' said the shopman, putting the men back into the box unceremoniously and handing it to Gip. 'Now,' said the shopman, and in a moment Gip had made them all alive again.

'You'll take that box?' asked the shopman.

'We'll take that box,' said I, 'unless you charge its full value. In which case it would need a Trust Magnate –'

'Dear heart! *No!*' and the shopman swept the little men back again, shut the lid, waved the box in the air, and there it was, in brown paper, tied up and – *with Gip's full name and address on the paper!*

The shopman laughed at my amazement.

'This is the genuine magic,' he said. 'The real thing.'

'It's almost too genuine for my taste,' I said again.

After that he fell to showing Gip tricks, odd tricks, and still odder the way they were done. He explained them, he turned them inside out, and there was the dear little chap nodding his busy bit of a head in the sagest manner.

I did not attend as well I might. 'Hey, presto!' said the Magic Shopman, and then would come the clear, small 'Hey, presto!' of the boy. But I was distracted by other things. It was being borne in upon me just how tremendously rum this place was; it was, so to speak, inundated by a sense of rumness. There was something vaguely rum about the fixtures even, about the ceiling, about the floor, about the casually distributed chairs. I had a queer feeling that whenever I wasn't looking at them straight they went askew, and moved about, and played a noiseless puss-in-the-corner behind my back. And the cornice had a serpentine design with mask – masks altogether too expressive for proper plaster.

Then abruptly my attention was caught by one of the odd-looking assistants. He was some way off and evidently unaware of my presence – I saw a sort of three-quarter length of him over a pile of toys and through an arch – and, you know, he was leaning against a pillar in an idle sort of way doing the most horrid things with his features. The particular horrid thing he did was with his nose. He did it just as though he was idle and wanted to amuse himself. First of all it was a short, blobby nose, and then suddenly he shot it out like a telescope, and then out it flew and became thinner and thinner until it was like a long, red, flexible whip. Like a thing in a nightmare it was! He flourished it about and flung it forth as a fly-fisher flings his line.

My instant thought was that Gip mustn't see him. I turned about, and there was Gip quite preoccupied with the shopman, and thinking no evil. They were whispering together and looking at me. Gip was standing on a stool, and the shopman was holding a sort of big drum in his hand.

'Hide and seek, Dad!' cried Gip. 'You're He!'

And before I could do anything to prevent it, the shopman had clapped the big drum over him.

I saw what was up directly. 'Take that off,' I cried, 'this instant! You'll frighten the boy. Take it off!'

The shopman with the unequal ears did so without a word, and held the big cylinder towards me to show its emptiness. And the stool was vacant! In that instant my boy had utterly disappeared! . . .

You know, perhaps, that sinister something that comes like a hand out of the unseen and grips your heart about. You know it takes your commonsense away and leaves you tense and deliberate, neither slow nor hasty, neither angry nor afraid. So it was with me.

I came up to this grinning shopman and kicked his stool aside.

'Stop this folly!' I said. 'Where is my boy?'

'You see,' he said, still displaying the drum's interior, 'there is no deception –'

I put out my hand to grip him, and he eluded me by a dexterous movement. I snatched again, and he turned from me and pushed open a door to escape. 'Stop!' I said, and he laughed, receding. I leapt after him – into utter darkness.

Thud!

'Lor' bless my 'eart! I didn't see you coming, sir!'

I was in Regent Street, and I had collided with a decent-looking working man; and a yard away, perhaps, and looking extremely perplexed with himself, was Gip. There was some sort of apology, and then Gip had turned and come to me with a bright little smile, as though for a moment he had missed me.

And he was carrying four parcels in his arm!

He secured immediate possession of my finger.

For the second I was rather at a loss. I stared round to see the door of the magic shop, and; behold, it was not there! There was no door, no shop, nothing, only the common pilaster between the shop where they sell pictures and the window with the chicks!

I did the only thing possible in that mental tumult; I walked straight to the kerbstone and held up my umbrella for a cab.

''Ansoms,' said Gip, in a note of culminating exultation.

I helped him in, recalled my address with an effort, and got in also. Something unusual proclaimed itself in my tailcoat pocket, and I felt and discovered a glass ball. With a petulant expression I flung it into the street.

Gip said nothing.

For a space neither of us spoke.

'Dad!' said Gip, at last, 'that *was* a proper shop!'

I came round with that to the problem of just how the whole thing had seemed to him. He looked completely undamaged – so far, good; he was neither scared nor unhinged, he was simply tremendously satisfied with the afternoon's entertainment, and there in his arms were the four parcels.

Confound it what could be in them?

'Um!' I said. 'Little boys can't go to shops like that every day.'

He received this with his usual stoicism, and for a moment I was sorry I was his father and not his mother, and so couldn't suddenly there, *coram publico*, in our hansom, kiss him. After all, I thought, the thing wasn't so very bad.

But it was only when we opened the parcels that I really began to be reassured. Three of them contained boxes of soldiers, quite ordinary lead soldiers, but of so good a quality as to make Gip altogether forget that originally these parcels had been Magic Tricks of the only genuine sort, and the fourth contained a kitten, a little living white kitten, in excellent health and appetite and temper.

I saw this unpacking with a sort of provisional relief. I hung about in the nursery for quite an unconscionable time . . .

That happened six months ago. And now I am beginning to believe it is all right. The kitten had only the magic natural to all kittens, and the soldiers seem as steady a company as any colonel could desire. And Gip?

The intelligent parent will understand that I have to go cautiously with Gip.

But I went so far as this one day. I said, 'How would you like your soldiers to come alive, Gip, and march about by themselves?'

'Mine do,' said Gip. 'I just have to say a word I know before I open the lid.'

'Then they march about alone?'

'Oh, *quite*, Dad. I shouldn't like them if they didn't do that.'

I displayed no unbecoming surprise, and since then I have taken occasion to drop in upon him once or twice, unannounced, when the soldiers were about, but so far I have never discovered them performing in anything like a magical manner . . .

It's so difficult to tell.

There's also a question of finance. I have an incurable habit of paying bills. I have been up and down Regent Street several times, looking for that shop. I am inclined to think, indeed, that in that matter honour is satisfied, and that, since Gip's name and address are known to them, I may very well leave it to these people, whoever they may be, to send in their bill in their own time.

*   *   *

H. G. WELLS actually grew up as the son of a small shopkeeper in Bromley, Kent and from his childhood was fascinated by science and tales of fantasy. He was still a student at the Normal School of Science in London when he wrote his first story, 'The

Chronic Argonauts', about time travel, published in 1888. He was for a time a teacher, but writing stories was already his obsession and in the space of less than four years he produced three classic novels that earned him the accolade of 'The Father of Modern Science Fiction': *The Time Machine* (1895), a complete re-working of his earlier story; the weird tale of *The Invisible Man* (1897); and the first novel of an alien invasion of the Earth, *The War of the Worlds* (1898). Magic and the supernatural can be found in several of H. G. Wells' short stories, notably 'The Man Who Could Work Miracles' (1898) which was made into an early special effects film in 1936, and 'The Truth About Pyecraft' (1903) featuring a spell that makes a man weightless. 'The Magic Shop' is equally significant, I think, because it allies magic with science in the form of a supernatural creature – the small, angry, red demon – and an invention that was unheard of at the time: a train that runs without steam.

THE MAGIC BONBONS

L. Frank Baum

Doctor Daws also has his own magic shop across the Atlantic in Boston. He is a wise old man who practises what he calls 'chemical sorcery' and makes up secret potions to help his customers fulfil their most heartfelt wishes. But unlike most magicians whose pills always taste nasty and whose lotions smell disgusting, the good Doctor ensures that his preparations are always pleasant – especially those that are to be eaten, sucked or drunk. When one of Dr Daws' customers accidentally leaves a packet of magic sweets behind on his counter, the parcel is mistakenly taken home by little Bessie Bostwick who has no idea of their power. And when Bessie pops the bonbons into the family sweet dish, she and her parents are soon unexpectedly – and hilariously – finding their wishes coming true . . .

*   *   *

There lived in Boston a wise and ancient chemist by the name of Dr. Daws, who dabbled somewhat in magic. There also lived in Boston a young lady by the name of Claribel Sudds, who was possessed of much money, little wit and an intense desire to go upon the stage.

So Claribel went to Dr. Daws and said:

'I can neither sing nor dance; I cannot recite verse nor play upon the piano; I am no acrobat nor leaper nor high kicker; yet I wish to go upon the stage. What shall I do?'

'Are you willing to pay for such accomplishments?' asked the wise chemist.

'Certainly,' answered Claribel, jingling her purse.

'Then come to me to-morrow at two o'clock,' said he.

All that night he practiced what is known as chemical sorcery; so that when Claribel Sudds came next day at two o'clock he showed her a small box filled with compounds that closely resembled French bonbons.

'This is a progressive age,' said the old man, 'and I flatter myself your Uncle Daws keeps right along with the procession. Now, one of your old-fashioned sorcerers would have made you some nasty, bitter pills to swallow; but I have consulted your taste and convenience. Here are some magic bonbons. If you eat this one with the lavender color you can dance thereafter as lightly and gracefully as if you had been trained a lifetime. After you consume the pink confection you will sing like a nightingale. Eating the white one will enable you to become the finest elocutionist in the land. The chocolate piece will charm you into playing the piano better than Rubenstein, while after eating you lemon-yellow bonbon you can easily kick six feet above your head.'

'How delightful!' exclaimed Claribel, who was truly enraptured. 'You are certainly a most clever sorcerer as well as a considerate compounder,' and she held out her hand for the box.

'Ahem!' said the wise one; 'a cheque please.'

'Oh, yes; to be sure! How stupid of me to forget it,' she returned.

He considerately retained the box in his own hand while she signed a cheque for a large amount of money, after which he allowed her to hold the box herself.

'Are you sure you have made them strong enough?' she inquired, anxiously; 'it usually takes a great deal to affect me.'

'My only fear,' replied Dr. Daws, 'is that I have made them too strong. For this is the first time I have ever been called upon to prepare these wonderful confections.'

'Don't worry,' said Claribel; 'the stronger they act the better I shall act myself.'

She went away, after saying this, but stopping in at a dry goods store to shop, she forgot the precious box in her new interest and left it lying on the ribbon counter.

Then little Bessie Bostwick came to the counter to buy a hair ribbon and laid her parcels beside the box. When she went away she gathered up the box with her other bundles and trotted off home with it.

Bessie never knew, until after she had hung her coat in the hall closet and counted up her parcels, that she had one too many. Then she opened it and exclaimed:

'Why, it's a box of candy! Someone must have mislaid it. But it is too small a matter to worry about; there are only a few pieces.' So she dumped the contents of the box into a bonbon dish that stood upon the hall table and picking out the chocolate piece – she was fond of chocolates – ate it daintily while she examined her purchases.

These were not many, for Bessie was only twelve years old and was not yet trusted by her parents to spend much money at the stores. But while she tried on the hair ribbon she suddenly felt a great desire to play upon the piano, and the desire at last became so overpowering that she went into the parlor and opened the instrument.

The little girl had, with infinite pains, contrived to learn two 'pieces' which she usually executed with a jerky movement of her right hand and a left hand that forgot to keep up and so made dreadful discords. But under the influence of the chocolate bonbon she sat down and ran her fingers lightly over the keys producing such exquisite harmony that she was filled with amazement at her own performance.

That was the prelude, however. The next moment she dashed into Beethoven's seventh sonata and played it magnificently.

Her mother, hearing the unusual burst of melody, came downstairs to see what musical guest had arrived; but when she discovered it was her own little daughter who was playing so divinely she had an attack of palpitation of the heart (to which she was subject) and sat down upon a sofa until it should pass away.

Meanwhile Bessie played one piece after another with untiring energy. She loved music, and now found that all she need do was to sit at the piano and listen and watch her hands twinkle over the keyboard.

Twilight deepened in the room and Bessie's father came home and hung up his hat and overcoat and placed his umbrella in the rack. Then he peeped into the parlor to see who was playing.

'Great Caesar!' he exclaimed. But the mother came to him softly with her finger on her lips and whispered: 'Don't interrupt her, John. Our child seems to be in a trance. Did you ever hear such superb music?'

'Why, she's an infant prodigy!' gasped the astounded father. 'Beats Blind Tom all hollow! It – it's wonderful!'

As they stood listening the senator arrived, having been invited to dine with them that evening. And before he had taken off his coat the Yale professor – a man of deep learning and scholarly attainments – joined the party.

Bessie played on; and the four elders stood in a huddled but silent and amazed group, listening to the music and waiting for the sound of the dinner gong.

Mr. Bostwick, who was hungry, picked up the bonbon dish that lay on the table beside him and ate the pink confection. The professor was watching him, so Mr. Bostwick courteously held the dish toward him. The professor ate the lemon-yellow piece and the senator reached out his hand and took the lavender piece. He did not eat it, however, for, chancing to remember that it might spoil his dinner, he put it in his vest pocket. Mrs. Bostwick, still intently listening to her precocious daughter, without thinking what she did, took the remaining piece, which was the white one, and slowly devoured it.

The dish was now empty, and Claribel Sudds' precious bonbons had passed from her possession forever!

Suddenly Mr. Bostwick, who was a big man, began to sing in a shrill, tremolo soprano voice. It was not the same song Bessie was playing, and the discord was shocking that the professor smiled, the senator put his hands to his ears and Mrs. Bostwick cried in a horrified voice:

'William!'

Her husband continued to sing as if endeavoring to emulate the famous Christine Nillson, and paid no attention whatever to his wife or his guests.

Fortunately the dinner gong now sounded, and Mrs. Bostwick dragged Bessie from the piano and ushered her guests into the dining-room. Mr. Bostwick followed, singing 'The Last Rose of Summer' as if it had been an encore demanded by a thousand delighted hearers.

The poor woman was in despair at witnessing her husband's undignified actions and wondered what she might do to control him. The professor seemed more grave than usual; the senator's face wore an offended expression, and Bessie kept moving her fingers as if she still wanted to play the piano.

Mrs. Bostwick managed to get them all seated, although her husband had broken into another aria; and then the maid brought in the soup.

When she carried a plate to the professor, he cried, in an excited voice:

'Hold it higher! Higher – I say!' And springing up he gave it a sudden kick that sent it nearly to the ceiling, from whence the dish descended to scatter soup over Bessie and the maid and to smash in pieces upon the crown of the professor's bald head.

At this atrocious act the senator rose from his seat with an exclamation of horror and glanced at his hostess.

For some time Mrs. Bostwick had been staring straight ahead, with a dazed expression; but now, catching the senator's eye, she bowed gracefully and began reciting 'The Charge of the Light Brigade' in forceful tones.

The senator shuddered. Such disgraceful rioting he had never seen nor heard before in a decent private family. He felt that his reputation was at stake, and, being the only sane person, apparently, in the room, there was no one to whom he might appeal.

The maid had run away to cry hysterically in the kitchen; Mr. Bostwick was singing 'O Promise Me'; the professor was trying to kick the globes off the chandelier; Mrs. Bostwick had switched her recitation to 'The Boy Stood on the Burning Deck,' and Bessie had stolen into the parlor and was pounding out the overture from the 'Flying Dutchman.'

The senator was not at all sure he would not go crazy himself, presently; so he slipped away from the turmoil, and, catching up his had and coat in the hall, hurried from the house.

That night he sat up late writing a political speech he was to deliver the next afternoon at Faneuil Hall, but his experiences at the Bostwicks' had so unnerved him that he could scarcely collect his thoughts, and often he would pause and shake his head pityingly as he remembered the strange things he had seen in that usually respectable home.

The next day he met Mr. Bostwick in the street, but passed him by with a stony glare of oblivion. He felt he really could not afford to know this gentleman in the future. Mr. Bostwick was naturally indignant at the direct snub; yet in his mind lingered a faint memory of some quite unusual occurrences at his dinner party the evening before, and he hardly knew whether he dared resent the senator's treatment or not.

The political meeting was the feature of the day, for the senator's eloquence was well known in Boston. So the big hall was crowded with people, and in one of the front rows sat the Bostwick family, with the learned Yale professor beside them. They all looked tired and pale, as if they had passed a rather dissipated evening, and the senator was rendered so nervous by seeing them that he refused to look in their direction a second time.

While the mayor was introducing him the great man sat fidgeting in his chair; and, happening to put his thumb and finger into his vest pocket, he found the lavender-colored bonbon he had placed there the evening before.

'This may clear my throat,' thought the senator, and slipped the bonbon into his mouth.

A few minutes afterwards he arose before the vast audience, which greeted him with enthusiastic plaudits.

'My friends,' began the senator, in a grave voice, 'this is a most impressive and important occasion.'

Then he paused, balanced himself upon his left foot, and kicked his right leg into the air in the way favored by ballet-dancers!

There was a hum of amazement and horror from the spectators, but the senator appeared not to notice it. He whirled around upon the tips of his toes, kicked right and left in a graceful manner, and startled a bald-headed man in the front row by casting a languishing glance in his direction.

Suddenly Claribel Sudds, who happened to be present, uttered a scream and sprang to her feet. Pointing an accusing finger at the dancing senator, she cried in a loud voice:

'That's the man who stole my bonbons! Seize him! Arrest him! Don't let him escape!'

But the ushers rushed her out of the hall, thinking she had gone suddenly insane; and the senator's friends seized him firmly and carried him out the stage entrance to the street, where they put him into an open carriage and instructed the driver to take him home.

The effect of the magic bonbon was still powerful enough to control the poor senator, who stood upon the rear seat of the carriage and danced energetically all the way home, to the delight of the crowd of small boys who followed the carriage and the grief of the sober-minded citizens, who shook their heads sadly and whispered that 'another good man had gone wrong.'

It took the senator several months to recover from the shame and humiliation of this escapade; and, curiously enough, he never had the slightest idea what had induced him to act in so extraordinary a manner. Perhaps it was fortunate the last bonbon had now been eaten, for they might easily have caused considerably more trouble than they did.

Of course Claribel went again to the wise chemist and signed a cheque for another box of magic bonbons; but she must have taken better care of these, for she is now a famous vaudeville actress.

*   *   *

L. (for Lyman) FRANK BAUM is famous as the creator of the magical land of Oz, the first fantasy world in American literature. After having no luck fulfilling his own dreams as an actor or journalist, in

1900 he came up with the idea of a story for his four young sons, *The Wonderful Wizard of Oz,* and such was the success of the tale of a young girl's quest to find the master magician and his fabulous kingdom, that Baum wrote a series of over forty sequels including *Dorothy and the Wizard of Oz* (1908), *The Emerald City of Oz* (1910) and *The Magic of Oz* (1919). The first book in the series was adapted for a short, animated film, followed by several stage versions and then in 1939 the classic full-length movie starring Judy Garland. For a while Frank Baum tried unsuccessfully to establish an 'Oz Land' in Hollywood – long before Disneyland – as well as writing another popular saga, the 'Little Wizard Series'. Magic and wizardry are to be found in several of his other works including *The Enchanted Island of Yew* (1903) and *Queen Zizi of Ix, or The Story of the Magic Cloak* (1905), plus a number of short stories, notably 'The Magic Bonbons' which was filmed in 1915 starring Violet Macmillan.

THE DAY BOY AND THE NIGHT GIRL

George MacDonald

Watho is a witch of great power. She is not, though, a traditional old wizened crone, but a tall, graceful figure with striking white skin, red hair and black eyes that flash with a red fire from deep within. Her driving ambition is for knowledge and she is the embodiment of an old saying that 'in the hearts of witches love and hate lie close together and often tumble over each other.' She has used her magical powers to kidnap a boy and girl and raise them in her castle – the one to know only daylight and the other only darkness. As they grow, the youngsters begin to wonder what lies beyond their prison and dream of going exploring. When Watho falls ill, the boy and girl seize their chance – only to find themselves at the mercy of the witch's ill-temper and her ability to plot terrible evil against them . . .

1. Watho

There was once a witch who desired to know everything. But the wiser a witch is, the harder she knocks her head against the wall when she comes to it. Her name was Watho, and she had a wolf in her mind. She cared for nothing in itself – only for knowing it. She was not naturally cruel, but the wolf had made her cruel.

She was tall and graceful, with a white skin, red hair, and black eyes, which had a red fire in them. She was straight and strong, but now and then would fall bent together, shudder, and sit for a moment with her head turned over her shoulder, as if the wolf had got out of her mind on to her back.

2. Aurora

This witch got two ladies to visit her. One of them belonged to the court, and her husband had been sent to a far and difficult embassy. The other was a young widow whose husband had lately died, and who had since lost her sight. Watho lodged them in different parts of her castle, and they did not know of each other's existence.

The castle stood on the side of a hill sloping gently down into a narrow valley, in which was a river, with a pebbly channel and a continual song. The garden went down to the bank of the river, enclosed by high walls, which crossed the river and there stopped. Each wall had a double row of battlements, and between the rows was a narrow walk.

In the topmost story of the castle the Lady Aurora occupied a spacious apartment of several large rooms looking southward. The windows projected oriel-wise over the garden below, and there was a splendid view from them both up and down and across the river. The opposite side of the valley was steep, but not very high. Far away snow-peaks were visible. These rooms Aurora seldom left, but their airy spaces, the brilliant landscape and sky, the plentiful sunlight, the musical instruments, books, pictures, curiosities, with the company of Watho, who made herself charming, precluded all dulness. She had venison and feathered game to eat, milk and pale sunny sparkling wine to drink.

She had hair of the yellow gold, waved and rippled; her skin was fair, not white like Watho's, and her eyes were of the blue of the heavens when bluest; her features were delicate but strong, her mouth large and finely curved, and haunted with smiles.

3. Vesper

Behind the castle the hill rose abruptly; the north-eastern tower, indeed, was in contact with the rock, and communicated with the interior of it. For in the rock was a series of chambers, known only to Watho and the one servant whom she trusted, called Falca. Some former owner had constructed these chambers after the tomb of an Egyptian king, and probably with the same design, for in the centre of one of them stood what could only be a sarcophagus, but that and others were walled off. The sides and roofs of them were carved in low relief, and curiously painted. Here the witch lodged the blind lady, whose name was Vesper. Her eyes were black, with long black lashes; her skin had a look of darkened silver, but was of purest tint and grain; her hair was black and fine and straight-flowing; her features were exquisitely formed, and if less beautiful yet more lovely from sadness; she always looked as if she wanted to lie down and not rise again. She did not know she was lodged in a tomb, though now and then she wondered she never touched a window. There were many couches, covered with richest silk, and soft as her own cheek, for her to lie upon; and the carpets were so thick, she might have cast herself down anywhere – as befitted a tomb. The place was dry and warm, and cunningly pierced for air, so that it was always fresh, and lacked only sunlight. There the witch fed her upon milk, and wine dark as a carbuncle, and pomegranates, and purple grapes, and birds that dwell in marshy places; and she played to her mournful tunes, and caused wailful violins to attend her, and told her sad tales, thus holding her ever in an atmosphere of sweet sorrow.

4. Photogen

Watho at length had her desire, for witches often get what they want: a splendid boy was born to the fair Aurora. Just as the sun rose, he opened his eyes. Watho carried him immediately to a distant part of the castle, and persuaded the mother that he never cried but once, dying the moment he was born. Overcome with grief, Aurora left the castle as soon as she was able, and Watho never invited her again.

And now the witch's care was that the child should not know darkness. Persistently she trained him until at last he never slept during the day, and never woke during the night. She never let him see anything black, and even kept all dull colours out of his way. Never, if she could help it, would she let a shadow fall upon him, watching against shadows as if they had been live things that would hurt him. All day he basked in the full splendour of the sun, in the same large rooms his mother had occupied. Watho used him to the sun, until he could bear more of it than any dark-blooded African. In the hottest of every day, she stript him and laid him in it, that he might ripen like a peach; and the boy rejoiced in it, and would resist being dressed again. She brought all her knowledge to bear on making his muscles strong and elastic and swiftly responsive – that his soul, she said laughing, might sit in every fibre, be all in every part, and awake the moment of call. His hair was of the red gold, but his eyes grew darker as he grew, until they were as black as Vesper's. He was the merriest of creatures, always laughing, always loving, for a moment raging, then laughing afresh. Watho called him Photogen.

5. Nycteris

Five or six months after the birth of Photogen, the dark lady also gave birth to a baby: in the windowless tomb of a blind mother, in the dead of night, under the feeble rays of a lamp in an alabaster globe, a girl came into the darkness with a wail. And just as she was born for the first time, Vesper was born for the second, and passed into a world as unknown to her as this was to her child – who would have to be born yet again before she could see her mother.

Watho called her Nycteris, and she grew as like Vesper as possible – in all but one particular. She had the same dark skin, dark eyelashes and brows, dark hair, and gentle sad look; but she had just the eyes of Aurora, the mother of Photogen, and if they grew darker as she grew older, it was only a darker blue. Watho, with the help of Falca, took the greatest possible care of her – in every way consistent with her plans, that is – the main point in which was that she should never see any light but what came from the lamp. Hence her optic nerves, and indeed her whole apparatus for seeing, grew both larger and more sensitive; her eyes, indeed, stopped short only of being too large. Under her dark hair and forehead and eyebrows, they looked like two breaks in a cloudy night-sky, through which peeped the heaven where the stars and no clouds live. She was a sadly dainty little creature.

No one in the world except those two was aware of the being of the little bat. Watho trained her to sleep during the day, and wake during the night. She taught her music, in which she was herself a proficient, and taught her scarcely anything else.

6. How Photogen Grew

The hollow in which the castle of Watho lay, was a cleft in a plain rather than a valley among hills, for at the top of its steep sides, both north and south, was a table-land, large and wide. It was covered with rich grass and flowers, with here and there a wood, the outlying colony of a great forest. These grassy plains were the finest hunting grounds in the world. Great herds of small, but fierce cattle, with humps and shaggy manes, roved about them, also antelopes and gnus, and the tiny roedeer, while the woods were swarming with wild creatures. The tables of the castle were mainly supplied from them. The chief of Watho's huntsmen was a fine fellow, and when Photogen began to outgrow the training she could give him, she handed him over to Fargu. He with a will set about teaching him all he knew. He got him pony after pony, larger and larger as he grew, every one less manageable than that which had preceded it, and advanced him from pony to horse, and from horse to horse, until he was equal to anything in that kind which the country produced. In similar fashion he trained him to the use of bow and arrow, substituting every three months a stronger bow and longer arrows; and soon he became, even on horseback, a wonderful archer. He was but fourteen when he killed his first bull, causing jubilation among the huntsmen, and, indeed, through all the castle, for there too he was the favourite. Every day, almost as soon as the sun was up, he went out hunting, and would in general be out nearly the whole of the day. But Watho had laid upon Fargu just one commandment, namely, that Photogen should on no account, whatever the plea, be out until sundown, or so near it as to wake in him the desire of seeing what was going to happen; and this commandment Fargu was anxiously careful not to break; for, although he would not have trembled had a whole herd of bulls come down upon him, charging at full speed across the level, and not an arrow left in his quiver, he was more than afraid of his mistress. When she looked at him in a certain way, he felt, he said, as if his heart turned to ashes in his breast, and what ran in his veins was no longer blood, but milk and water. So that, ere long, as Photogen grew older, Fargu began to tremble, for he found it steadily growing harder to restrain him. So full of life was he, as Fargu said to his mistress, much to her content, that he was more like a live thunderbolt than a human being. He did not know what fear was, and that not because he did not know danger; for he had had a severe laceration from the razor-like tusk of a boar – whose spine, however, he had severed with one blow of his hunting-knife, before Fargu could reach him with defence. When he would spur his horse into the midst of a herd of bulls, carrying only his bow and his short sword, or shoot an arrow into a herd, and go after it as if to reclaim it for a runaway shaft, arriving in time to follow it with a spear-thrust before the wounded animal knew which way to charge, Fargu thought with terror how it would be when he came to know the temptation of the huddle-spot leopards, and the knife-clawed lynxes, with which the forest was haunted. For the boy had been so steeped in the sun, from childhood so saturated with his influence, that he looked upon every danger from a sovereign height of courage. When, therefore, he was ap-proaching his sixteenth year, Fargu ventured to beg of Watho that she would lay her commands upon the youth himself, and release him from responsibility for him. One might as soon hold a tawny-maned lion as Photogen, he said. Watho called the youth, and in the presence of Fargu laid her command upon him never to be out when the rim of the sun should touch the horizon, accompanying the prohibition with hints of consequences, none the less awful that they were obscure. Photogen listened respectfully, but, knowing neither the taste of fear nor the temptation of the night, her words were but sounds to him.

7. How Nycteris Grew

The little education she intended Nycteris to have, Watho gave her by word of mouth. Not meaning she should have light enough to read by, to leave other reasons unmentioned, she never put a book in her hands. Nycteris, however, saw so much better than Watho imagined, that the light she gave her was quite sufficient, and she managed to coax Falca into teaching her the letters, after which she taught herself to read, and Falca now and then brought her a child's book. But her chief pleasure was in her instrument. Her very fingers loved it, and would wander about over its keys like feeding sheep. She was not unhappy. She knew nothing of the world except the tomb in which she dwelt, and had some pleasure in everything she did. But she desired, nevertheless, something more or different. She did not know what it was, and the nearest she could come to expressing it to herself was – that she wanted more room. Watho and Falca would go from her beyond the shine of the lamp, and come again; therefore surely there must be more room somewhere. As often as she was left alone, she would fall to poring over the coloured bas-reliefs on the walls. These were intended to represent various of the powers of Nature under allegorical similitudes, and as nothing can be made that does not belong to the general scheme, she could not fail at least to imagine a flicker of relationship between some of them, and thus a shadow of the reality of things found its way to her.

There was one thing, however, which moved and taught her more than all the rest – the lamp, namely, that hung from the ceiling, which she always saw alight, though she never saw the flame, only the slight condensation towards the centre of the alabaster globe. And besides the operation of the light itself after its kind, the indefiniteness of the globe, and the softness of the light, giving her the feeling as if her eyes could go in and into its whiteness, were somehow also associated with the idea of space and room. She would sit for an hour together gazing up at the lamp, and her heart would swell as she gazed. She would wonder what had hurt her, when she found her face wet with tears, and then would wonder how she could have been hurt without knowing it. She never looked thus at the lamp except when she was alone.

8. The Lamp

Watho having given orders, took it for granted they were obeyed, and that Falca was all night long with Nycteris, whose day it was. But Falca could not get into the habit of sleeping through the day, and would often leave her alone half the night. Then it seemed to Nycteris that the white lamp was watching over her. As it was never permitted to go out – while she was awake at least – Nycteris, except by shutting her eyes, knew less about darkness than she did about light. Also, the lamp being fixed high overhead, and in the centre of everything, she did not know much about shadows either. The few there were fell almost entirely on the floor, or kept like mice about the foot of the walls.

Once, when she was thus alone, there came the noise of a far-off rumbling: she had never before heard a sound of which she did not know the origin, and here therefore was a new sign of something beyond these chambers. Then came a trembling, then a shaking; the lamp dropped from the ceiling to the floor with a great crash, and she felt as if both her eyes were hard shut and both her hands over them. She concluded that it was the darkness that had made the rumbling and the shaking, and rushing into the room, had thrown down the lamp. She sat trembling. The noise and the shaking ceased, but the light did not return. The darkness had eaten it up!

Her lamp gone, the desire at once awoke to get out of her prison. She scarcely knew what *out* meant; out of one room into another, where there was not even a dividing door, only an open arch, was all she knew of the world. But suddenly she remembered that she had heard Falca speak of the lamp *going out*: this must be what she had meant? And if the lamp had gone out, where had it gone? Surely where Falca went, and like her it would come again. But she could not wait. The desire to go out grew irresistible. She must follow her beautiful lamp! She must find it! She must see what it was about!

Now there was a curtain covering a recess in the wall, where some of her toys and gymnastic things were kept; and from behind that curtain Watho and Falca always appeared, and behind it they vanished. How they came out of solid wall, she had not an idea, all up to the wall was open space, and all beyond it seemed wall; but clearly the first and only thing she could do, was to feel her way behind the curtain. It was so dark that a cat could not have caught the largest of mice. Nycteris could see better than any cat, but now her great eyes were not of the smallest use to her. As she went she trod upon a piece of the broken lamp. She had never worn shoes or stockings, and the fragment, though, being of soft alabaster, it did not cut, yet hurt her foot. She did not know what it was, but as it had not been there before the darkness came, she suspected that it had to do with the lamp. She kneeled therefore, and searched with her hands, and bringing two large pieces together, recognized the shape of the lamp. Therewith it flashed upon her that the lamp was dead, that this brokenness was the death of which she had read without understanding, that the darkness had killed the lamp. What then could Falca have meant when she spoke of the lamp *going out?* There was the lamp – dead indeed, and so changed that she would never have taken it for a lamp but for the shape! No, it was not the lamp any more now it was dead, for all that made it a lamp was gone, namely, the bright shining of it. Then it must be the shine, the light, that had gone out! That must be what Falca meant – and it must be somewhere in the other place in the wall. She started afresh after it, and groped her way to the curtain.

Now she had never in her life tried to get out, and did not know how; but instinctively she began to move her hands about over one of the walls behind the curtain, half expecting them to go into it, as she supposed Watho and Falca did. But the wall repelled her with inexorable hardness, and she turned to the one opposite. In so doing, she set her foot upon an ivory die, and as it met sharply the same spot the broken alabaster had already hurt, she fell forward with her outstretched hands against the wall. Something gave way, and she tumbled out of the cavern.

9. Out

But alas! *out* was very much like *in*, for the same enemy, the darkness, was here also. The next moment, however, came a great gladness – a firefly, which had wandered in from the garden. She saw the tiny spark in the distance. With slow pulsing ebb and throb of light, it came pushing itself through the air, drawing nearer and nearer, with that motion which more resembles swimming than flying, and the light seemed the source of its own motion.

'My lamp! my lamp!' cried Nycteris. 'It is the shiningness of my lamp, which the cruel darkness drove out. My good lamp has been waiting for me here all the time! It knew I would come after it, and waited to take me with it.'

She followed the firefly, which, like herself, was seeking the way out. If it did not know the way, it was yet light; and, because all light is one, any light may serve to guide to more light. If she was mistaken in thinking it the Spirit of her lamp, it was of the same Spirit as her lamp – and had wings. The gold-green jet-boat, driven by light, went throbbing before her through a long narrow passage. Suddenly it rose higher, and the same moment Nycteris fell upon an ascending stair. She had never seen a stair before, and found going-up a curious sensation. Just as she reached what seemed the top, the firefly ceased to shine, and so disappeared. She was in utter darkness once more. But when we are following the light, even its extinction is a guide. If the firefly had gone on shining, Nycteris would have seen the stair turn, and would have gone up to Watho's bedroom; whereas now, feeling straight before her, she came to a latched door, which after a good deal of trying she managed to open – and stood in a maze of wondering perplexity, awe, and delight. What was it? Was it outside of her, or something taking place in her head? Before her was a very long and very narrow passage, broken up she could not tell how, and spreading out above and on all sides to an infinite height and breadth and distance – as if space itself

were growing out of a trough. It was brighter than
her rooms had ever been – brighter than if six
alabaster lamps had been burning in them. There
was a quantity of strange streaking and mottling
about it, very different from the shapes on her walls.
She was in a dream of pleasant perplexity, of delightful bewilderment. She could not tell whether she was
upon her feet or drifting about like the firefly, driven
by the pulses of an inward bliss. But she knew little as
yet of her inheritance. Unconsciously she took one
step forward from the threshold, and the girl who
had been from her very birth a troglodyte, stood in
the ravishing glory of a southern night, lit by a
perfect moon – not the moon of our northern clime,
but a moon like silver glowing in a furnace – a moon
one could see to be a globe – not far off, a mere flat
disc on the face of the blue, but hanging down
halfway, and looking as if one could see all round it
by a mere bending of the neck.

'It is my lamp,' she said, and stood dumb with
parted lips. She looked and felt as if she had been
standing there in silent ecstasy from the beginning.

'No, it is not my lamp,' she said after a while; 'it is
the mother of all the lamps.'

And with that she fell on her knees, and spread out
her hands to the moon. She could not in the least
have told what was in her mind, but the action was in
reality just a begging of the moon to be what she was
– that precise incredible splendour hung in the far-
off roof, that very glory essential to the being of poor
girls born and bred in caverns. It was a resurrection –
nay, a birth itself, to Nycteris. What the vast blue sky,
studded with tiny sparks like the heads of diamond
nails could be; what the moon, looking so absolutely

content with light – why, she knew less about them than you and I! But the greatest of astronomers might envy the rapture of such a first impression at the age of sixteen. Immeasurably imperfect it was, but false the impression could not be, for she saw with the eyes made for seeing, and saw indeed what many men are too wise to see.

As she knelt, something softly flapped her, embraced her, stroked her, fondled her. She rose to her feet, but saw nothing, did not know what it was. It was likest a woman's breath. For she knew nothing of the air even, had never breathed the still newborn freshness of the world. Her breath had come to her only through long passages and spirals in the rock. Still less did she know of the air alive with motion – of that thrice blessed thing, the wind of a summer night. It was like a spiritual wine, filling her whole being with an intoxication of purest joy. To breathe was a perfect existence. It seemed to her the light itself she drew into her lungs. Possessed by the power of the gorgeous night, she seemed at one and the same moment annihilated and glorified.

She was in the open passage or gallery that ran round the top of the garden walls, between the cleft battlements, but she did not once look down to see what lay beneath. Her soul was drawn to the vault above her, with its lamp and its endless room. At last she burst into tears, and her heart was relieved, as the night itself is relieved by its lightning and rain.

And now she grew thoughtful. She must hoard this splendour! What a little ignorance her gaolers had made of her! Life was a mighty bliss, and they had scraped hers to the bare bone! They must not know that she knew. She must hide her knowledge – hide it even from her own eyes, keeping it close in her bosom, content to know that she had it, even when she could not brood on its presence, feasting her eyes with its glory. She turned from the vision, therefore, with a sigh of utter bliss, and with soft quiet steps and groping hands, stole back into the darkness of the rock. What was darkness or the laziness of Time's feet to one who had seen what she had that night seen? She was lifted above all weariness – above all wrong.

When Falca entered, she uttered a cry of terror. But Nycteris called to her not to be afraid, and told her how there had come a rumbling and a shaking, and the lamp had fallen. Then Falca went and told her mistress, and within an hour a new globe hung in the place of the old one. Nycteris thought it did not look so bright and clear as the former, but she made no lamentation over the change; she was far too rich to heed it. For now, prisoner as she knew herself, her heart was full of glory and gladness; at times she had to hold herself from jumping up, and going dancing and singing about the room. When she slept, instead of dull dreams, she had splendid visions. There were times, it is true, when she became restless, and impatient to look upon her riches, but then she would reason with herself, saying, 'What does it matter if I sit here for ages with my poor pale lamp, when out there a lamp is burning at which ten thousand little lamps are glowing with wonder?'

She never doubted she had looked upon the day and the sun, of which she had read; and always when she read of the day and the sun, she had the night and the moon in her mind; and when she read of the night and the moon, she thought only of the cave and the lamp that hung there.

10. The Great Lamp

It was some time before she had a second opportunity of going out, for Falca since the fall of the lamp, had been a little more careful, and seldom left her for long. But one night, having a little headache, Nycteris lay down upon her bed, and was lying with her eyes closed, when she heard Falca come to her, and felt she was bending over her. Disinclined to talk, she did not open her eyes, and lay quite still. Satisfied that she was asleep, Falca left her, moving so softly that her very caution made Nycteris open her eyes and look after her – just in time to see her vanish – through a picture, as it seemed, that hung on the wall a long way from the usual place of issue. She jumped up, her headache forgotten, and ran in the opposite direction; got out, groped her way to the stair, climbed, and reached the top of the wall. Alas! the great room was not so light as the little one she had left! Why? Sorrow of sorrows! the great lamp was gone! Had its globe fallen and its lovely light gone out upon great wings, a resplendent firefly, oaring itself through a yet grander and lovelier room? She looked down to see if it lay anywhere broken to pieces on the carpet below; but she could not even see the carpet. But surely nothing very dreadful could have happened – no rumbling or shaking, for there were all the little lamps shining brighter than before, not one of them looking as if any unusual matter had befallen. What if each of those little lamps was growing into a big lamp, and after being a big lamp for a while, had to go out and grow a bigger lamp still – out there, beyond this *out*? Ah! here was the living thing that could not be seen, come to her again – bigger to-night! with such loving kisses, and such liquid strokings of her cheeks and forehead, gently tossing her hair, and delicately toying with it! But it ceased, and all was still. Had it gone out? What would happen next? Perhaps the little lamps had not to grow great lamps, but to fall one by one and go out first? With that, came from below a sweet scent, then another, and another. Ah, how delicious! Perhaps they were all coming to her only on their way out after the great lamp! Then came the music of the river, which she had been too absorbed in the sky to note the first time. What was it? Alas! alas! another sweet living thing on its way out. They were all marching slowly out in long lovely file, one after the other, each taking its leave of her as it passed! It must be so: here were more and more sweet sounds, following and fading! The whole of the *Out* was going out again; it was all going after the great lovely lamp! She would be left the only creature in the solitary day! Was there nobody to hang up a new lamp for the old one, and keep the creatures from going? – She crept back to her rock very sad. She tried to comfort herself by saying that anyhow there would be room out there; but as she said it she shuddered at the thought of *empty* room.

When next she succeeded in getting out, a half-moon hung in the east; a new lamp had come, she thought, and all would be well.

It would be endless to describe the phases of feeling through which Nycteris passed, more numer-ous and delicate than those of a thousand changing moons. A fresh bliss bloomed in her soul with every varying aspect of infinite nature. Ere long she began to suspect that the new moon was the old moon, gone out and come in again like herself; also that, unlike herself, it wasted and grew again; that it was indeed a live thing, subject like herself to caverns, and keepers, and solitudes, escaping and shining when it could. Was it a prison like hers it was shut in and did it grow dark when the lamp left it? Where could be the way into it? With that first she began to look below, as well as above and around her; and then first noted the tops of the trees between her and the floor. There were palms with their red-fingered hands full of fruit; eucalyptus trees crowded with little boxes of powder-puffs; oleanders with their half-caste roses; and orange trees with their clouds of young silver stars, and their aged balls of gold. Her eyes could see colours invisible to ours in the moon-light, and all these she could distinguish well, though at first she took them for the shapes and colours of the carpet of the great room. She longed to get down among them, now she saw they were real creatures, but she did not know how. She went along the whole length of the wall to the end that crossed the river, but found no way of going down. Above the river she stopped to gaze with awe upon the rushing water. She knew nothing of water but from what she drank and what she bathed in; and, as the moon shone on the dark, swift stream, singing lustily as it flowed, she did not doubt the river was alive, a swift rushing serpent of life, going – out? – whither? And then she wondered if what was brought into her rooms had been killed that she might drink it, and have her bath in it.

Once when she stepped out upon the wall, it was into the midst of a fierce wind. The trees were all roaring. Great clouds were rushing along the skies, and tumbling over the little lamps: the great lamp had not come yet. All was in tumult. The wind seized her garments and hair, and shook them as if it would tear them from her. What could she have done to make the gentle creature so angry? Or was this another creature altogether – of the same kind, but hugely bigger and of a very different temper and behaviour? But the whole place was angry! Or was it that the creatures dwelling in it, the wind, and the trees, and the clouds, and the river, had all quarrelled, each with all the rest? Would the whole come to confusion and disorder? But, as she gazed wondering and disquieted, the moon, larger than ever she had seen her, came lifting herself above the horizon to look, broad and red, as if she, too, were swollen with anger that she had been roused from her rest by their noise, and compelled to hurry up to see what her children were about, thus rioting in her absence, lest they should rack the whole frame of things. And as she rose, the loud wind grew quieter and scolded less fiercely, the trees grew stiller and moaned with a lower complaint, and the clouds hunted and hurled themselves less wildly across the sky. And if she were pleased that her children obeyed her very presence, the moon grew smaller as she ascended the heavenly stair; her puffed cheeks sank, her complexion grew clearer, and a sweet smile spread over her countenance, as peacefully she rose and rose. But there was treason and rebellion in her court; for, ere she reached the top of her great stairs, the clouds had assembled, forgetting their late wars, and very still they were as they laid their heads together and conspired. Then combining, and lying silently in wait until she came near, they threw themselves upon her, and swallowed her up. Down from the roof came spots of wet, faster and faster, and they wetted the cheeks of Nycteris; and what could they be but the tears of the moon, crying because her children were smothering her? Nycteris wept too, and not knowing what to think, stole back in dismay to her room.

The next time, she came out in fear and trembling. There was the moon still away in the west – poor, indeed, and old, and looking dreadfully worn, as if all the wild beasts in the sky had been gnawing at her – but there she was, alive still, and able to shine!

11. The Sunset

Knowing nothing of darkness, or stars, or moon, Photogen spent his days in hunting. On a great white horse he swept over the grassy plains, glorying in the sun, fighting the wind, and killing the buffaloes.

One morning, when he happened to be on the ground a little earlier than usual, and before his attendants, he caught sight of an animal unknown to him, stealing from a hollow into which the sunrays had not yet reached. Like a swift shadow it sped over the grass, slinking southward to the forest. He gave chase, noted the body of a buffalo it had half eaten, and pursued it the harder. But with great leaps and bounds the creature shot farther and farther ahead of him, and vanished. Turning therefore defeated, he met Fargu, who had been following him as fast as his horse could carry him.

'What animal was that, Fargu?' he asked. 'How he did run!'

Fargu answered he might be a leopard, but he rather thought from his pace and look that he was a young lion.

'What a coward he must be!' said Photogen.

'Don't be too sure of that,' rejoined Fargu. 'He is one of the creatures the sun makes uncomfortable. As soon as the sun is down, he will be brave enough.'

He had scarcely said it, when he repented; nor did he regret it the less when he found that Photogen made no reply. But alas what was said was said.

'Then,' said Photogen to himself, 'that contemptible beast is one of the terrors of sundown, of which Madame Watho spoke!'

He hunted all day, but not with his usual spirit. He did not ride so hard, and did not kill one buffalo. Fargu to his dismay observed also that he took every pretext for moving farther south, nearer to the forest. But all at once, the sun now sinking in the west, he seemed to change his mind, for he turned his horse's head, and rode home so fast that the rest could not keep him in sight. When they arrived, they found his horse in the stable, and concluded that he had gone into the castle. But he had in truth set out again by the back of it. Crossing the river a good way up the valley, he reascended to the ground they had left, and just before sunset reached the skirts of the forest.

The level orb shone straight in between the bare stems, and saying to himself he could not fail to find the beast, he rushed into the wood. But even as he entered, he turned, and looked to the west. The rim of the red was touching the horizon, all jagged with broken hills. 'Now,' said Photogen, 'we shall see;' but he said it in the face of a darkness he had not proved. The moment the sun began to sink among the spikes and saw-edges, with a kind of sudden flap at his heart a fear inexplicable laid hold of the youth; and as he had never felt anything of the kind before, the very fear itself terrified him. As the sun sank, it rose like the shadow of the world, and grew deeper and darker. He could not even think what it might be, so utterly did it enfeeble him. When the last flaming scimitar-edge of the sun went out like a lamp, his horror seemed to blossom into very madness. Like the closing lids of an eye – for there was no twilight, and this night no moon – the terror and the darkness rushed together, and he knew them for one. He was no longer the man he had known, or rather thought himself. The courage he had had was in no sense his own – he had only had courage, not been courageous; it had left him, and he could scarcely stand – certainly not stand straight, for not one of his joints could he make stiff or keep from trembling. He was but a spark of the sun, in himself nothing.

The beast was behind him – stealing upon him! He turned. All was dark in the wood, but to his fancy the darkness here and there broke into pairs of green eyes, and he had not the power even to raise his bow-hand from his side. In the strength of despair he strove to rouse courage enough – not to fight – that he did not even desire – but to run. Courage to flee home was all he could ever imagine, and it would not come. But what he had not, was ignominiously given him. A cry in the wood, half a screech, half a growl, sent him running like a boar-wounded cur. It was not even himself that ran, it was the fear that had come alive in his legs; he did not know that they moved. But as he ran he grew able to run – gained courage at least to be a coward. The stars gave a little light. Over the grass he sped, and nothing followed him. 'How fallen, how changed,' from the youth who had climbed the hill as the sun went down! A mere contempt to himself, the self that contemned was a coward with the self it contemned! There lay the shapeless black of a buffalo, humped upon the grass: he made a wide circuit, and swept on like a shadow driven in the wind. For the wind had arisen, and added to his terror: it blew from behind him. He reached the brow of the valley, and shot down the steep descent like a falling star. Instantly the whole upper country behind him arose and pursued him! The wind came howling after him, filled with screams, shrieks, yells, roars, laughter, and chattering, as if all the animals of the forest were careering with it. In his ears was a trampling rush, the thunder of the hoofs of the cattle, in career from every quarter of the wide plains to the brow of the hill above him. He fled straight for the castle, scarcely with breath enough to pant.

As he reached the bottom of the valley, the moon peered up over its edge. He had never seen the moon before – except in the daytime, when he had taken her for a thin bright cloud. She was a fresh terror to him – so ghostly! so ghastly! so gruesome! – so knowing as she looked over the top of her garden wall upon the world outside! That was the night itself! the darkness alive – and after him! the horror of horrors coming down the sky to curdle his blood, and turn his brain to a cinder! He gave a sob, and made straight for the river, where it ran between the two walls, at the bottom of the garden. He plunged in, struggled through, clambered up the bank, and fell senseless on the grass.

12. The Garden

Although Nycteris took care not to stay out long at a time, and used every precaution, she could hardly have escaped discovery so long, had it not been that the strange attacks to which Watho was subject had been more frequent of late, and had at last settled into an illness which kept her to her bed. But whether from an access of caution or from suspicion, Falca, having now to be much with her mistress both day and night, took it at length into her head to fasten the door as often as she went by her usual place of exit; so that one night, when Nycteris pushed, she found, to her surprise and dismay, that the wall pushed her again, and would not let her through; nor with all her searching could she discover wherein lay the cause of the change. Then first she felt the pressure of her prison-walls, and turning, half in despair, groped her way to the picture where she had once seen Falca disappear. There she soon found the spot by pressing upon which the wall yielded. It let her through into a sort of cellar, where was a glimmer of light from a sky whose blue was paled by the moon. From the cellar she got into a long passage, into which the moon was shining, and came to a door. She managed to open it, and, to her great joy found herself in *the other place*, not on the top of the wall, however, but in the garden she had longed to enter. Noiseless as a fluffy moth she flitted away into the covert of the trees and shrubs, her bare feet welcomed by the softest of carpets, which, by the very touch, her feet knew to be alive, whence it came that it was so sweet and friendly to them. A soft little wind was out among the trees, running now here, now there, like a child that had got its will. She went dancing over the grass, looking behind her at her shadow as she went. At first she had taken it for a little black creature that made game of her, but when she perceived that it was only where she kept the moon away, and that every tree, however great and grand a creature, had also one of these strange attendants, she soon learned not to mind it, and by and by it became the source of as much amusement to her, as to any kitten its tail. It was long before she was quite at home with the trees, however. At one time they seemed to disapprove of her; at another not even to know she was there, and to be altogether taken up with their own business. Suddenly, as she went from one to another of them, looking up with awe at the murmuring mystery of their branches and leaves, she spied one a little way off, which was very different from all the rest. It was white and dark, and sparkling, and spread like a palm – a small slender palm, without much head; and it grew very fast, and sang as it grew. But it never grew any bigger, for just as fast as she could see it growing, it kept falling to pieces. When she got close to it, she discovered that it was a water-tree – made of just such water as she washed with – only it was alive of course, like the river – a different sort of water from that, doubtless, seeing the one crept swiftly along the floor, and the other shot straight up, and fell, and swallowed itself, and rose again. She put her feet into the marble basin, which was the flower-pot in which it grew. It was full of real water, living and cool – so nice, for the night was hot!

But the flowers! ah, the flowers! she was friends with them from the very first. What wonderful creatures they were! – and so kind and beautiful – always sending out such colours and such scents –red scent, and white scent, and yellow scent – for the other creatures! The one that was invisible and everywhere, took such a quantity of their scents, and carried it away! yet they did not seem to mind. It was their talk, to show they were alive, and not painted like those on the walls of her rooms, and on the carpets.

She wandered along down the garden, until she reached the river. Unable then to get any further – for she was a little afraid, and justly, of the swift watery serpent – she dropped on the grassy bank, dipped her feet in the water, and felt it running and pushing against them. For a long time she sat thus, and her bliss seemed complete, as she gazed at the river, and watched the broken picture of the great lamp overhead, moving up one side of the roof, to go down the other.

13. Something Quite New

A beautiful moth brushed across the great blue eyes of Nycteris. She sprang to her feet to follow it – not in the spirit of the hunter, but of the lover. Her heart – like every heart, if only its fallen sides were cleared away – was an inexhaustible fountain of love: she loved everything she saw. But as she followed the moth, she caught sight of something lying on the bank of the river, and not yet having learned to be afraid of anything, ran straight to see what it was. Reaching it, she stood amazed. Another girl like herself! But what a strange-looking girl! – so curiously dressed too! – and not able to move! Was she dead? Filled suddenly with pity, she sat down, lifted Photogen's head, laid it on her lap, and began stroking his face. Her warm hands brought him to himself. He opened his black eyes, out of which had gone all the fire, and looked up with a strange sound of fear, half moan, half gasp. But when he saw her face, he drew a deep breath, and lay motionless – gazing at her: those blue marvels above him, like a better sky, seemed to side with courage and assuage his terror. At length, in a trembling, awed voice, and a half whisper, he said, 'Who are you?'

'I am Nycteris,' she answered.

'You are a creature of the darkness, and love the night,' he said, his fear beginning to move again.

' I may be a creature of the darkness,' she replied. 'I hardly know what you mean. But I do not love the night. I love the day – with all my heart; and I sleep all the night long.'

'How can that be?' said Photogen, rising on his elbow, but dropping his head on her lap again the moment he saw the moon; '– how can it be,' he repeated, 'when I see your eyes there – wide awake?'

She only smiled and stroked him, for she did not understand him, and thought he did not know what he was saying.

'Was it a dream then?' resumed Photogen, rubbing his eyes. But with that his memory came clear, and he shuddered, and cried, 'Oh horrible! horrible! to be turned all at once into a coward! a shameful, contemptible, disgraceful coward! I am ashamed – ashamed – and *so* frightened! It is all so frightful!'

'What is so frightful ?' asked Nycteris, with a smile like that of a mother to her child waked from a bad dream.

'All, all,' he answered; 'all this darkness and the roaring.'

My dear,' said Nycteris, 'there is no roaring. How sensitive you must be! What you hear is only the walking of the water, and the running about of the sweetest of all the creatures. She is invisible, and I call her Everywhere, for she goes through all the other creatures, and comforts them. Now she is amusing herself, and them too, with shaking them and kissing them, and blowing in their faces. Listen: do you call that roaring? You should hear her when she is rather angry though! I don't know why, but she is some-times, and then she does roar a little.'

'It is so horribly dark!' said Photogen, who, listen-ing while she spoke, had satisfied himself that there was no roaring.

'Dark!' she echoed. 'You should be in my room when an earthquake has killed my lamp. I do not understand. How *can* you call this dark? Let me see: yes, you have eyes, and big ones, bigger than Madam Watho's or Falca's – not so big as mine, I fancy – only I never saw mine. But then – oh yes! – I know now what is the matter! You can't see with them because they are so black. Darkness can't see, of course. Never mind: I will be your eyes, and teach you to see. Look here – at these lovely white things in the grass, with red sharp points all folded together into one. Oh, I love them so! I could sit looking at them all day, the darlings!'

Photogen looked close at the flowers, and thought he had seen something like them before, but could not make them out. As Nycteris had never seen an open daisy, so had he never seen a closed one.

Thus instinctively Nycteris tried to turn him away from his fear; and the beautiful creature's strange lovely talk helped not a little to make him forget it.

'You call it dark! she said again, as if she could not get rid of the absurdity of the idea; 'why, I could count every blade of the green hair – I suppose it is what the books call grass – within two yards of me! And just look at the great lamp! It is brighter than usual to-day, and I can't think why you should be frightened, or call it dark!'

As she spoke, she went on stroking his cheeks and hair, and trying to comfort him. But oh how miserable he was and how plainly he looked it! He was on the point of saying that her great lamp was dreadful to him, looking like a witch, walking in the sleep of death; but he was not so ignorant as Nycteris, and knew even in the moonlight that she was a woman, though he had never seen one so young or so lovely before; and while she comforted his fear, her presence made him the more ashamed of it. Besides, not knowing her nature, he might annoy her, and make her leave him to his misery. He lay still therefore, hardly daring to move: all the little life he had seemed to come from her, and if he were to move, she might move; and if she were to leave him, he must weep like a child.

'How did you come here?' asked Nycteris, taking his face between her hands.

'Down the hill,' he answered.

'Where do you sleep?' he asked.

He signed in the direction of the house. She gave a little laugh of delight.

'When you have learned not to be frightened, you will always be wanting to come out with me,' she said.

She thought with herself she would ask her presently, when she had come to herself a little, how she had made her escape, for she must, of course, like herself, have got out of a cave, in which Watho and Falco had been keeping her.

'Look at the lovely colours,' she went on, pointing to a rose-bush, on which Photogen could not see a single flower. 'They are far more beautiful – are they not? – than any of the colours upon your walls. And then they are alive, and smell so sweet!'

He wished she would not make him keep opening his eyes to look at things he could not see; and every other moment would start and grasp tight hold of her, as some fresh pang of terror shot into him.

'Come, come, dear!' said Nycteris, 'you must not go on this way. You must be a brave girl, and–'

'A girl!' shouted Photogen, and started to his feet in wrath. 'If you were a man, I should kill you.'

'A man?' repeated Nycteris : 'what is that? How could I be that? We are both girls – are we not?'

'No, I am not a girl,' he answered '– although,' he added, changing his tone, and casting himself on the ground at her feet, 'I have given you too good reason to call me one.'

'Oh, I see!' returned Nycteris. 'No, of course – you can't be a girl: girls are not afraid – without reason. I understand now: it is because you are not a girl that you are so frightened.'

Photogen twisted and writhed upon the grass.

'No, it is not,' he said sulkily: 'it is this horrible darkness that creeps into me, goes all through me, into the very marrow of my bones – that is what makes me behave like a girl. If only the sun would rise!'

'The sun what is it?' cried Nycteris, now in her turn conceiving a vague fear.

Then Photogen broke into a rhapsody, in which he vainly sought to forget his.

'It is the soul, the life, the heart, the glory of the universe,' he said. 'The worlds dance like motes in his beams. The heart of man is strong and brave in his light, and when it departs his courage grows from him – goes with the sun, and he becomes such as you see me now.'

'Then that is not the sun?' said Nycteris, thoughtfully, pointing up to the moon.

'That!' cried Photogen, with utter scorn; 'I know nothing about *that*, except that it is ugly and horrible. At best it can be only the ghost of a dead sun. Yes, that is it! That is what makes it look so frightful.'

'No,' said Nycteris, after a long, thoughtful pause; 'you must be wrong there. I think the sun is the ghost of a dead moon, and that is how he is so much more splendid as you say. Is there, then, another big room, where the sun lives in the roof?'

'I do not know what you mean,' replied Photogen. 'But you mean to be kind, I know, though you should not call a poor fellow in the dark a girl. If you will let me lie here, with my head in your lap, I should like to sleep. Will you watch me, and take care of me?'

'Yes, that I will,' answered Nycteris, forgetting all her own danger.

So Photogen fell asleep.

14. The Sun

There Nycteris sat, and there the youth lay all night long, in the heart of the great cone-shadow of the earth, like two Pharaohs in one Pyramid. Photogen slept, and slept; and Nycteris sat motionless lest she should wake him, and so betray him to his fear.

The moon rode high in the blue eternity; it was a very triumph of glorious night; the river ran babble-murmuring in deep soft syllables; the fountain kept rushing moonward, and blossoming momently to a great silvery flower, whose petals were for ever falling like snow, but with a continuous musical clash, into the bed of its exhaustion beneath; the wind woke, took a run among the trees, went to sleep, and woke again; the daisies slept on their feet at hers, but she did not know they slept; the roses might well seem awake, for their scent filled the air, but in truth they slept also, and the odour was that of their dreams; the oranges hung like gold lamps in the trees, and their silvery flowers were the souls of their yet unembodied children; the scent of the acacia blooms filled the air like the very odour of the moon herself.

At last, unused to the living air, and weary with sitting so still and so long, Nycteris grew drowsy. The air began to grow cool. It was getting near the time when she too was accustomed to sleep. She closed her eyes just a moment, and nodded – opened them suddenly wide, for she had promised to watch.

In that moment a change had come. The moon had got round, and was fronting her from the west, and she saw that her face was altered, that she had grown pale, as if she too were wan with fear, and from her lofty place espied a coming terror. The light seemed to be dissolving out of her; she was dying – she was going out! And yet everything around looked strangely clear – clearer than ever she had seen anything before; how could the lamp be shedding more light when she herself had less? Ah, that was just it! See how faint she looked! It was because the light was forsaking her, and spreading itself over the room, that she grew so thin and pale! She was giving up everything! She was melting away from the roof like a bit of sugar in water.

Nycteris was fast growing afraid, and sought refuge with the face upon her lap. How beautiful the creature was – what to call it she could not think, for it had been angry when she called it what Watho called her. And, wonder upon wonder now, even in the cold change that was passing upon the great room, the colour as of a red rose was rising in the wan cheek. What beautiful yellow hair it was that spread over her lap! What great huge breaths the creature took! And what were those curious things it carried? She had seen them on her walls, she was sure.

Thus she talked to herself while the lamp grew paler and paler, and everything kept growing yet clearer. What could it mean? The lamp was dying – going out into the other place of which the creature in her lap had spoken, to be a sun! But why were the things growing clearer before it was yet a sun? That was the point. Was it her growing into a sun that did it? Yes! yes! it was coming death! She knew it, for it was coming upon her also! She felt it coming! What was she about to grow into? Something beautiful, like the creature in her lap? It might be! Anyhow, it must be death; for all her strength was going out of her, while all around her was growing so light she could not bear it! She must be blind soon! Would she be blind or dead first?

For the sun was rushing up behind her. Photogen woke, lifted his head from her lap, and sprang to his feet. His face was one radiant smile. His heart was full of daring – that of the hunter who will creep into the tiger's den. Nycteris gave a cry, covered her face with her hands, and pressed her eyelids close. Then blindly she stretched out her arms to Photogen, crying, 'Oh, I am *so* frightened! What is this? It must be death! I don't wish to die yet. I love this room and the old lamp. I do not want the other place. This is terrible. I want to hide. I want to get into the sweet, soft, dark hands of all the other creatures. Ah me! ah me!'

'What is the matter with you, girl?' said Photogen, with the arrogance of all male creatures until they have been taught by the other kind. He stood looking down upon her over his bow, of which he was examining the string. 'There is no fear of anything now, child! It is day. The sun is all but up. Look he will be above the brow of yon hill in one moment more! Good-bye. Thank you for my night's lodging. I'm off. Don't be a goose. If ever I can do anything for you – and all that, you know!'

'Don't leave me; oh, don't leave me!' cried Nycteris. 'I am dying! I am dying! I cannot move. The light sucks all the strength out of me. And oh, I am so frightened!'

But already Photogen had splashed through the river, holding high his bow that it might not get wet. He rushed across the level, and strained up the opposing hill. Hearing no answer, Nycteris removed her hands. Photogen had reached the top, and the same moment the sunrays alighted upon him; the glory of the king of day crowded blazing upon the golden-haired youth. Radiant as Apollo, he stood in mighty strength, a flashing shape in the midst of flame. He fitted a glowing arrow to a gleaming bow. The arrow parted with a keen musical twang of the bowstring, and Photogen darting after it, vanished with a shout. Up shot Apollo himself, and from his quiver scattered astonishment and exultation. But the brain of poor Nycteris was pierced through and through. She fell down in utter darkness. All around her was a flaming furnace. In despair and feebleness and agony, she crept back, feeling her way with doubt and difficulty and enforced persistence to her cell. When at last the friendly darkness of her chamber folded her about with its cooling and consoling arms, she threw herself on her bed and fell fast asleep. And there she slept on, one alive in a tomb, while Photogen, above in the sun-glory, pursued the buffaloes on the lofty plain, thinking not once of her where she lay dark and forsaken, whose presence had been his refuge, her eyes and her hands his guardians through the night. He was in his glory and his pride; and the darkness and its disgrace had vanished for a time.

15. The Coward Hero

But no sooner had the sun reached the noonstead, than Photogen began to remember the past night in the shadow of that which was at hand, and to remember it with shame. He had proved himself – and not to himself only, but to a girl as well – a coward! – one bold in the daylight, while there was nothing to fear, but trembling like any slave when the night arrived. There was, there must be, something unfair in it! A spell had been cast upon him! He had eaten, he had drunk something that did not agree with courage! In any case he had been taken unprepared! How was he to know what the going down of the sun would be like? It was no wonder he should have been surprised into terror, seeing it was what it was – in its very nature so terrible! Also, one could not see where danger might be coming from! You might be torn in pieces, carried off, or swallowed up, without even seeing where to strike a blow! Every possible excuse he caught at, eager as a self-lover to lighten his self-contempt. That day he astonished the huntsmen – terrified them with his reckless daring – all to prove to himself he was no coward. But nothing eased his shame. One thing only had hope in it – the resolve to encounter the dark in solemn earnest, now that he knew something of what it was. It was nobler to meet a recognized danger than to rush contemptuously into what seemed nothing – nobler still to encounter a nameless horror. He could conquer fear and wipe out disgrace together. For a marksman and swordsman like him, he said, one with his strength and courage, there was but danger. Defeat there was not. He knew the darkness now, and when it came he would meet it as fearless and cool as now he felt himself. And again he said, 'We shall see!'

He stood under the boughs of a great beech as the sun was going down, far away over the jagged hills: before it was half down, he was trembling like one of the leaves behind him in the first sigh of the night-wind. The moment the last of the glowing disc vanished, he bounded away in terror to gain the valley, and his fear grew as be ran. Down the side of the hill, an abject creature, he went bounding and rolling and running; fell rather than plunged into the river, and came to himself, as before, lying on the grassy bank in the garden.

But when he opened his eyes, there were no girl-eyes looking down into his; there were only the stars in the waste of the sunless Night – the awful all-enemy he had again dared, but could not encounter. Perhaps the girl was not yet come out of the water! He would try to sleep, for he dared not move, and perhaps when he woke he would find his head on her lap, and the beautiful dark face, with its deep blue eyes, bending over him. But when he woke he found his head on the grass, and although he sprang up with all his courage, such as it was, restored, he did not set out for the chase with such an *elan* as the day before; and, despite the sun-glory in his heart and veins, his hunting was this day less eager; he ate little, and from the first was thoughtful even to sadness. A second time he was defeated and disgraced! Was his courage nothing more than the play of the sunlight on his brain? Was he a mere ball tossed between the light and the dark? Then what a poor contemptible creature he was! But a third chance lay before him. If he failed the third time, he dared not foreshadow what he must then think of himself! It was bad enough now – but then!

Alas! it went no better. The moment the sun was down, he fled as if from a legion of devils.

Seven times in all, he tried to face the coming night in the strength of the past day, and seven times he failed – failed with such increase of failure, with such a growing sense of ignominy, overwhelming at length all the sunny hours and joining night to night, that, what with misery, self-accusation, and loss of confidence, his daylight courage too began to fade, and at length, from exhaustion, from getting wet, and then lying out of doors all night, and night after night, – worst of all, from the consuming of the deathly fear, and the shame of shame, his sleep forsook him, and on the seventh morning, instead of going to the hunt, he crawled into the castle, and went to bed. The grand health, over which the witch had taken such pains, had yielded, and in an hour or two he was moaning and crying out in delirium.

16. An Evil Nurse

Watho was herself ill, as I have said, and was the worse tempered; and, besides, it is a peculiarity of witches, that what works in others to sympathy, works in them to repulsion. Also, Watho had a poor, helpless, rudimentary spleen of a conscience left, just enough to make her uncomfortable, and therefore more wicked. So, when she heard that Photogen was ill, she was angry. Ill, indeed after all she had done to saturate him with the life of the system, with the solar might itself! He was a wretched failure, the boy! And because he was *her* failure, she was annoyed with him, began to dislike him, grew to hate him. She looked on him as a painter might upon a picture, or a poet upon a poem, which he had only succeeded in getting into an irrecoverable mess. In the hearts of witches, love and hate lie close together, and often tumble over each other. And whether it was that her failure with Photogen foiled also her plans in regard to Nycteris, or that her illness made her yet more of a devil's wife, certainly Watho now got sick of the girl too, and hated to know her about the castle.

She was not too ill, however, to go to poor Photogen's room and torment him. She told him she hated him like a serpent, and hissed like one as she said it, looking very sharp in the nose and chin, and flat in the forehead. Photogen thought she meant to kill him, and hardly ventured to take anything brought him. She ordered every ray of light to be shut out of his room; but by means of this he got a little used to the darkness. She would take one of his arrows, and now tickle him with the feather end of it, now prick him with the point till the blood ran down. What she meant finally I cannot tell, but she brought Photogen speedily to the determination of making his escape from the castle: what he should do then he would think afterwards. Who could tell but he might find his mother somewhere beyond the forest! If it were not for the broad patches of darkness that divided day from day, he would fear nothing!

But now, as he lay helpless in the dark, ever and anon would come dawning through it the face of the lovely creature who on that first awful night nursed him so sweetly: was he never to see her again? If she was as he had concluded, the nymph of the river, why had she not reappeared? She might have taught him not to fear the night, for, plainly she had no fear of it herself! But then, when the day came, she did seem frightened – why was that, seeing there was nothing to be afraid of then? Perhaps one so much at home in the darkness, was correspondingly afraid of the light! Then his selfish joy at the rising of the sun, blinding him to her condition, had made him behave to her, in ill return for her kindness, as cruelly as

Watho behaved to him! How sweet and dear and lovely she was! If there were wild beasts that came out only at night, and were afraid of the light, why should there not be girls too, made the same way – who could not endure the light, as he could not bear the darkness? If only he could find her again! Ah, how differently he would behave to her! But alas perhaps the sun had killed her – melted her – burned her up – dried her up – that was it, if she was the nymph of the river!

17. Watho's Wolf

From that dreadful morning Nycteris had never got to be herself again. The sudden light had been almost death to her; and now she lay in the dark with the memory of a terrific sharpness – a something she dared scarcely recall, lest the very thought of it should sting her beyond endurance. But this was as nothing to the pain which the recollection of the rudeness of the shining creature whom she had nursed through his fear caused her; for, the moment his suffering passed over to her, and he was free, the first use he made of his returning strength had been to scorn her! She wondered and wondered; it was all beyond her comprehension.

Before long, Watho was plotting evil against her. The witch was like a sick child weary of his toy: she would pull her to pieces, and see how she liked it. She would set her in the sun, and see her die, like a jelly from the salt ocean cast out on a hot rock. It would be a sight to soothe her wolf-pain. One day, therefore, a little before noon, while Nycteris was in her deepest sleep, she had a darkened litter brought to the door, and in that she made two of her men carry her to the plain above. There they took her out, laid her on the grass, and left her.

Watho watched it all from the top of her high tower, through her telescope; and scarcely was Nycteris left, when she saw her sit up, and the same moment cast herself down again with her face to the ground.

'She'll have a sunstroke,' said Watho, 'and that'll be the end of her.'

Presently, tormented by a fly, a huge-humped buffalo, with great shaggy mane, came galloping along, straight for where she lay. At sight of the thing on the grass, he started, swerved yards aside, stopped dead, and then came slowly up, looking malicious. Nycteris lay quite still, and never even saw the animal.

'Now she'll be trodden to death!' said Watho. 'That's the way those creatures do.'

When the buffalo reached her, he sniffed at her all over, and went away; then came back, and sniffed again; then all at once went off as if a demon had him by the tail.

Next came a gnu, a more dangerous animal still, and did much the same; then a gaunt wild boar. But no creature hurt her, and Watho was angry with the whole creation.

At length, in the shade of her hair, the blue eyes of Nycteris began to come to themselves a little, and the first thing they saw was a comfort. I have told already how she knew the night-daisies, each a sharp-pointed little cone with a red tip; and once she had parted the rays of one of them, with trembling fingers, for she was afraid she was dreadfully rude, and perhaps was hurting it; but she did want, she said to herself, to see what secret it carried so carefully hidden; and she found its golden heart. But now, right under her eyes, inside the veil of her hair, in the sweet twilight of whose blackness she could see it perfectly, stood a daisy with its red tip opened wide into a carmine ring, displaying its heart of gold on a platter of silver. She did not at first recognize it as one of those cones come awake, but a moment's notice revealed what it was. Who then could have been so cruel to the lovely little creature, as to force it open like that, and spread it heart-bare to the terrible death- lamp? Whoever it was, it must be the same that had thrown her out there to be burned to death in its fire! But she had her hair, and could hang her head, and make a small sweet night of her own about her! She tried to bend the daisy down and away from the sun, and to make its petals hang about it like her hair, but she could not. Alas! it was burned and dead already! She did not know that it could not yield to her gentle force because it was drinking life, with all the eagerness of life, from what she called the death-lamp. Oh, how the lamp burned her!

But she went on thinking – she did not know how; and by and by began to reflect that, as there was no roof to the room except that in which the great fire went rolling about, the little Red-tip must have seen the lamp a thousand times, and must know it quite well! and it had not killed it! Nay, thinking about farther, she began to ask the question whether this, in which she now saw it, might not be its more perfect condition. For not only now did the whole seem perfect, as indeed it did before, but every part showed its own individual perfection as well, which perfection made it capable of combining with the rest into the higher perfection of a whole. The flower was a lamp itself! The golden heart was the light, and the silver border was the alabaster globe, skilfully broken, and spread wide to let out the glory. Yes, the radiant shape was plainly its perfection! If, then, it was the lamp which had opened it into that shape, the lamp could not be unfriendly to it, but must be of its own kind, seeing it made it perfect! And again, when she thought of it, there was clearly no little resemblance between them. What if the flower then was the little great-grandchild of the lamp, and he was loving it all the time? And what if the lamp did not mean to hurt her, only could not help it? The red tips looked as if the flower had some time or other been hurt: what if the lamp was making the best it could of her – opening her out somehow like the flower? She would bear it patiently, and see. But how coarse the colour of the grass was! Perhaps, however, her eyes not being made for the bright lamp, she did not see them as they were! Then she remembered how different were the eyes of the creature that was not a girl and was afraid of the darkness! Ah, if the darkness would only come again, all arms, friendly and soft everywhere about her! She would wait and wait, and bear, and be patient.

She lay so still that Watho did not doubt she had fainted. She was pretty sure she would be dead before the night came to revive her.

18. Refuge

Fixing her telescope on the motionless form, that she might see it at once when the morning came, Watho went down from the tower to Photogen's room. He was much better by this time, and before she left him, he had resolved to leave the castle that very night. The darkness was terrible indeed, but Watho was worse than even the darkness, and he could not escape in the day. As soon, therefore, as the house seemed still, he tightened his belt, hung to it his hunting-knife, put a flask of wine and some bread in his pocket, and took his bow and arrows. He got from the house, and made his way at once up to the plain. But what with his illness, the terrors of the night, and his dread of the wild beasts, when he got to the level he could not walk a step further, and sat down, thinking it better to die than to live. In spite of his fears, however, sleep contrived to overcome him, and he fell at full length on the soft grass.

He had not slept long when he woke with such a strange sense of comfort and security, that he thought the dawn at least must have arrived. But it was dark night about him. And the sky – no, it was not the sky, but the blue eyes of his naiad looking down upon him! Once more he lay with his head in her lap, and all was well, for plainly the girl feared the darkness as little as he the day.

'Thank you,' he said. 'You are like live armour to my heart; you keep the fear off me. I have been very ill since then. Did you come up out of the river when you saw me cross?'

'I don't live in the water,' she answered. 'I live under the pale lamp, and I die under the bright one.'

'Ah, yes! I understand now,' he returned. 'I would not have behaved as I did last time if I had understood; but I thought you were mocking me; and I am so made that I cannot help being frightened at the darkness. I beg your pardon for leaving you as I did, for, as I say, I did not understand. Now I believe you were really frightened. Were you not?'

'I was, indeed,' answered Nycteris, 'and shall be again. But why you should be, I cannot in the least understand. You must know how gentle and sweet the darkness is, how kind and friendly, how soft and velvety! It holds you to its bosom and loves you. A little while ago, I lay faint and dying under your hot lamp. What is it you call it?'

'The sun,' murmured Photogen: 'how I wish he would make haste!'

'Ah! do not wish that. Do not, for my sake, hurry him. I can take care of you from the darkness, but I have no one to take care of me from the light. – As I was telling you, I lay dying in the sun. All at once I drew a deep breath. A cool wind came and ran over my face. I looked up. The torture was gone, for the death-lamp itself was gone. I hope he does not die and grow brighter yet. My terrible headache was all gone, and my sight was come back. I felt as if I were new made. But I did not get up at once, for I was tired still. The grass grew cool about me, and turned soft in colour. Something wet came upon it, and it was now so pleasant to my feet, that I rose and ran about. And when I had been running about a long time, all at once I found you lying, just as I had been lying a little while before. So I sat down beside you to take care of you, till your life – and my death – should come again.'

'How good you are, you beautiful creature! Why, you forgave me before ever I asked you!' cried Photogen.

Thus they fell a talking, and he told her what he knew of his history, and she told him what she knew of hers, and they agreed they must get away from Watho as far as ever they could.

'And we must set out at once,' said Nycteris.

'The moment the morning comes,' returned Photogen.

'We must not wait for the morning,' said Nycteris, 'for then I shall not be able to move, and what would you do the next night? Besides Watho sees best in the daytime. Indeed, you must come now, Photogen. You must.'

'I can not; I dare not,' said Photogen. 'I cannot move. If I but lift my head from your, lap, the very sickness of terror seizes me.'

'I shall be with you,' said Nycteris, soothingly. 'I will take care of you till your dreadful sun comes, and then you may leave me, and go away as fast as you can. Only please put me in a dark place first, if there is one to be found.'

'I will never leave you again, Nycteris,' cried Photogen. 'Only wait till the sun comes, and brings me back my strength, and we will go away together, and never, never part any more.'

No, no,' persisted Nycteris; 'we must go now. And you must learn to be strong in the dark as well as in the day, else you will always be only half brave. I have begun already – not to fight your sun, but to try to get at peace with him, and understand what he really is, and what he means with me – whether to hurt me or to make the best of me. You must do the same with my darkness.'

'But you don't know what mad animals there are away there towards the south,' said Photogen. 'They have huge green eyes, and they would eat you up like a bit of celery, you beautiful creature!'

'Come, come you must,' said Nycteris, 'or I shall have to pretend to leave you, to make you come. I have seen the green eyes you speak of, and I will take care of you from them.'

'You! How can you do that? If it were day now, I could take care of you from the worst of them. But as it is, I can't even see them for this abominable darkness. I could not see your lovely eyes but for the light that is in them; that lets me see straight into heaven through them. They are windows into the very heaven beyond the sky. I believe they are the very place where the stars are made.'

'You come then, or I shall shut them,' said Nycteris, 'and you shan't see them any more till you are good. Come. If you can't see the wild beasts, I can.'

'You can and you ask me to come!' cried Photogen.

'Yes,' answered Nycteris. 'And more than that, I see them long before they can see me, so that I am able to take care of you.'

'But how?' persisted Photogen. 'You can't shoot with bow and arrow, or stab with a hunting knife.'

'No, but I can keep out of the way of them all. Why, just when I found you, I was having a game with two or three of them at once, I see, and scent them too, long before they are near me – long before they can see or scent me.'

'You don't see or scent any now, do you?' said Photogen, uneasily, rising on his elbow.

'No – none at present. I will look,' replied Nycteris, and sprang to her feet.

'Oh, oh! do not leave me – not for a moment,' cried Photogen, straining his eyes to keep her face in sight through the darkness.

'Be quiet, or they will hear you,' she returned. 'The wind is from the south, and they cannot scent us. I have found out all about that. Ever since the dear dark came, I have been amusing myself with them, getting every now and then just into the edge of the wind, and letting one have a sniff of me.'

'Oh, horrible!' cried Photogen. 'I hope you will not insist on doing so any more. What was the consequence?'

'Always, the very instant, he turned with flashing eyes, and bounded towards me – only he could not see me, you must remember. But my eyes being so much better than his, I could see him perfectly well, and would run away round him until I scented him, and then I knew he could not find me anyhow. If the wind were to turn, and run the other way now, there might be a whole army of them down upon us, leaving no room to keep out of their way. You had better come.'

She took him by the hand. He yielded and rose, and she led him away. But his steps were feeble, and as the night went on, he seemed more and more ready to sink.

'Oh dear! I am so tired! and so frightened!' he would say.

'Lean on me,' Nycteris would return, putting her arm round him, or patting his cheek. 'Take a few steps more. Every step away from the castle is clear gain. Lean harder on me. I am quite strong and well now.'

So they went on. The piercing night-eyes of
Nycteris saw not a few pairs of green ones gleaming
like holes in the darkness, and many a round she
made to keep far out of their way; but she never said
to Photogen she saw them. Carefully she kept him off
the uneven places, and on the softest and smoothest
of the grass, talking to him gently all the way as they
went – of the lovely flowers and the stars – how
comfortable the flowers looked, down in their green
beds, and how happy the stars up in their blue
beds!

When the morning began to come, he began to
grow better, but was dreadfully tired with walking
instead of sleeping, especially after being so long ill.
Nycteris too, what with supporting him, what with
growing fear of the light which was beginning to ooze
out of the east, was very tired. At length, both equally
exhausted, neither was able to help the other. As if by
consent they stopped. Embracing each the other,
they stood in the midst of the wide grassy land,
neither of them able to move a step, each supported
only by the leaning weakness of the other, each ready
to fall if the other should move. But while the one
grew weaker still, the other had begun to grow
stronger. When the tide of the night began to ebb,
the tide of the day began to flow; and now the sun
was rushing to the horizon, borne upon its foaming
billows. And ever as he came, Photogen revived. At
last the sun shot up into the air, like a bird from the
hand of the Father of Lights. Nycteris gave a cry of
pain, and hid her face in her hands.

'Oh me!' she sighed; 'I am *so* frightened! The
terrible light stings so!'

But the same instant, through her blindness, she

heard Photogen give a low exultant laugh, and the next felt herself caught up: she who all night long had tended and protected him like a child, was now in his arms, borne along like a baby, with her head lying on his shoulder. But she was the greater, for suffering more, she feared nothing.

19. The Werewolf

At the very moment when Photogen caught up Nycteris, the telescope of Watho was angrily sweeping the table-land. She swung it from her in rage, and running to her room, shut herself up. There she anointed herself from top to toe with a certain ointment; shook down her long red hair, and tied it round her waist; then began to dance, whirling round and round faster and faster, growing angrier and angrier, until she was foaming at the mouth with fury. When Falca went looking for her, she could not find her anywhere.

As the sun rose, the wind slowly changed and went round, until it blew straight from the north. Photogen and Nycteris were drawing near the edge of the forest, Photogen still carrying Nycteris, when she moved a little on his shoulder uneasily, and murmured in his ear,

'I smell a wild beast – that way, the way the wind is coming.'

Photogen turned, looked back towards the castle, and saw a dark speck on the plain. As he looked, it grew larger: it was coming across the grass with the speed of the wind. It came nearer and nearer. It looked long and low, but that might be because it was running at a great stretch. He set Nycteris down under a tree, in the black shadow of its bole, strung his bow, and picked out his heaviest, longest, sharpest arrow. Just as he set the notch on the string, he saw that the creature was a tremendous wolf, rushing straight at him. He loosened his knife in its sheath, drew another arrow half-way from the quiver, lest the first should fail, and took his aim – at a good distance, to leave time for a second chance. He shot. The arrow rose, flew straight, descended, struck the beast, and started again into the air, doubled like a letter V. Quickly Photogen snatched the other, shot, cast his bow from him, and drew his knife. But the arrow was in the brute's chest, up to the feather; it tumbled heels over head with a great thud of its back on the earth, gave a groan, made a struggle or two, and lay stretched out motionless.

'I've killed it, Nycteris,' cried Photogen. 'It is a great red wolf.'

'Oh, thank you!' answered Nycteris feebly from behind the tree. 'I was sure you would. I was not a bit afraid.'

Photogen went up to the wolf. It was a monster! But he was vexed that his first arrow had behaved so badly, and was the less willing to lose the one that had done him such good service: with a long and a strong pull, he drew it from the brute's chest. Could he believe his eyes? There lay – no wolf, but Watho, with her hair tied round her waist! The foolish witch had made herself invulnerable, as she supposed, but had forgotten that, to torment Photogen therewith, she had handled one of his arrows. He ran back to Nycteris and told her.

She shuddered and wept, and would not look.

20. All is well

There was now no occasion to fly a step farther. Neither of them feared any one but Watho. They left her there, and went back. A great cloud came over the sun, and rain began to fall heavily, and Nycteris was much refreshed, grew able to see a little, and with Photogen's help walked gently over the cool wet grass.

They had not gone far before they met Fargu and the other huntsmen. Photogen told them he had killed a great red wolf, and it was Madam Watho. The huntsmen looked grave, but gladness shone through.

'Then,' said Fargu, 'I will go and bury my mistress.'

But when they reached the place, they found she was already buried – in the maws of sundry birds and beasts which has made their breakfast of her.

Then Fargu, overtaking them, would, very wisely, have Photogen go to the king, and tell him the whole story. But Photogen, yet wiser than Fargu, would not set out until he had married Nycteris. 'For then,' he said, 'the king himself can't part us; and if ever two people couldn't do the one without the other, those two are Nycteris and I. She has got to teach me to be a brave man in the dark, and I have got to look after her until she can bear the heat of the sun, and he helps her to see, instead of blinding her.'

They were married that very day. And the next day they went together to the king, and told him the whole story. But whom should they find at the court but the father and mother of Photogen, both in high favour with the king and queen. Aurora nearly died for joy, and told them all how Watho had lied, and made her believe her child was dead.

No one knew anything of the father or mother of Nycteris; but when Aurora saw in the lovely girl her own azure eyes shining through night and its clods, it made her think strange things, and wonder how even the wicked themselves may be a link to join together the good. Through Watho, the mothers, who had never seen each other, had changed eyes in their children.

The king gave them the castle and lands of Watho, and there they lived and taught each other for many years that were not long. But hardly had one of them passed, before Nycteris had come to love the day best, because it was the clothing and crown of Photogen, and she saw that the day was greater than the night, and the sun more lordly than the moon; and Photogen had come to love the night best, because it was the mother and home of Nycteris.

'But who knows,' Nycteris would say to Photogen, 'that, when we go out, we shall not go into a day as much greater than your day as your day is greater than my night?'

*   *   *

GEORGE MACDONALD has been described as one of the most remarkable writers of the nineteenth century and his pioneer fantasy novels were deeply influential on J.R.R. Tolkien and C.S. Lewis who wrote; 'I regarded him as my master – his imaginative works are both magical and terrifying.' MacDonald's fascination with magic was evident in his first book, *Phantastes, A Faerie Romance for Men and Women*

(1858), in which he expressed his philosophy of writing 'for people who, afraid of the risks and suffering involved in becoming adult, refuse to grow up'. Witches and wise women appeared in several of his other novels, notably *At The Back of the North Wind* (1871) featuring the 'Witch Who Got Her Power From Wickedness' and speaks in 'the tone of a dry axle'. There is also the enchanting heroine of *The Wise Woman* (1890) and the fractious Old Mother Wotherwop in *The Princess and the Curdie* (1883). George MacDonald was among the earliest children's authors to feature a vampire in his novel, *Lilith* (1895), and certainly the first to use that other creature of nightmare, a werewolf in 'The Day Boy and the Night Girl'. The tale was also a favourite of Lewis Carroll who gave the manuscript of his own book, *Alice's Adventures in Wonderland* (1865), to MacDonald for his opinion. Apparently, the Scotsman read it instead to his children who – he said later – 'greeted each chapter rapturously'.

THE MAGIC CHILD-KILLER

Roald Dahl

The Grand High Witch has also long given up the old-fashioned idea of wearing a black hat and cloak and riding about on a broomstick. In fact, for much of the time, she lives as an ordinary woman, wearing ordinary clothes and – as far as most people are concerned – doing ordinary things. Secretly though, she spends her time plotting the great objective of all modern witches: to kill children! For if there is one thing they all hate it is boys and girls and they are determined to live up to their motto, 'Squish them and squiggle them and make them disappear!' To aid the witches in this bloodthirsty quest, they all have magic fingers that can turn anything into stone and make tongues of flame leap from nowhere. Every year, they all gather for their annual meeting to hear what the Grand High Witch has planned to help them achieve their objective. This year, it seems, she is going to use magic to make things even more dangerous for kids than ever before . . .

*   *   *

'Children are rrree-volting!' screamed The Grand High Witch. 'Vee vill vipe them all avay! Vee vill scrrrub them off the face of the earth! Vee vill flush them down the drain!'

'Yes, yes!' chanted the audience. 'Wipe them away! Scrub them off the earth! Flush them down the drain!'

'Children are foul and filthy!' thundered The Grand High Witch.

'They are! They are!' chorused the English witches. 'They are foul and filthy!'

'Children are dirty and stinky!' screamed The Grand High Witch.

'Dirty and stinky!' cried the audience, getting more and more worked up.

'Children are smelling of dogs' drrroppings!' screeched The Grand High Witch.

'Pooooooo!' cried the audience. 'Pooooooo! Pooooooo! Pooooooo!'

'They are vurse than dogs' drrroppings!' screeched The Grand High Witch. 'Dogs' drrroppings is smelling like violets and prrrimroses compared vith children!'

'Violets and primroses!' chanted the audience. They were clapping and cheering almost every word spoken from the platform. The speaker seemed to have them completely under her spell.

'To talk about children is making me sick!' screamed The Grand High Witch. 'I am feeling sick even *thinking* about them! Fetch me a basin!'

The Grand High Witch paused and glared at the mass of eager faces in the audience. They waited, wanting more.

'So now!' barked The Grand High Witch. 'So now I am having a plan! I am having a giganticus plan for getting rrrid of every single child in the whole of Inkland!'

The witches gasped. They gaped. They turned and gave each other ghoulish grins of excitement.

'Yes!' thundered The Grand High Witch. 'Vee shall svish them and svollop them and vee shall make to

disappear every single smelly little brrrat in Inkland
in vun strrroke!'

'Whoopee!' cried the witches, clapping their
hands. 'You are brilliant, O Your Grandness! You are
fantabulous!'

'Shut up and listen!' snapped The Grand High
Witch. 'Listen very carefully and let us not be having
any muck-ups!'

The audience leaned forward, eager to learn how
this magic was going to be performed.

'Each and every vun of you', thundered The
Grand High Witch, 'is to go back to your home towns
immediately and rrree-sign from your jobs. Rrree-
sign! Give notice! Rrree-tire!'

'We will!' they cried. 'We will resign from our
jobs!'

'And after you have rrree-signed from your jobs,'
The Grand High Witch went on, 'each and every vun
of you vill be going out and you vill be buying . . .'
She paused.

'What will we be buying?' they cried. 'Tell us, O
Brilliant One, what is it we shall be buying?'

'Sveet-shops!' shouted The Grand High Witch.

'Sveet-shops!' they cried. 'We are going to buy
sweet-shops! What a frumptious wheeze!'

'Each of you vill be buying for herself a sveetshop.
You vill be buying the very best and most rrree-
spectable sveet-shops in Inkland.'

'We will! We will!' they answered. Their dreadful
voices were like a chorus of dentists' drills all grind-
ing away together.

'I am vonting no tuppenny-ha'penny crrrummy
little tobacco-selling-newspaper-sveet-shops!' shouted
The Grand High Witch. 'I am vonting you to get only

the very best shops filled up high vith piles and piles of luscious sveets and tasty chocs!'

'The best!' they cried. 'We shall buy the best sweet-shops in town!'

'You vill be having no trouble in getting vot you vont,' shouted The Grand High Witch, 'because you vill be offering four times as much as a shop is vurth and nobody is rrree-fusing an offer like that! Money is not a prrroblem to us vitches as you know very vell. I have brrrought vith me six trrunks stuffed full of Inklish banknotes, all new and crrrisp. And all of them,' she added with a fiendish leer, 'all of them homemade.'

The witches in the audience grinned, appreciating this joke.

At that point, one foolish witch got so excited at the possibilities presented by owning a sweet-shop that she leapt to her feet and shouted, 'The children will come flocking to my shop and I will feed them poisoned sweets and poisoned chocs and wipe them all out like weasels!'

The room became suddenly silent. l saw the tiny body of The Grand High Witch stiffen and then go rigid with rage. 'Who spoke?' she shrieked. 'It vos *you*! You over there!'

The culprit sat down fast and covered her face with her clawed hands.

'You blithering bumpkin!' screeched The Grand High Witch. 'You brrrainless bogvumper! Are you not rrree-alising that if you are going rrround poisoning little children you vill be caught in five minutes flat? Never in my life am I hearing such a boshvolloping suggestion coming from a vitch!'

The entire audience cowered and shook. I'm quite sure they all thought, as l did, that the terrible white-hot sparks were about to start flying again.

Curiously enough, they didn't.

'If such a tomfiddling idea is all you can be coming up vith,' thundered The Grand High Witch, 'then it is no vunder Inkland is still svorming with rrrotten little children!'

There was another silence. The Grand High Witch glared at the witches in the audience. 'Do you not know', she shouted at them, 'that vee vitches are vurrrking only with magic?'

'We know, Your Grandness!' they all answered. 'Of course we know!'

The Grand High Witch grated her bony gloved hands against each other and cried out, 'So each of you is owning a magnificent sveet-shop! The next move is that each of you vill be announcing in the vindow of your shop that on a certain day you vill be having a Great Gala Opening vith frree sveets and chocs to every child!'

'That will bring them in, the greedy little brutes!' cried the audience. 'They'll be fighting to get through the doors!'

'Next,' continued The Grand High Witch, 'you vill prepare yourselves for this Great Gala Opening by filling every choc and every sveet in your shop vith my very latest and grrreatest magic formula! This is known as FORMULA 86 DELAYED ACTION MOUSE-MAKER!'

'Delayed Action Mouse-Maker!' they chanted. 'She's done it again! Her Grandness has concocted yet another of her wondrous magic child-killers! How do we make it, O Brilliant One?'

'Exercise patience,' answered The Grand High

Witch. 'First, I am explaining to you how my Formula 86 Delayed Action Mouse-Maker is vurrrking. Listen carefully.'

'We are listening!' cried the audience who were now jumping up and down in their chairs with excitement.

'Delayed Action Mouse-Maker is a green liqvid,' explained The Grand High Witch, 'and vun droplet in each choc or sveet vill be qvite enough. So here is vot happens:

'Child eats choc vich has in it Delayed Action Mouse-Maker liqvid . . .

'Child goes home feeling fine . . .

'Child goes to bed, still feeling fine . . .

'Child vakes up in the morning still okay . . .

'Child goes to school still feeling fine . . .

'Formula, you understand, is *delayed action*, and is not vurrrking yet.'

'We understand, O Brainy One!', cried the audience. 'But when does it start working?'

'It is starting to vurrrk at exactly nine o'clock, vhen the child is arriving at school!' shouted The Grand High Witch triumphantly. 'Child arrives at school. Delayed Action Mouse-Maker immediately starts to vurrrk. Child starts to shrrrink. Child is starting to grow fur. Child is starting to grow tail. All is happening in prrreecisely twenty-six seconds. After tventy-six -seconds, child is not a child any longer. It is a mouse!'

'A mouse!' cried the witches. 'What a frumptious thought!'

'Classrooms vill all be svorrrming vith mice!' shouted The Grand High Witch. 'Chaos and pande-monium vill be rrreigning in every school in Inkland! Teachers vill be hopping up and down! Vimmen teachers vill be standing on desks and holding up skirts and yelling, "Help, help, help!" '

'They will! They will!' cried the audience.

'And vot', shouted The Grand High Witch, 'is happening next in every school?'

'Tell us!' they cried. 'Tell us, O Brainy One!'

The Grand High Witch stretched her stringy neck forward and grinned at the audience, showing two rows of pointed teeth, slightly blue. She raised her voice louder than ever and shouted, '*Mouse-trrraps is coming out!*'

'Mouse-traps!' cried the witches.

'And cheese!' shouted The Grand High Witch. 'Teachers is all rrrushing and rrrunning out and getting mouse-trrraps and baiting them vith cheese and putting them down all over school! Mice is nibbling cheese! Mouse-trrraps is going off! All over school, mouse-trrraps is going *snappety-snap* and mouse-heads is rrrolling across the floors like marbles! All over Inkland, in everrry school in Inkland, noise of snapping mouse-trrraps vill be heard!'

At this point, the disgusting old Grand High Witch began to do a sort of witch's dance up and down the platform, stamping her feet and clapping her hands. The entire audience joined in the clapping and the foot-stamping. They were making such a tremendous racket that I thought surely Mr Stringer would hear it and come banging at the door. But he didn't.

Then, above all the noise, I heard the voice of The Grand High Witch screaming out some sort of an awful gloating song,

'Down vith children! Do them in!
Boil their bones and fry their skin!
Bish them, sqvish them, bash them, mash them!
Brrreak them, shake them, slash them, smash
    them!
Offer chocs vith magic powder!
Say 'Eat up!' then say it louder.
Crrram them full of sticky eats,
Send them home still guzzling sveets.
And in the morning little fools
Go marching off to separate schools.
A girl feels sick and goes all pale.
She yells, 'Hey look! I've grrrown a tail!'
A boy who's standing next to her
Screams, 'Help! I think I'm grrrowing fur!'
Another shouts, 'Vee look like frrreaks!
There's viskers growing on our cheeks!'
A boy who vos extremely tall
Cries out, 'Vot's wrong? I'm grrrowing small!'
Four tiny legs begin to sprrrout
From everybody rrround about.
And all at vunce, all in a trrrice,
There are no children! Only MICE!
In every school is mice galore
All rrrunning rrround the school-rrroom floor!
And all the poor demented teachers
Is yelling, 'Hey, who are these crrreatures?'
They stand upon the desks and shout,
'Get out, you filthy mice! Get out!
Vill someone fetch some mouse-trrraps, please!
And don't forrrget to bring the cheese!'
Now mouse-trrraps come and every trrrap
Goes *snippy-snip* and *snappy-snap*.
The mouse-trrraps have a powerful spring,

The springs go *crack* and *snap* and *ping*!
Is lovely noise for us to hear!
Is music to a vitch's ear!
Dead mice is every place arrround,
Piled two feet deep upon the grrround,
Vith teachers searching left and rrright,
But not a single child in sight!
The teachers- cry, 'Vot's going on?
Oh vhere have all the children gone?
Is half-past nine and as a rrrule
They're never late as this for school!'
Poor teachers don't know vot to do.
Some sit and rrread, and just a few
Amuse themselves throughout the day
By sveeping all the mice avay.
AND ALL US VITCHES SHOUT HOORAY!'

*   *   *

ROALD DAHL once said that he had a magic garden where he used to dream up grisly and entertaining tales. In fact, he used to sit in an old shed at the end of his garden to write his novels and short stories. It is true, though, that the idea for his very first book for younger readers, *James and the Giant Peach* (1961), came to him in the garden after he had planted a peach tree that, despite all his loving attention, refused to grow. Instead, the idea of an enormous peach grew in his imagination and inspired him to write that first book. Roald Dahl started his career writing for adults and produced several collections of fantasy and horror stories, all with a twist in the tale. But after the success of *James and the Giant Peach*, he devoted his efforts almost entirely to children's books and produced several classics including, *Charlie and the Chocolate Factory* (1964), *Danny, the Champion of the World* (1975) and my favourite that I have read to my own children several times, *The Magic Finger* (1966).

THE APRIL WITCH

Ray Bradbury

Cecy Elliott is an American witch – but she is a teenager and, if anything, more clever and certainly much nicer than the Grand High Witch and her evil clan of English witches. Cecy, who thinks of herself as a bit 'plain and odd', belongs to a strange family who all possess supernatural powers. They live secretly alongside ordinary people in Illinois, but actually have ambitions and emotions that are very similar to us human beings. Cecy herself has remarkable magic powers: she can fly, read the thoughts of other people and put herself into anything from 'a pebble, a crocus or a preying mantis'. Despite these unique talents, the one human emotion she most wants to experience is love *– although she knows that if she marries an ordinary man she will loose all her magic powers. Undeterred, Cecy decides to try to fall in love through someone who already has an admirer – but her choice of Ann Leary creates complications she could not for a moment have imagined . . .*

*   *   *

Into the air, over the valleys, under the stars, above a river, a pond, a road, flew Cecy. Invisible as new spring winds, fresh as the breath of clover rising from twilight fields, she flew. She soared in doves as soft as white ermine, stopped in trees and lived in blossoms, showering away in petals when the breeze blew. She perched in a lime-green frog, cool as mint by a shining pool. She trotted in a brambly dog and barked to hear echoes from the sides of distant barns. She lived in new April grasses, in sweet clear liquids rising from the musky earth.

It's spring, thought Cecy. I'll be in every living thing in the world tonight.

Now she inhabited neat crickets on the tar-pool roads, now prickled in dew on an iron gate. Hers was an adaptably quick mind flowing unseen upon Illinois winds on this one evening of her life when she was just seventeen.

'I want to be in love,' she said.

She had said it at supper. And her parents had widened their eyes and stiffened back in their chairs. 'Patience,' had been their advice. 'Remember, you're remarkable. Our whole family is odd and remark-able. We can't mix or marry with ordinary folk. We'd lose our magical powers if we did. You wouldn't want to lose your ability to "travel" by magic, would you? Then be careful. Be careful!'

But in her high bedroom, Cecy had touched perfume to her throat and stretched out, trembling and apprehensive, on her four-poster, as a moon the color of milk rose over Illinois country, turning rivers to cream and roads to platinum.

'Yes,' she sighed. 'I'm one of an odd family. We sleep days and fly nights like black kites on the wind. If we want, we can sleep in moles through the winter, in the warm earth. I can live in anything at all – a pebble, a crocus, or a praying mantis. I can leave my plain, bony body behind and send my mind far out for adventure. Now!'

The wind whipped her away over fields and meadows.

She saw the warm spring lights of cottages and farms glowing with twilight colors.

If I can't be in love, myself, because I'm plain and odd, then I'll be in love through someone else, she thought.

Outside a farmhouse in the spring night a dark-haired girl, no more than nineteen, drew up water from a deep stone well. She was singing.

Cecy fell – a green leaf – into the well. She lay in the tender moss of the well, gazing up through dark coolness. Now she quickened in a fluttering, invisible amoeba. Now in a water droplet! At last, within a cold cup, she felt herself lifted to the girl's warm lips. There was a soft night sound of drinking.

Cecy looked out from the girl's eyes.

She entered into the dark head and gazed from the shining eyes at the hands pulling the rough rope. She listened through the shell ears to this girl's world. She smelled a particular universe through these delicate nostrils, felt this special heart beating, beating. Felt this strange tongue move with singing.

Does she know I'm here? thought Cecy.

The girl gasped. She stared into the night meadows.

'Who's there?'

No answer.

'Only the wind,' whispered Cecy.

'Only the wind.' The girl laughed at herself, but shivered.

It was a good body, this girl's body. It held bones of finest slender ivory hidden and roundly fleshed. This brain was like a pink tea rose, hung in darkness, and there was cider-wine in this mouth. The lips lay firm on the white, white teeth and the brows arched neatly at the world, and the hair blew soft and fine on her milky neck. The pores knit small and close. The nose tilted at the moon and the cheeks glowed like small fires. The body drifted with feather-balances from one motion to another and seemed always singing to itself. Being in this body, this head, was like basking in a hearth fire, living in the purr of a sleeping cat, stirring in warm creek waters that flowed by night to the sea.

I'll like it here, thought Cecy.

'What?' asked the girl, as if she'd heard a voice.

'What's your name' asked Cecy carefully.

'Ann Leary.' The girl twitched. 'Now why should I say that out loud?'

'Ann, Ann,' whispered Cecy. 'Ann, you're going to be in love.'

As if to answer this, a great roar sprang from the road, a clatter and a ring of wheels on gravel. A tall man drove up in a rig, holding the reins high with his monstrous arms, his smile glowing across the yard.

'Ann!'

'Is that you, Tom?'

'Who else?' Leaping from the rig, he tied the reins to the fence.

'I'm not speaking to you!' Ann whirled, the bucket in her hands slopping.

'No!' cried Cecy.

Ann froze. She looked at the hills and the first spring stars. She stared at the man named Tom. Cecy made her drop the bucket.

'Look what you've done!'

Tom ran up.

'Look what you *made* me do!'

He wiped her shoes with a kerchief, laughing.

'Get away!' She kicked at his hands, but he laughed again, and gazing down on him from miles away, Cecy saw the turn of his head, the size of his skull, the flare of his nose, the shine of his eye, the girth of his shoulder, and the hard strength of his hands doing this delicate thing with the handkerchief. Peering down from the secret attic of this lovely head, Cecy yanked a hidden copper ventriloquist's wire and the pretty mouth popped wide: 'Thank you!'

'Oh, so you *have* manners?' The smell of leather on his hands, the smell of the horse rose from his clothes into the tender nostrils, and Cecy, far, far away over night meadows and flowered fields, stirred as with some dream in her bed.

'Not for you, no!' said Ann.

'Hush, speak gently,' said Cecy. She moved Ann's fingers out toward Tom's head. Ann snatched them back.

'I've gone mad!'

'You have.' He nodded, smiling but bewildered. 'Were you going to touch me then?'

'I don't know. Oh, go away!' Her cheeks glowed with pink charcoals.

'Why don't you run? I'm not stopping you.' Tom got up. 'Have you changed your mind? Will you go to the dance with me tonight? It's special. Tell you why later.'

'No,' said Ann.

'Yes!' cried Cecy. 'I've never danced. I want to dance. I've never worn a long gown, all rustly. I want that. I want to dance all night. I've never known what it's like to be in a woman, dancing; Father and Mother would never permit it. Dogs, cats, locusts, leaves, everything else in the world at one time or another I've known, but never a woman in the spring, never on a night like this. Oh, please – we *must* go to that dance!'

She spread her thought like the fingers of a hand within a new glove.

'Yes,' said Ann Leary, 'I'll go. I don't know why, but I'll go to the dance with you tonight, Tom.'

'Now inside, quick!' cried Cecy. 'You must wash, tell your folks, get your gown ready, out with the iron, into your room!'

'Mother,' said Ann, 'I've changed my mind!'

The rig was galloping off down the pike, the rooms of the farmhouse jumped to life, water was boiling for a bath, the coal stove was heating an iron to press the gown, the mother was rushing about with a fringe of hairpins in her mouth. 'What's come over you, Ann? You don't like Tom!'

'That's true.' Ann stopped amidst the great fever.

But it's spring! thought Cecy.

'It's spring,' said Ann.

And it's a fine night for dancing, thought Cecy.

'. . . for dancing,' murmured Ann Leary.

Then she was in the tub and the soap creaming on her white seal shoulders, small nests of soap beneath her arms, and the flesh of her warm breasts moving in her hands and Cecy moving the mouth, making the smile, keeping the actions going. There must be no pause, no hesitation, or the entire pantomime might fall in ruins! Ann Leary must be kept moving, doing, acting, wash here, soap there, now out! Rub with a towel! Now perfume and powder!

'You!' Ann caught herself in the mirror, all white-ness and pinkness like lilies and carnations. 'Who are you tonight?'

'I'm a girl seventeen.' Cecy gazed from her violet eyes. 'You can't see me. Do you know I'm here?'

Ann Leary shook her head. 'I've rented my body to an April witch, for sure.'

'*Close*, very close!' laughed Cecy. 'Now, on with your dressing.'

The luxury of feeling good clothes move over an ample body! And then the halloo outside.

'Ann, Tom's back!'

'Tell him to wait.' Ann sat down suddenly. 'Tell him I'm not going to that dance.'

'What?' said her mother, in the door.

Cecy snapped back into attention. It had been a fatal relaxing, a fatal moment of leaving Ann's body for only an instant. She had heard the distant sound of horses' hoofs and the rig rambling through moon-lit spring country. For a second she thought, I'll go find Tom and sit in his head and see what it's like to be in a man of twenty-two on a night like this. And so she had started quickly across a heather field, but now, like a bird to a cage, flew back and rustled and beat about in Ann Leary's head.

'Ann!'

'Tell him to go away!'

'Ann!' Cecy settled down and spread her thoughts.

But Ann had the bit in her mouth now. 'No, no, I hate him!'

I shouldn't have left – even for a moment. Cecy poured her mind into the hands of the young girl, into the heart, into the head, softly, softly. *Stand up*, she thought.

Ann stood.

Put on your coat!

Ann put on her coat.

Now, march!

No! thought Ann Leary.

March!

'Ann,' said her mother, 'don't keep Tom waiting another minute. You get on out there now and no nonsense. What's come over you?'

'Nothing, Mother. Good night. We'll be home late.'

Ann and Cecy ran together into the spring evening.

A room full of softly dancing pigeons ruffling their quiet, trailing feathers, a room full of peacocks, a room full of rainbow eyes and lights. And in the center of it, around, around, around, danced Ann Leary.

'Oh, it *is* a fine evening,' said Cecy.

'Oh, it's a fine evening,' said Ann.

'You're odd,' said Tom.

The music whirled them in dimness, in rivers of song; they floated, they bobbed, they sank down, they arose for air, they gasped, they clutched each other like drowning people and whirled on again, in fan motions, in whispers and sighs, to 'Beautiful Ohio.'

Cecy hummed. Ann's lips parted and the music came out.

'Yes, I'm odd,' said Cecy.

'You're not the same,' said Tom.

'No, not tonight.'

'You're not the Ann Leary I knew.'

'No, not at all, at all,' whispered Cecy, miles and miles away. 'No, not at all,' said the moved lips.

'I've the funniest feeling,' said Tom.

'About what?'

'About you.' He held her back and danced her and looked into her glowing face, watching for something. 'Your eyes,' he said, 'I can't figure it.'

'Do you see *me*?' asked Cecy.

'Part of you's here, Ann, and part of you's not.' Tom turned her carefully, his face uneasy.

'Yes.'

'Why did you come with me?'

'I didn't want to come,' said Ann.

'Why, then?'

'Something made me.'

'What?'

'I don't know.' Ann's voice was faintly hysterical.

'Now, now, hush, hush,' whispered Cecy. 'Hush, that's it. Around, around.'

They whispered and rustled and rose and fell away in the dark room, with the music moving and turning them.

'But you *did* come to the dance,' said Tom.

'I did,' said Cecy.

'Here.' And he danced her lightly out an open door and walked her quietly away from the hall and the music and the people.

They climbed up and sat together in the rig.

'Ann,' he said, taking her hands, trembling. 'Ann.' But the way he said her name it was as if it wasn't her name. He kept glancing into her pale face, and now her eyes were open again. 'I used to love you, you know that,' he said.

'I know.'

'But you've always been fickle and I didn't want to be hurt.'

'It's just as well, we're very young,' said Ann.

'No, I mean to say, I'm sorry,' said Cecy.

'What *do* you mean?' Tom dropped her hands and stiffened.

The night was warm and the smell of the earth shimmered up all about them where they sat, and the fresh trees breathed one leaf against another in a shaking and rustling.

'I don't know,' said Ann.

'Oh, but *I* know,' said Cecy. 'You're tall and you're the finest-looking man in all the world. This is a good evening; this is an evening I'll always remember, being with you.' She put out the alien cold hand to find his reluctant hand again and bring it back, and warm it and hold it very tight.

'But,' said Tom, blinking, 'tonight you're here, you're there. One minute one way, the next minute another. I wanted to take you to the dance tonight for old times' sake. I meant nothing by it when I first asked you. And then, when we were standing at the well, I knew something had changed, really changed, about you. You were different. There was something new and soft, something . . .' He groped for a word. 'I don't know, I can't say. The way you looked. Something about your voice. And I know I'm in love with you again.'

'No,' said Cecy. 'With me, with *me.*'

'And I'm afraid of being in love with you,' he said. 'You'll hurt me again.'

'I might,' said Ann.

No, no, I'd love you with all my heart! thought Cecy. Ann, say it to him, say it for me. Say you'd love him with all your heart.

Ann said nothing.

Tom moved quietly closer and put his hand up to hold her chin.

'I'm going away. I've got a job a hundred miles from here. Will you miss me?'

'Yes,' said Ann and Cecy.

'May I kiss you good-by, then?'

'Yes,' said Cecy before anyone else could speak.

He placed his lips to the strange mouth. He kissed the strange mouth and he was trembling.

Ann sat like a white statue.

'Ann!' said Cecy. 'Move your arms, *hold* him!'

She sat like a carved wooden doll in the moonlight.

Again he kissed her lips.

'I do love you,' whispered Cecy. 'I'm here, it's me you saw in her eyes, it's me, and I love you if she never will.'

He moved away and seemed like a man who had run a long distance. He sat beside her. 'I don't know what's happening. For a moment there . . .'

'Yes?' asked Cecy.

'For a moment I thought –' He put his hands to his eyes: 'Never mind. Shall I take you home now?'

'Please,' said Ann Leary.

He clucked to the horse, snapped the reins tiredly, and drove the rig away. They rode in the rustle and slap and motion of the moonlit rig in the still early, only eleven o'clock spring night, with the shining meadows and sweet fields of clover gliding by.

And Cecy, looking at the fields and meadows,

thought, It would be worth it, it would be worth everything to be with him from this night on. And she heard her parents' voices again, faintly, 'Be careful. You wouldn't want to lose your magical powers, would you – married to a mere mortal? Be careful. You wouldn't want that.'

Yes, yes, thought Cecy, even that I'd give up, here and now, if he would have me. I wouldn't need to roam the spring nights then, I wouldn't need to live in birds and dogs and cats and foxes, I'd need only to be with him. Only him. Only him.

The road passed under, whispering.

'Tom,' said Ann at last.

'What?' He stared coldly at the road, the horse, the trees, the sky, the stars.

'If you're ever, in years to come, at any time, in Green Town Illinois, a few miles from here, will you do me a favour?'

'Perhaps.'

'Will you do me the favour of stopping and seeing a friend of mine?' Ann Leary said this haltingly, awkwardly.

'Why?'

'She's a good friend. I've told her of you. I'll give you her address. Just a moment.' When the rig stopped at her farm she drew forth a pencil and paper from her small purse and wrote in the moonlight, pressing the paper to her knee. 'There it is. Can you read it?'

He glanced at the paper and nodded bewilderedly.

'Cecy Elliott, 12 Willow Street, Green Town, Illinois,' he said.

'Will you visit her someday?' asked Ann.

'Someday,' he said.

'Promise?'

'What has this to do with us?' he cried savagely. 'What do I want with names and papers?' He crumpled the paper into a tight ball and shoved it in his coat.

'Oh, please promise!' begged Cecy.

'. . . promise . . .' said Ann.

'All right, all right, now let me be!' he shouted.

I'm tired, thought Cecy. I can't stay. I have to go home. I'm weakening. I've only the power to stay a few hours out like this in the night, traveling, traveling. But before I go . . .

'. . . before I go,' said Ann.

She kissed Tom on the lips.

'This is *me* kissing you,' said Cecy.

Tom held her off and looked at Ann Leary and looked deep, deep inside. He said nothing, but his face began to relax slowly, very slowly, and the lines vanished away, and his mouth softened from its hardness, and he looked deep again into the moonlit face held here before him.

Then he put her off the rig and without so much as good night was driving swiftly down the road.

Cecy let go.

Ann Leary, crying out, released from prison, it seemed, raced up the moonlit path to her house and slammed the door.

Cecy lingered for only a little while. In the eyes of a cricket she saw the spring night world. In the eyes of a frog she sat for a lonely moment by a pool. In the eyes of a night bird she looked downs from a tall, moon-haunted elm and saw the lights go out in two farmhouses, one here, one a mile away. She thought of herself and her family, and her strange power, and the fact that no one in the family could ever marry any one of the people in this vast world out here beyond the hills.

'Tom?' Her weakening mind flew in a night bird under the trees and over deep fields of wild mustard. 'Have you still got the paper, Tom? Will you come by someday, some year, sometime, to see me? Will you know me then? Will you look in my face and remember then where it was you saw me last and know that you love me as I love you, with all my heart for all time?'

She paused in the cool night air, a million miles from towns and people, above farms and continents and rivers and hills. 'Tom?' Softly.

Tom was asleep. It was deep night; his clothes were hung on chairs or folded neatly over the end of the bed. And in one silent, carefully upflung hand upon the white pillow, by his head, was a small piece of paper with writing on it. Slowly, slowly, a fraction of an inch at a time, his fingers closed down upon and held it tightly. And he did not even stir or notice when a blackbird, faintly, wondrously, beat softly for a moment against the clear moon crystals of the windowpane, then, fluttering quietly, stopped and flew away toward the east, over the sleeping earth.

*   *   *

RAY BRADBURY is one of the leading writers of fantasy fiction in the world today and has frequently used his own childhood in the rural Midwest of America as the inspiration for his most memorable stories. From his earliest days in Waukegan, Ray loved to go to magic shows and the circus and never forgot characters he met there like Blackstone the Magician and 'Mr Electrico', an extraordinary man who wore a black velvet cape, sat in an electric chair and made blue flames spurt from his fingertips, nostrils and teeth. When, later, Ray Bradbury met the showman, he told him his ambition was to be a great magician. Instead, the youngster and his family moved to Los Angeles where he began writing and drawing on the magical events of his boyhood in short stories like 'Corpse Carnival', 'The Black Ferris' and 'The Last Circuit', his novels *The Illustrated Man* (1951) and *Something Wicked This Way Comes* (1962) and two books written especially for younger readers, *Switch on the Night* (1955) and *The Halloween Tree* (1972). It is no surprise that Ray Bradbury has been called by his admirers 'a magician with words'.

MS WIZ, SUPERMODEL

Terence Blacker

Ms Wiz wears a purple T-shirt and jeans and explains to anyone who asks about her special powers: 'I go wherever magic is needed.' With her bright green eyes and long black hair, not to mention her china cat, Hecate, a magic rat and a rather rude owl, none of the pupils at St Barnabas School had ever seen anyone like her when she first arrived to be teacher of Class Three. They thought she must be either a hippy or a witch. Those who decided on the later were nearer the truth – although Ms Wiz, real name Miss Wisdom, insists that witch is an old-fashioned name and she is actually a 'Paranormal Operative'. She soon reveals her talent to magic people into anything and even makes a School Inspector lose his trousers! All the kids in Class Three decide Ms Wiz is cool, especially when she includes magic-making and spell-casting in her lessons. Natalie, especially, gets the chance to see her teacher's powers at work when she admits to being too embarrassed to dress up for the school's Easter Parade and finds herself getting a visit from the extraordinary 'Ghost of the Easter Bunny' . . .

*   *   *

'Shy, Natalie?' The voice of Mr Bailey, the teacher of Class Three, echoed around the classroom.

'Shy? Why?'

'Shy, why, don't cry,' said Jack from the back of the room as the rare moment of silence was broken.

Mr Bailey closed his eyes wearily. Class Three was known as the problem class of St Barnabas and there was no time when the children were more of a problem than at the end of term.

'Right!' He snapped open his eyes. 'I will tell you one more time.' He looked around the classroom, daring anyone to speak. 'Next week is the annual St Barnabas Easter Parade. As usual, there will be a fancy dress competition and, as usual, each class will enter three children. This year the prizes are going to be awarded by a real celebrity.'

'Mr Brown, the mayor,' groaned Jack quietly. 'As usual.'

'Someone really famous,' Mr Bailey continued. 'A mystery supermodel.'

'Mrs Brown, the mayor's wife,' said Jack.

'So here are the three children I have selected to take part,' said Mr Bailey. 'Caroline will go as an Easter rabbit.'

'Yes!' Caroline punched the air.

'Peter will be the Easter egg.' The fattest boy in Class Three, known to his friends as Podge, stood up and bowed.

'And, wearing a special Easter bonnet, will be Natalie Sawyer. Eh, Natalie?' The class was silent as Natalie stared at her hands.

'Go on, Nat.' Humphrey, the boy who shared a desk with her and copied all her work, nudged her in the ribs. 'You're our best hope of winning.'

Natalie nodded slowly. 'All right,' she said.

But, of course, it wasn't all right. Later that day, after school, Natalie sat in her room at home, thinking of ways to get out of appearing at the St Barnabas Easter Parade.

'All the other parents will be at the parade,' she said quietly to herself. 'And Mum and Dad will be at work as usual.'

'Not necessarily.'

'What?' Natalie looked up in surprise. The voice had seemed to come from a pile of dolls that were lying on the pillow of her bed.

'Not necessarily,' it repeated.

Nervously, Natalie moved the dolls. At the bottom of the pile was a small woollen rabbit she had never seen before. She was about to pick it up when the rabbit said, 'Hang on.'

A faint humming noise filled the room. Before Natalie's eyes, the rabbit grew and changed shape, until – in a matter of seconds – a woman with dark hair, wearing a purple T-shirt and jeans, sat on the bed.

'That's better,' said the woman, shaking out her hair. 'How d'you do?' She held out her hand. 'My name's Ms Wiz.'

Natalie hesitated, then shook the stranger's hand. It was oddly cold. 'Ms Wiz,' she said quietly. 'I've heard the children of Class Three talking about you. Aren't you a –' She paused, not wanting to be rude. 'Well, aren't you a bit of a witch?'

'Certainly not,' said Ms Wiz with a flash of her green eyes. 'Witches are silly, old-fashioned things. I am extremely modern. A paranormal operative is what I am.'

'What's a paranormal operative for?' asked Natalie.

Ms Wiz sighed impatiently. 'Everything has to be for something these days, doesn't it? Magic can't just be magic. Oh no, it has to produce something.'

'Sorry,' said Natalie quietly.

'Anyway, enough about me,' said Ms Wiz. 'I'm here to solve your problems. l heard that you didn't want to appear at the Easter parade. Why's that'?'

'I'm embarrassed.' In a quiet voice, Natalie explained to Ms Wiz how both of her parents worked late into the evening. How they were always too busy to come to school events. How she was looked after by a series of nannies who were more interested in their boyfriends than anything she was doing.

'I see,' said Ms Wiz. 'So if your mum and dad were at the parade, you'd be happy to appear in it.'

'But they won't be.' Tears filled Natalie's eyes. 'Mum's acting in a play and Dad's too busy at his office.'

Ms Wiz stood up. 'Leave this to me,' she said.

The humming sound returned to the room as the dark-haired stranger grew fainter and fainter, until she was just a blur, like a picture on a television with a faulty aerial. Then she disappeared, leaving Natalie alone.

'I . . . shall . . . return,' said a distant voice. 'I just have to make a few calls.'

Natalie's mother, Mrs Sawyer, was in her dressing room. The rehearsals for the new play were going really well. That afternoon, the director had told her she was wonderful no less than four times, which was twice more than anyone else in the cast.

As she sat in front of a big mirror, inspecting her makeup, she sang quietly to herself, 'There's no business like show business, you smile when you are –'

She stopped. Something reflected in the comer of

the mirror had caught her attention. She turned in
her seat – and gasped.

A large rabbit about the size of a slightly plump
child, was crouching in the comer of the room.

'Stop singing,' it ordered in a strange croaky
voice.

Mrs Sawyer pinched herself.

'Must be those stress pills I've been taking
recently,' she muttered. 'I'll be seeing pink elephants
next.'

'I am no dream,' said the rabbit. 'I am the ghost of
the Easter Bunny.'

'G-g-ghost?' whispered Mrs Sawyer. 'B-b-bunny?'

'You got it, lady,' said the rabbit, taking a
hop closer to her. 'And I have a message for you. It's
all about someone you seem to have forgotten
recently . . .'

Natalie's father, Mr Sawyer, was sitting in his office. It
had been a good day. He had worked hard. The
market had been kind. He had made lots of money.
There was, he thought just enough time to make a
couple more deals before he went home. Or even a
couple of couple more deals.

He turned to the computer on his desk and tapped
a few keys. A faint humming sound filled the room.

On the screen appeared a message written in large
letters. 'WHAT ABOUT YOUR DAUGHTER, MR
SAWYER?'

'Funny.' Mr Sawyer pressed a few more keys on the
computer. 'Must be some sort of malfunction.'

'THE ONLY MALFUNCTION AROUND HERE IS
YOU, BUSTER.'

'What?' Mr Sawyer felt sweat breaking out around his neck. 'Who are you?'

'THIS IS THE EASTER BUNNY HERE. OR RATHER THE GHOST OF THE EASTER BUNNY.'

Mr Sawyer glanced over his shoulder. What would happen if the boss walked in and found out he was receiving computer messages from some weird rabbity ghost?

'THE ST BARNABAS EASTER PARADE IS NEXT WEEK.' The letters were appearing on the screen so quickly he hardly had time to read them. 'YOU WILL BE THERE, WONT YOU?'

'Well, I have a rather urgent meeting with –'

'YOU . . . WILL . . . BE . . . THERE . . . WON'T YOU?'

'Yes, er, I will.'

'GOOD. NOW, GO HOME.'

'Fine, right.' Mr Sawyer stood up and put on his jacket 'Er, goodnight Bunny.'

'MR BUNNY TO YOU.'

'Mr Bunny.' Mr Sawyer switched off the computer and walked quickly to the door.

'Hi, darling!'

'Hi, darling!'

Natalie looked up in surprise to see her mum and dad standing at her bedroom door. She glanced at the clock beside her bed. It was only just past six o'clock.

'Hi.' She kissed them both. 'You're home really early.'

'I missed you,' said Mrs Sawyer. 'All of a sudden.'

'Me too,' said Mr Sawyer. 'It suddenly occurred to

me that it must almost be time for the annual St Barnabas Easter Parade.'

'Next week,' said Natalie. 'I'm going as an Easter bonnet. Podge will be an Easter egg. And Caroline's an Easter bunny.'

Suddenly her parents seemed to have turned pale.

'B-b-bunny?' said Mrs Sawyer.

'Mr Bunny?' said Mr Sawyer.

'That's right,' said Natalie. 'Is something wrong?'

A week later, the head teacher of St Barnabas, Mr Gilbert, stood behind the microphone in the school hall. He looked worried.

'Welcome to the St Barnabas Easter Fashion Parade,' he announced. 'I'm so glad so many parents with busy schedules were able to be here.'

In the front row, Mr and Mrs Sawyer smiled at one another.

Two rows behind them sat Jack and Katrina, who had just wished Podge, Caroline and Natalie luck as they left to get changed for the parade.

'I hope Podge managed to get into his Easter egg,' whispered Katrina.

Jack laughed. 'He's the only person I know who's had to go on a diet to be an Easter egg.'

'Now I have good news and bad news,' Mr Gilbert was saying into the microphone. 'The bad news is that unfortunately the mystery supermodel we booked has had to fly to Paris for an emergency Save-the-Whale film premiere.'

There were groans around the room.

'The good news is that Mr Brown, the mayor, has agreed to be our special guest.'

Mr Gilbert smiled at the small, plump man, who sat beside him.

'Told you,' said Jack rather loudly.

'So, on with the show,' said Mr Gilbert. 'First on is –'

There was a crash from the back of the hall as the double doors were flung open. Silhouetted against the sunlight was a tall, glamorous creature in an elegant, skimpy purple dress.

'Hi, y'all.' The woman ambled down the aisle, wobbling slightly on her high heels. 'I'm your super-model for the day.'

There was a stunned silence as she climbed the steps to the platform. 'Yes sirree, ah'm here to present your prizes. The name's Miss Wisteria.'

'Ah. Thank you, er, Miss Wisteria,' said Mr Gilbert 'How very kind you are.'

The tall woman looked the head teacher up and down. 'You're kinda cute yourself,' she said. In the nearby seat, the mayor was looking displeased. 'Aren't you a bit . . . mature to be a supermodel?' he asked loudly. 'I thought they were meant to be young and skinny.'

The woman's green eyes flashed angrily. 'Mature's in, honey – skinny's out. Who wants to look like an eating disorder on legs anyway?'

'I don't think she's a model at all,' said the mayor grumpily. 'I think she's a parent dressed up.'

Jack was looking closely at the supermodel. 'Miss Wisteria,' he whispered to Katrina. 'Are you thinking what I'm thinking?'

Katrina smiled. 'Well, she has got black nail var-nish,' she said.

'This could be interesting,' said Jack.

The Easter Parade began. There were children dressed as daffodils and mad March hares and spring lambs and spring onions. Caroline hopped across the stage as the rabbit. Podge got a special cheer in his Easter egg suit – particularly when the audience noticed that his bottom seemed to be hatching from the back of it.

When Natalie entered in her wide-rimmed Easter bonnet, covered with primroses, Mr and Mrs Sawyer clapped wildly. She stood centre stage and, as if by magic, a flock of yellow butterflies appeared and fluttered among the flowers.

After the parade, Mr Gilbert stood up again. 'I shall now ask Miss Wisteria to judge the competition,' he announced.

'Third was the Easter bunny,' said Miss Wisteria.

'That was Caroline of Class Three,' said Mr Gilbert.

'Second was the brilliant Easter egg,' said Miss Wisteria.

Mr Gilbert looked slightly surprised. 'Peter. Also of Class Three.'

'And the winner.' Miss Wisteria smiled down at the front row. 'The Easter bonnet!'

The room erupted with cheers.

'Another Class Three contestant,' shouted the head teacher above the din. 'Natalie!'

As Natalie, Podge and Caroline stepped back on to the stage, the mayor suddenly leapt to his feet. 'This is no supermodel,' he said pointing at Miss Wisteria. 'This is a . . . quack.' He tried again, but the only sound that came out of his mouth was an odd quacking noise.

'Well hot dog, the mayor seems to be talking duck language.' Miss Wisteria stepped forward. 'And I was so looking forward to his speech and all.' She picked up the Easter Parade Cup from the table and handed it to Natalie.

Mr Gilbert was scratching his head. 'It's very odd,' he murmured. 'Class Three haven't won so many prizes since we had that strange teacher here called –' Suddenly he looked at Miss Wisteria who was stepping down from the stage to talk to Jack and Katrina. 'l know who you are,' he shouted.

'Nice one, Ms Wiz,' Jack was saying. 'But that's the worst American accent I've ever heard.'

'How did you know about Natalie?' asked Katrina.

Ms Wiz smiled at Natalie who was being congratulated by her parents.

'An Easter bunny told me.'

Mr Gilbert was pushing his way through the crowd. 'You're that Ms Wiz who's always causing trouble,' he called out.

'Time for rapid fade,' said Ms Wiz, glancing in his direction as a faint humming noise filled the hall.

'Stop her!' shouted the mayor whose voice had suddenly returned.

'I . . . shall . . . return,' said a distant voice.

'Where's that woman?' said Mr Gilbert. 'Where's Ms Wiz?'

'She felt a bit faint,' said Jack.

'You know how it is with supermodels,' said Katrina.

'Why's she never here when I need to talk to her?' muttered the head teacher angrily.

Natalie joined the group, her Easter bonnet in her hands. 'Maybe she's a bit shy,' she said.

*   *   *

TERENCE BLACKER has created a spellbinding character in Ms Wiz and she has now appeared in over a dozen adventures. The author was born in Suffolk and after studying at Cambridge University tried his luck as an amateur steeplechase jockey, bike messenger and book salesman in Paris before working in publishing for several years. In 1983 he took up writing full-time and found an enthusiastic audience among younger readers for his series of 'Hotshots' football books. This was followed by the first of the Ms Wiz titles that began in 1987 with *Ms Wiz Spells Trouble*. The book was short-listed for the Children's Book Award and selected for the Children's Book of the Year in 1989. Subsequent stories of the sharp and cool Miss Wisdom have taken her through a variety of adventures where her magical powers have proved essential – especially a romance with a vampire in *Ms Wiz Loves Dracula* (1996). There are plans for a Ms Wiz film which Terence Blacker believes should be a musical. 'Maybe she will be the new *Mary Poppins*,' he says, 'she would be a sort of Mary Poppins with attitude!'

WORKS LIKE MAGIC

Jacqueline Wilson

Rose is a girl with a very unusual magical skill – just by thinking and giving a flick of her thumb she can rewind or fast-forward her life, just the same as she as does when she watches a video. The first sign things are about to happen is when her hand begins to glow – and after that the magic takes over and sends her into all sorts of situations that either happened earlier in her life or could happen tomorrow. Rose discovered she had this magic power the day the family TV broke down just as she was about to watch her favourite film, The Wizard of Oz, *for about the five hundredth time. The strange little repairman who came to fix the set also gave Rose the sort of magic power anyone would just love to have. However, when she uses it at school during one of Mrs Mackay's boring lessons, the result is not at all what she expects . . .*

*   *   *

Rose's cheeriness chilled a little as she went into her classroom. She wasn't enjoying school very much nowadays. She had a horrible strict teacher called Mrs Mackay who kept clapping her hands and saying 'That's quite enough, Rose. Now just sit down and stop showing off.' Mrs Mackay didn't let them talk much in class, and they had to do proper lessons like Arithmetic and English. Mrs Mackay even spoilt the fun lessons like Art and Music and Movement. Rose wasn't allowed to paint lovely sploshy pictures of flying elephants and wicked witches. She had to paint incredibly boring things like A Spring Day or An Autumn Wood, and Mrs Mackay nagged if she went over the lines. Rose couldn't make up her own swirly swooshy dances in Music and Movement. Mrs Mackay wanted them to learn special steps and the boys could march but the girls had to be on their tippy-toes. Rose snorted in disgust.

'Good morning, Rose,' said Mrs Mackay, eyebrows raised. 'Are you doing a pig impersonation?'

The children giggled and Rose burned.

'No Mrs Mackay,' she mumbled.

'Then stop that silly snorting, please. Now sit down and get out your Arithmetic book.'

Rose sighed deeply. She looked at her hands. Maybe she could fast forward herself through lessons to playtime? But then it was PE and now they were in Mrs Mackay's class they had to play Rounders, and Rose could never hit the silly ball or catch it either come to that. She'd have to fast forward PE too. In fact if she didn't watch out she'd be fast forwarding steadily right though the Juniors and she'd be at Secondary School before it was time to go home.

Rose wasn't too sure about Secondary School. Some of the boys in her brother Rick's gang were already at the Comprehensive and they kept telling horrible tales about your lunch being nicked by other kids and if you made a fuss you got beaten up in the toilets. Rose wasn't convinced they were telling the truth, but she wasn't terribly keen to find out one way or another. Changing schools was certainly going to be a big step. Going up into the Juniors from the Infants school had just been a little hop.

Rose had loved life in the Infants, especially the first baby class. There were no proper lessons and you could talk all you wanted. She'd had a lovely teacher called Miss Flower who'd made a special fuss of Rose because she had a flowery name too. Miss Flower pinned Rose's paintings up on the wall. Miss Flower asked Rose to sing a song because she had a good loud voice. Miss Flower laughed and clapped when Rose made up a little dance to make listening to the song more interesting. Miss Flower *never* said 'That's quite enough, Rose. Now just sit down and stop showing off.'

I wish I was back in the Infants, Rose thought.

Then she thought some more. She looked at her left hand. She wondered if there was some way of locking it into position so she could whizz back into the past in a matter of seconds. Her hand started glowing at the thought. Of its own accord her thumb tucked in tight and she had an overwhelming urge to press it hard. It looked like she'd worked out the way.

But what if it didn't work properly? What if she zapped herself too far back? She really didn't fancy being a baby again, wearing soggy nappies and only able to say goo-goo gargle-gargle like baby Robbie. You couldn't have a snack whenever you got peckish, you had to yell your head off until Mum got the message and stuck a bottle in your mouth. And even if you got fat from all the feeds you were still little. It was a long time before Rose got big enough to hold her own against Rick. In fact it was sometimes still a struggle nowadays. Maybe it would be better to stay firmly in the present?

'Now, we're going to do some Problems in Arithmetic today,' said Mrs Mackay. 'Rose, come up to the blackboard.'

Rose had a serious problem tackling Problems. If it took six men three hours to dig a hole in a field it took one girl half a second to clench her fist tightly over her thumb and whizz herself back to the past.

'W-h-e-e-e-e-e-e,' Rose squeaked, as she went whirling backwards, so fast this time that she couldn't possibly keep track, she couldn't stop, she couldn't change her mind, she couldn't even think, she just unspooled through her past life until suddenly her thumb shot out of her fist, her hand opened and she was shaken right back into her five year old self.

'What's the matter, Rose?' said a gentle voice, and a sweetly familiar figure in a soft blue frock bent down by the tiny chair.

'It really is you, Miss Flower!' said Rose. She looked down at herself and saw her own soppy little checked frock and her long-ago red shoes with straps and when she shook her bead she felt the two wispy plaits she'd once worn bounce about on her shoulders.

'Of course, it's me,' said Miss Flower. 'I think you must have fallen asleep for a minute, Rose! Wake up now, poppet.'

Rose was wide awake now and raring to go.

'I'm really in the Infants class,' she said, looking round the bright friendly room with the finger-painting easels and the water trough and the play-house in the corner and the pink dough – oh, she'd forgotten all about the pleasures of playing with pink dough!

She settled herself at the dough table and stuck her fingers into the lovely squashy ball of dough. Her fingers were small and fat and five-years old, but her mind was still her own and had sophisticated ideas. She wasn't going to make boring old sausages or snakes or necklaces like the other children. She stroked the pink dough, sniffing its strange smell. She decided to model a rose. Yes, a beautiful pink rose, with a tight bud and curling petals. She could feel it blooming beneath her fingers.

She set to work fashioning a petal. But her hands were hopelessly clumsy now. When she tried to roll the dough into thin strips her fingers bunched and botched. When she tried to curl the edge of a petal it broke off completely. When she tried to stick several petals together she pressed too hard and the rose got squashed into a shapeless lump.

Rose groaned, despairing. She found she had baby tears in her eyes.

'What's the matter, Rose?' asked Miss Flower.

'I can't make the dough work,' said Rose, sniffing and snorting.

'Yes, you can, dear. Why, that's lovely! A dear little pig.'

A pig, indeed! She couldn't seem to get away from pigs today.

'How about doing some finger painting now?' Miss Flower suggested tactfully, as Rose crossly flattened the pig-rose into a pancake.

Rose pulled on an apron, fiddling with the fasteners for ages before they would pop into place. She stood at the easel, dipped a finger into the pot of paint, and started on a self portrait. She wanted to paint her plaits with ribbons and her check frock and her red shoes with straps. But her finger wouldn't paint what she wanted. It drew a stupid round shape with spidery arms and legs. It didn't even manage a head, let alone hair. It smeared two blobby eyes right in the middle of the chest, and a smiley mouth straight across the stomach.

Rose stamped her red shoes.

'What's the matter, Rose?' said Miss Flower yet again.

'I can't make the paint work either,' Rose moaned.

'Oh dear, you are having trouble today,' said Miss Flower. She came and looked at Rose's picture. 'But it's a beautiful painting, you funny girl.'

'What is it?' said Rose. She peered up at Miss Flower.

Miss Flower hesitated. She looked at the painting intently.

'It's not another pig,' said Rose.

'Of course it's not,' Miss Flower agreed. 'It's a picture of you.' It was probably just a lucky guess.

'It's a picture of me looking like a pig,' said Rose, and she couldn't feel proud when Miss Flower pinned the silly painting on the wall.

Perhaps it wasn't such fun being an Infant again after all. Rose's hands were so helpless. She didn't have much luck weaving a little raffia mat and though she could manage to thread big beads onto a piece of string it soon became terribly boring. She tried chatting to the other children in her class, but they just prattled on about baby things.

Rose brightened when Miss Flower clapped her hands and told them to sit in a circle because it was story time. Rose recognised the little girl and boy on the cover of the book.

'Oh, it's Topsy and Tim. I remember! I read that ages and ages ago,' Rose said.

'Did you, Rose?' said Miss Flower. Her eyebrows were raised and her blue eyes were twinkling. She obviously thought Rose was telling stories herself.

'I did, really I did. I read all the Topsy and Tim books,' Rose insisted.

'Well. I expect you've looked at the pictures,' said Miss Flower.

'No, I can read! It's easy-peasy,' said Rose, and she went and stood next to Miss Flower, looking at the book on her lap.

She'd show her. She'd read it right through to the whole class. She might be back in her five year old body but she could still remember how to read, for goodness sake.

Or could she? She looked at the squiggly black shapes on the page. She could pick out an 'a' here, an 'e' there . . . but that was all! She looked at a big letter that might be a T but she didn't even know whether it was T for Topsy or T for Tim. She felt so silly standing there in front of the whole class. She clenched her fat little fists. She was tired of being little and stupid. She tucked her right thumb tight inside her fist. The circle of children seemed to start spinning. Miss Flower's kind face faded. Rose suddenly rushed forwards, hurtling through time, round and round so quickly that when she suddenly stopped with a jerk and found herself standing at the blackboard feeling silly all over again she staggered and nearly fell, the chalk in her hand squeaking all the way down the board.

Mrs Mackay thought she'd fainted. Rose was hurried off to the school sickroom. The secretary tucked her up on the sofa and gave her a cup of sweet tea and a digestive biscuit. Rose managed to miss the entire arithmetic lesson after all. This Little Piggy Rose went hee-hee-hee all the way home.

*   *   *

JACQUELINE WILSON sells almost as many books as J.K. Rowling and certainly has millions of readers who enjoy her stories every bit as much as the Harry Potter novels. She started writing stories when she was a child in Somerset and knew she wanted to be an author from the age of about six! In fact, she started her working life on magazine – including the girls' weekly, *Jackie,* which was named after her because everyone at the publishers thought the name was just right – before becoming a great success as a writer of gritty and uncompromising stories about resourceful girls living on poor estates or from broken homes. Especially popular among her books have been *The Story of Tracy Beaker* (1991), focusing on a girl in care who longs for a real family; *Bad Girls* (1997) about Mandy's struggles with school bullies; and *The Illustrated Mum* (1999) in which Star and Dolphin have to cope with a manic-depressive mother. To date she has written over seventy books and several of these have won prestigious awards. In 2002, Jacqueline Wilson was awarded an OBE for services to literature. She says she delights in meeting children in schools and libraries and loves to dress in black with pointed 'witchy' boots and wear lots of chunky silver rings. 'The rings seem to mesmerise the children,' she says, 'and they can always try them on!'

FEEL FREE

Alan Garner

*Charon is one of the earliest characters to be found in the
history of the supernatural – an old man possessed of
magical powers whose job is to ferry the souls of the dead
across the River Acheron into the Underworld. Tales about
him are to be found in Greek mythology and these say that he
was probably a very ancient god who misused his power and
was sentenced to serve for eternity as a ferryman of corpses.
Charon was, though, permitted to charge each person he
carried in his boat and it soon became a tradition in Greece
for people to be buried with a coin placed in their mouths to
pay for their passage. More than 2,000 years later, this
legend fascinates Brian who comes across a dish illustrated
with a picture of Charon in a museum and decides to sketch
it as part of his school project. While he is drawing, Brian
becomes friendly with Tosh, the museum's cranky old care-
taker, who somewhat reluctantly allows him to handle the
dish – and by so doing propels the boy, as if by magic, into
the weirdest situation of his life . . .*

*   *   *

The line of sight from Tosh's den to Brian went
under the Giant Panda's belly, between the gilded
coffin of Bak-en-Mut and the town stocks, through
the Taj Mahal and over Lady Henrietta Maria's dyed
bodice. The first morning when Brian had started his
drawing the Taj Mahal had blocked Tosh's view, but

when Brian came back from his dinner three doors had opened to give a clear run through, and whenever he looked Tosh's eye was on him.

Tosh kept to his den, where he brewed tea and filled in his coupon, unless he was on patrol. He patrolled every hour, on the hour, up one side, across the back and down the other side, which meant that he came upon Brian from behind. He said nothing the first day, but stood at ease, lifting his heels and lowering them; click; click; click; and he sucked his teeth. Then he patrolled back to his den. There were no visitors to the museum all day, all week.

'What are you on?' said Tosh half-way through the second afternoon.

'Eh up.' said Brian. 'It talks.'

'None of your lip,' said Tosh. His medal ribbons bristled.

But on the third day Tosh patrolled with a mug of hot brown water thickened with condensed milk. 'Cuppertea,' he said.

Brian put down his drawing board. 'Thanks, Tosh.'

'Yer welcome.'

'How's trade?' said Brian.

'Average.' said Tosh. 'For the season.'

'Been pretty quiet here, hasn't it?' said Brian. 'Since they built the Holiday Camp, I mean. The old park just can't compete, can it?'

'We have our regulars,' said Tosh. 'And our aberlutions is still second to none.'

'It's Open Day up the Camp,' said Brian. 'Anyone can go, free.'

'It's all kidology,' said Tosh. 'There's nowt free in this world, lad.'

'There is today.' said Brian. 'I'm going, anyroad.'

'What are you on here?' said Tosh.

'It's my Project for school,' said Brian. 'Last term it was Compost: this term it's Pottery.'

The next time round Tosh said, 'What you got to do with this malarky?'

'I'm trying to draw that Ancient Greek dish from all sides and see if I can copy it.'

'What for?'

'Greek pottery's supposed to be the best, so I thought I'd start at the top.'

'Fancy it, do you?'

'Yes,' said Brian. 'It's funny, is that. I seem to be quite knacky with it, though I've only just started. I may go and do evening classes.'

'I'm partial to a bit of art, meself.' said Tosh. 'Signwriting: but painting's favourite. Not yon modern stuff, though: more traditional – dogs and flowers and that. It makes you realise how much work they put in, them fellers. Same as him there.' Tosh pointed to the Egyptian coffin. 'Yon Back-in-a-Minute. The gold leaf and stuff, all them little pictures – that wasn't done on piece work. Eh? Not on piece work.'

'Not this dish. neither,' said Brian. 'That's why I'm having such a sweat over the drawing. Every line's perfect.'

'Ah,' said Tosh. 'They had time in them days. They had all the time there is. All the time in the world.'

The dish stood alone in its case, a typed label on the glass: 'Attic Krater, 5th Century BC, Artist Unknown. The scene depicts Charon, ferryman of the dead, conveying a soul across the river Acheron in the Underworld.'

At first Brian had thought the design was too

wooden and formal. The old boatman Charon crouched with bent knees, and the dead man was as blank as any traveller. The waves curled in solid, regular spirals and the rest of the design was geometry – squares, crosses, leaf patterns without life. But as he worked Brian found a balance and a rhythm in the dish. Nothing was there without a reason, and its place in the design was so accurately fixed that to move it was like playing a wrong note. And all this Brian had found in two days from a red and black dish in a glass case.

'Have you done, then?' said Tosh an hour later.

Brian sat with his hands in his pockets, glaring at the dish.

'No. Eh, Tosh: let's have the case open. I want to cop hold of that dish.'

'Not likely,' said Tosh. 'It's more than my job's worth. Can't you see all you want from here?'

'Seeing's not enough. That's why these drawings don't work. They're on the flat, and the dish is curved. Pattern and shape are all part of it – you can't have one without the other. My drawing's like sucking sweets with the wrapper on.'

'What if you bust it, though?' said Tosh.

'It'd mend. It's been bust before. Come on, Tosh, be a pal.'

Tosh went to his den and came back with a key. 'I know nowt about this,' he said.

Brian moved his fingers along the surfaces of the dish. 'That's it,' he kept saying. 'That's it. Yes. That's it. Eh, Tosh, the man as made this was a blooming marvel. It's perfect. It's like I don't know what, it's like – it's – heck, it's like flying.'

'Ay, well, one thing's for sure,' said Tosh. 'The feller as made yon: his head doesn't ache. How old is it?'

'A good two thousand year,' said Brian. 'Two thousand year. He sat and worked this out, these curves and lines and colours and patterns, and then he made it. Two thousand year. Heck. And it's come all that way. To me. So as I know what he was thinking. Two thousand . . .'

'Ay, his head doesn't ache any more, right enough,' said Tosh.

Brian turned the cup over to examine the base.

'It'd do for a cake stand, would that,' said Tosh. 'For Sundays.'

'Tosh, look!' Brian nearly dropped the dish. On the base was a clear thumb print fired hard as the rest of the clay.

'There he is,' whispered Brian.

The change from the case to the outside air had put a mist on the surface of the dish, and Brian set his own fingers against the other hand.

'Two thousand year, Tosh. That's nothing. Who was he?'

'No, he'll not have a headache.'

Brian stared at his own print and the fossilled clay. 'Tosh,' he said. 'they're the same. That thumb print and mine. What do you make of it?'

'They're not,' said Tosh. 'No two people ever has the same tabs.'

'These are.'

'They can't be,' said Tosh. 'I went on courses down London when I was a constable.'

'These are the same.'

'You might think so, but you'd be wrong. It's been

proved as how every man, woman and child is born
with different finger prints from anyone else.'

'How's it been proved?' said Brian.

'Because the same prints have never turned up
twice. Why, men have been hanged on the strength
of that, and where would be the sense if it wasn't
true?'

'Look for yourself,' said Brian.

Tosh put on his glasses. For a while he said
nothing. then, 'Ah. Very good. Very close, I'll allow,
but see at yon line across the other feller's thumb.
That's a scar. You haven't got one.'

'But a scar's something that happens.' said Brian.
'It's nothing to do with what you're born like. If he
hadn't gashed his thumb, they'd be the same.'

'But they're not, are they?' said Tosh. 'And it was a
long time ago. so what's the odds?'

Brian finished his drawings early. He was taking
Sandra to the Open Day at the Camp, and he wanted
to have a shave. They met at the bus stop.

'There's that Beryl Fletcher,' said Sandra.

'What about her?' said Brian.

'She only left school last week, and she's cracking
on she's dead sophisticated.'

'Give over,' said Brian. 'You're jealous.'

Two buses came and went.

'Do you like me dress?' said Sandra.

'Yes.'

'Just "yes"?'

'It's all right,' said Brian. 'Smashing.'

'You never noticed,' said Sandra.

'I did. It's nice – better than Beryl Fletcher's.'

Sandra laughed. 'You'd never notice, you great cloth-head. What's up? You've not had two words to say for yourself.'

'Sorry,' said Brian. 'l was thinking about that dish I've been working on all week at the museum.'

'What's her name?'

'I don't know her name, but she's very mature.'

'How old is she?' said Sandra.

'Two-and-a-bit-thousand year.'

A bus came and they got on.

'You know Tosh, the head Parky, him as looks after the museum?' said Brian.

'Yes. He's our kid's wife's uncle.'

'Was he ever a bobby?'

'He used to be a sergeant,' said Sandra.

Three stops later Sandra said. 'You're quiet.'

'Am I? Sorry.'

'What's to do, love? What's wrong?'

'Have you ever hidden something to chance it being found again years and years later – perhaps long after you're dead?'

'No,' said Sandra.

'I have,' said Brian. 'I was a great one for filling screwtop bottles with junk and then burying them. I put notes inside, and pieces out of the newspaper. You're talking to somebody you'll never meet, never know: but if they find the bottle they'll know you. There's bits of you in the bottle, waiting all this time, see, in the dark, and as soon as the bottle's opened – time's nothing – and – and –'

'Eh up.' said Sandra, 'people are looking. You do get some ideas, Brian Walton!'

'It's that dish at the museum,' said Brian.

'I thought it was a crummy old pot, but when I started to sort it out I found what was inside it.'

'What? A message?' said Sandra.

'No. Better than that. This fellow as made it over two thousand years ago – he knew nothing about me, but he worked out how to fit the picture and the shape together. When you look at it you don't see how clever he was, but when you touch it, and try to copy it, you're suddenly with him – same as if you're watching over his shoulder and he's talking to you, showing you. So when I do a pot next, he'll be helping. It'll be his pot. And he's been dead two thousand year! What about that, eh?'

'Fancy.' said Sandra.

The bus had arrived at the camp. Sandra was about to step down from the platform when she tipped forward at the waist. Her eyes widened and she clutched at the rail.

'What's the matter?' said Brian.

'It's me shoe!' she hissed. 'It's fast!' The stiletto heel had jammed between the ridges of the platform, and Sandra had to take her shoe off to get it free. 'Oh, it's scratched!' she said. 'First time out, and all.'

'Come on,' said Brian. 'If you will be sophistic-ated . . .'

'Hello! Hello! Hello!' said the loudspeaker. 'This is Open Day, friends, and it's free, free, free! Walk in! Have fun!'

Where do you want to start?' said Brian.

'I don't know,' said Sandra. 'Let's see what there is.'

'Hello! Hello! Hello! This is Your Day and Your Camp. The Camp with a Difference, friends and neighbours, Where Only You Matter. This is the Camp with Only One Rule – Feel Free! Feel free, friends!'

Brian and Sandra danced to two of the five resident tape recordings, drove a motor boat on the Marine Lake, spun their own candy floss . . .

'Hello! Hello! Hello! Feel free, friends! This is the Lay-Say-Fair Holiday Camp, a totally new concept in Family Camping, adding a new dimension to leisure, where folk come to stay, play, make hay, or relax in the laze-away-days that you find only at the Lay-Say-Fair Holiday Camp. Yes! And it's all free, friends. Thanks to the All-in L.S.F. Tariff, which you pay when you reserve your chalet. There are no hidden extras: this once-and-for-all payment is your passport to delight. Yes! Remember! L.S.F. saves Pounds! Now!'

'Me feet are killing me,' said Sandra.

They sat on a bench in the Willow Pattern Garden. Brian stroked the head of a Chinese bronze dragon, from which the Camp's music tinkled. The sun was low, the day at its best after the heat.

'Isn't it dreamy?' said Sandra. 'Better than the old park. These banks and banks of flowers and rock gardens: and the bees buzzing.'

'It's hard luck on the bees,' said Brian. 'They'll be dead by morning.'

'You're proper cheerful today, you are,' said Sandra. 'Why will they be dead?'

'Selective weedkiller,' said Brian. 'You couldn't keep the soil as clean as that, else. They spray it on, and nobody bothers to tell the bees.'

'How do you know?'

'I read quite a lot about it last term,' said Brian.

'When I was doing Compost. There's a lot in soil; you may not think it, but there is.'

'We're off,' said Sandra.

'No. Look,' said Brian, and leant backwards to gather a handful of earth from a rockery flower bed. 'Soil isn't muck, it's . . . well, I'll be . . . Sandra? This here soil's plastic!'

Smooth, clean granules rolled between his fingers.

'The whole blooming lot's plastic – grass flowers, and all!'

'Now that's what I call sensible. It helps to keep the cost down,' said Sandra. 'And it doesn't kill bees.'

'Ay.' said Brian. 'Bees. Surely they're not that daft.'

He climbed up the rockery, and he soon found the bees. They were each mounted on a quivering hair spring, the buzzer plugged in to a time switch.

'Hello! Hello! Hello!' said the bronze dragon. 'Lay-Say-Fair, The Camp with a Difference. Have you visited the Pleasureteria yet, friends? The L.S.F. Pleasureteria is the only Do-it-Yourself Fun-Drome in existence: all the fun of the fair for free! Free! Now!'

'We'll have a stab at that, shall we?' said Brian. They rode on the Big Wheel, the Dodgems, the Roller Coaster, the Dive Bomber, the Octopus. The equipment was automatically controlled. Lights winked, recorded voices gave instructions, bells rang.

In the Pally-Palais Sandra battled with sudden air jets from the floor, and clung to Brian on the Cake Walk. It was late dusk when they came out of the Palais. They laughed a lot.

'Well, something's made you buck up at last,' said Sandra. 'I thought I was landed with pottery and compost for the night.'

'What shall we go on now?' said Brian.

'There's the Tunnel of Love, if you're feeling romantic,' said Sandra.

'You never know till you try, do you?' said Brian.

They walked on to the stage by the water channel; There was a gate across the channel with a notice saying: 'Passengers wait here. Pull illuminated handle for boat. Do not board boat until boat has stopped. Do not stand up in boat. Passengers must be seated when bell rings. No smoking.'

' "Feel free, friends",' said Brian.

Beyond the gate was a grotto of plaster stalactites and stalagmites, and the channel rushed among them to a black tunnel.

'Queer green light there, isn't it?' said Sandra. 'Ever so eerie.'

'Special paint,' said Brian. 'It shows up luminous in ultra-violet light. Remember that Bottom of the Sea Spectacular in "Goldilocks on Ice" at the Opera House last year? Same thing in this grotto.'

Brian pulled the lever and a boat came out of the darkness upstream. Its prow was shaped to fit in a recess in the gate, which kept it firm.

'Passengers board now,' said a recorded voice. 'Take your seats immediately. Passengers board now. Take your seats immediately. Do not stand.'

Brian climbed into the boat and turned to help Sandra. She put one foot on the seat, then twisted awkwardly.

'Hurry up,' said Brian.

'It's me heel again. It's caught in something. On the stage.'

They began to laugh. Brian tried to lift Sandra into the boat but had nothing to brace himself against.

'Kick your shoe off.'

'I can't.'

They pushed and pushed. A bell rang. 'All passengers sit. Stand clear. Do not try to board. Stand clear.'

The bell rang again, and the gate flew open.

Sandra was still laughing, but Brian felt the water take the boat, and he knew he could not hold it. Already he was being dragged off balance.

'Get back,' he said. 'You'll fall in. Get back.'

'I can't. I'm stuck.'

'I'm going to shove you,' said Brian. 'Shove you. Ready? On three. One. Two. Three. . . .!'

He pushed Sandra as hard as he could, and she fell back on to the stage. He lurched in the boat and grabbed at the stern to save himself. For a moment the boat hung level with Sandra, who was three feet away, but dry, as she scrambled up, still laughing.

'Enjoy yourself!' she shouted. The boat bobbed away on the race, and Brian stood watching. Now he was in the grotto, and Sandra was distant in another light.

'Sit down. Brian! Coo-ee! Have a nice trip, love, and if you can't be good be careful! Shall I see you next time round? Coo-ee!'

She was swinging away from him, a tiny figure lost among stalactites. He stood, looking, looking, and slowly lifted his hand off the nail that had worked loose at the edge of the stern. He had not felt its sharpness, but now the gash throbbed across the ball of his thumb. The boat danced towards the tunnel.

*   *   *

ALAN GARNER has been described by *The Times* as 'the Wizard of Cheshire' because of his series of novels, the 'Alderley Edge' books – *the Weirdstone of Brisingamen* (1960), *The Moon of Gomrath* (1963) and *Elidor* (1965) – which feature magic and magicians in the district around the well-known Cheshire landmark. His fascination with magic can be traced back to his childhood when poor health confined him to bed for long periods and he loved dreaming up imaginary worlds. After taking a degree in classics at Oxford, Garner began writing tales mixing the mundane world of today with ancient myths: indeed he once claimed that he never invents stories but 'finds' them in landscapes and the artefacts of ancient history. Since his Alderley sequence featuring the adventures of Colin and Susan and the great wizard, Cadellin Silverbrow, in their quest to prevent the premature awakening of 140 heroic knights asleep in the underworld, Alan Garner has enhanced his reputation with several more milestones of fantasy fiction including *The Owl Service* (1967) and *Red Shift* (1973) not forgetting several collections of outstanding fairy stories. He has also been single-minded in his dedication to writing for readers between the ages of ten and eighteen who, he believes, are the most important of all and make the best audience for books. 'Few adults,' he claimed not so long ago, 'read with comparable involvement'. This is a sentiment he also shares with Philip Pullman and which I, too, hope has been satisfied by this collection.

ACKNOWLEDGEMENTS

The editor and publishers are grateful to the following authors, their publishers and agents for permission to include copyright stories in this collection:

'Doctor Cadaverezzi's Magic Show' by Philip Pullman from *Count Karlstein* published by Doubleday. Reprinted by permission of the Random House Group Ltd.
'The Magician of Karakosk' by Peter S. Beagle from *The Magician of Karakosk* published by Souvenir Press and reprinted with their permission.
'Elphenor and Weasel' by Sylvia Townsend Warner from *Kingdoms of Elphin* published by Chatto & Windus. Reprinted by permission of The Random House Group Ltd.
'The Rule of Names' by Ursula K. Le Guin. Copyright © 1964, 1992 by Ursula K. Le Guin. First published in *Fantastic*; from *The Wind's Twelve Quarters*; reprinted by permission of the author and the author's agents, the Virginia Kidd Agency Inc.
'The Magic Shop' by H. G. Wells. Published by permission of A. P. Watt Ltd on behalf of the Literary Executors of the Estate of H. G. Wells.
'The Magic Child-Killer' by Roald Dahl from *The Witches* published by Jonathan Cape Ltd and Penguin Books Ltd. Reprinted by permission of David Higham Associates Ltd.

'The April Witch' by Ray Bradbury from *The Golden Apples of the Sun* published by Rupert Hart-Davis. Reprinted by permission of Abner Stein.

'Ms Wiz Supermodel' by Terence Blacker published by Macmillan. Reprinted by permission of Macmillan Children's Books.

'Works Like Magic' by Jacqueline Wilson from *Video Rose* published by Blackie Children's Books. Reprinted by permission of David Higham Associates Ltd.

'Feel Free' by Alan Garner © 1968 from *Ghostly Experiences* published by Armada Lion Books, Harper-Collins. Reprinted by permission of Sheil Land Associates Ltd.

With special thanks to Philip Pullman, Ray Bradbury, Catherine Trippett and members of staff of the British Museum and London Library for their help in the compiling of this anthology.